Majestik One

by

Dr. James Denito, D. C.

RoseDog Books
PITTSBURGH, PENNSYLVANIA 15222

RoseDog Books
701 Smithfield Street
Pittsburgh, PA 15222
Visit our website at www.rosedogbookstore.com

ISBN: 978-1-4349-3055-2
eISBN: 978-1-4349-7124-1

CHAPTERS

Prologue

It is a time when time feels short. Hundreds of prophesies have come and gone for humans, but one remained, looming in different forms, in diverse cultures and now felt by nearly everyone. It was determined that in 2012, specifically the end of that year, the world would face its greatest change since the extinction of the dinosaurs. Sure, civilizations had come and gone, leaving behind clues ranging from massive stone monuments seemingly impossible to build to small artifacts that constantly shuffled the story of who was here before us. These mysterious ancestors of ours existed all right, but now they were so far in the past we found it hard to learn from their lives what we needed to know. Why were they gone? Was it their fault or something bigger than them, from nature itself? The archeologists argued and the anthropologists plotted, but then there were the geologists and all those other scientists. The pieces never could be made to fit if you believed in your story enough. So, everyone argued as usual, and before you knew it, 2012 was here.

The year came and went, but the biggest change was there were no more prophesies once it passed. Sure it was a bad year, but was it really worse than any other? The human race was alive, 7 billion strong and packed into the cities like never before, dependent on smaller numbers of bigger corporations for every resource that could make a profit. Yet a veil began to rise from the collective conscious, clearing the path to a future that finally seemed worth living for. What do we do now that we are no longer doomed? We of course went where we always wanted to go, to the sky.

Economists realized it was right there all along; the new frontier was off mother earth. Countries worked together on everything from space hotels to new propulsion systems that made a mockery of what held us back before. It was all about gravity. We knew it held us in this reality, yet never knew it was so simple to master until we listened to the crazy people who tinkered in their garages. Bill Gates was one of them long ago and look what he gave us, so why not give the other guys a chance? Seems our governments had built all kinds of devices with their own secret methods, and we finally got to see where hundreds of billions of taxpayer funds had disappeared to. One way or another, we were going to the stars and no one wanted to be left behind.

More years came and went, and if you thought orbit was full of junk before, space became a traffic jam in no time, punctuating the blackness with all the necessary waste. Private business showed once again why it ruled the planet. Unbridled from government at last, there was no better way to build a space Hyatt than the perfect mixture of risk and palm-rubbing profit. So in just a few decades, everything was possible, every-where was reachable, and everyone began to think that 2012 was indeed a turning point. How simple it all turned out. There was no need for something to come out of the heavens and kick our proverbial butts back into the Stone Age. It all worked perfectly well on just a bluff; our collective subconscious found a way to get our humanity restored on just a colossal nothing! Yes sir, life was good and we humans could now conquer the universe! ...Until that day, the day we realized we weren't wrong after all. The day the earth let out a mighty grunt and nearly succeeded in killing off the pesky human race. The planet apparently had been expanding all along in spite of the debate, and on this day, it grew too much for all who clung to her. On this day, it was one big step closer than ever; perched ready to start the next cycle of life yet again. What do you do now from your space hotel view? What do you do now looking up though the hazy ashen skies to those you love? What do you do to make today the day before tomorrow again?

CHAPTER ONE

The night had been unusually busy with medical emergencies. Now at last it seemed over. Drained and weary-eyed, I marshaled the strength to collapse respectfully into a stiff cushioned booth in, of all places, the East Lounge. A blue neon clock mocked back the time; 5:30 a.m.

The cold vinyl couldn't comfort me, so I wiggled up and leaned over the steamy herbal tea the waitress had just delivered. I inhaled the green brew's aroma. It offered energy to keep my eyes open a few more minutes, just long enough to glimpse the sunrise.

No matter how many times you've seen it, the sight of the sun breaking above the curved horizon of the earth imparts something to you. We need to experience sunrises to see past our pompous technological idealisms. The sunlight's daily appearance and departure has a way of reminding us about being mortal, about being back on earth.

The first signs suddenly appear. In moments the sublime amber glow bursts into a fiery orange-yellow nova, flaring outward with all the power and magnificence the universe has to offer. The new surface of the planet jumps to life as the shadowed edge of night runs away at incredible speed, traversing the revolving mass below. And suddenly, the sun is high enough to become blinding, and I turn my head respectfully away from her.

I close my eyes and sigh contently as I feel the solar warmth and energy course through my body. The tea now seems impotent compared to the sun's effects. Still old Sol is millions of miles away, just like the thoughts dancing through my head.

Remembering happier times, it all seems like a dream that I ended up in space, looking down on my place of birth from an orbiting hotel. But at least here my patients' maladies are far more interesting than those of my earthbound years. This concoction of artificial air, recycled water and vortex gravity doesn't engender the optimum health a human needs to be happy and sane.

And it never will as far as I'm concerned. Yet they sent me here to improve all that. Someone felt I was the answer, I just don't know who.

All these guests are nothing more than pawns in one last grand experiment at being human, but nonetheless they come, knowing the risks. Their hope is that one day we'll learn enough about the Universe to conquer our own destructive traits.

Before something so enchanted is realized, we must first survive our present circumstances. I guess that's all they really want from me; answers to impossible questions. So, I do many things; sort of a jack-of-all-trades you might say. However, they all boil down to ensuring we all stay alive up here. If I'm not fixing bodies, I'm modifying food in the hotel's laboratories or helping the engineers solve the latest problem. Just never enough damn time, if only I had the time!

By now the sun is fully exposed and the window panels are automatically tinting darker, commanded by some computer far away in the structure. I watch as the massive solar panels unfold from the bellies of the hotel's support cogs, reaching out like hungry flowers towards the light. The thought amused me that it took some imported expert; someone like me, to suggest that storing the panels during the nightly eclipsing might reduce the costly cosmic dust damage to the delicate films. Sometimes they do listen.

The light charged the extended panels to a golden white, whose rays reflected like lasers towards the windows. I could see my reflection now off the pane. I squinted as I sunk back in my seat. I still felt terrible, too tired for what I knew the next shift might bring.

A familiar voice suddenly snapped me out of my contemplation, "Ray! Hey buddy, 'nother long one?" A warm hand plopped on my shoulder as I looked up to see my good friend Max, smiling his usual ear-to-ear self.

Through a stretch and feeble yawn I managed to ask as I looked back to the clock, "I know what I'm doing here at 6:00 a.m., but what's your excuse?"

He slid into the opposite seat and gave me one of his grinning logical looks, "Well, don't you remember, those cultures we put in the plasma flux are ripe today. It's harvest time!"

"Damn, I did forget. I don't suppose..."

"Never fear my friend, we've got you covered; again. You weren't in your room when I called, so I figured the clinic had beckoned you again last night. I talked Pamela into helping me run those tests this morning. You know how she just loves to work on her day off. Anyway, the two of us should have the harvest analysis done by lunch."

I stood up and gratefully patted Max on the back as I headed to get a little sleep. "Thanks pal, I owe you one!"

"No, you owe me six," he quipped back, "but who's counting!"

As I walked from the lounge I said back to him over my shoulder, "How about I buy lunch today, noon at the Orion Room?"

Max lit up and replied, "You're on. And I'll tell Pam you insisted she join us! You know, in gratitude for her helping today."

I smiled as I walked away, navigating to my room. Once in the hall outside my suite, I fumbled for my door access card. Funny, I remember putting it in my back pocket last night when I left. Hope I didn't lose it when that drunk was hanging all over me at the clinic. If they didn't allow alcohol up here, people like that wouldn't need to be treated for a bump on the head at 3:00 in the morning! Ahh..,here it is. Now how did it get in my shirt pocket?

The card clicked into place on the scanner, and after what seemed an eternity, the door finally slid open. Hmmm, have to get maintenance to check on this. As I walked past the illumination sensor, a blasting shock of discomfort shot up my leg, stopping me in my tracks. I respectfully refrained from screaming in pain and looked down to see what I had walked into. My heavy storage case lay there in the foyer! I immediately surveyed the room; it was such a mess I thought I was in the wrong place. Stupidly I leaned back into the hall to check the door number. It was my room, but it wasn't as I had left it.

Somebody had ransacked my room and left the scent of a cologne permeating the air, a scent I would never use! By now my heart was pounding as I realized they could still be here. Slowly I crept toward my weapon, eying every corner and dark space. Finally, in front of my private safe outside the bedroom, I lightly thumbed the sensor and the panel jumped open. My hand was immediately on my gun.

Epinephrine now had me shaking like a leaf, ready to kill the first thing that moved. It rapidly occurred to me I had no idea what I would do if someone were actually to confront me here. Sensibly I shoved the gun in my pants and dashed from the room, my sanity quickly returning. Halfway down the hall I grabbed the emergency phone and called security. I hurriedly returned to a post just outside my door to await reinforcements.

Ten minutes later an officer arrived, nonchalantly strolling from the elevator. I was furious as I ran toward him, "Everyone on this floor could have been murdered in the time it took you to get here!"

"What are you talking about?! Dr. Phillips, I'm sorry, but they gave me no indication this was an emergency. After all, it is only 6:15 a.m.!"

Grabbing hold of his arm, I led him to my door. "In there," bravely pulling out my gun again. He pulled his pistol with a disbelieving look at me, drew a deep breath and cautiously made his way in. Following closely at his heels, I could feel my whole body tensing again with each step. We both stopped instantly a few meters in when the sudden movement of a shadow in the bedroom caught our attention. The officer lunged into the bedroom and shouted, "Don't move or you're history!" His arms were locked extended, coldly aiming at the figure in front of him.

"Don't shoot, don't shoot!" screamed back an accented female voice. The officer dropped his arms and turned back to look at me, an expression of relief and irritation filled his face. I peered around the corner to see the maid standing by my bed, clutching one of my pillow cases.

"Señor, I am sorry. I saw the door open on my way to the linen room, so I popped in to grab your sheets. Also, the room was such a mess!" Tears were now welling in the little woman's eyes as she stood there cowering.

As I walked my gun back to my safe, I calmly asked her to leave and return during lunch to restore order to my room. Meanwhile the officer had poked his head in the other two rooms and returned to my side. He stood close to me as he stowed his weapon. "No signs of anyone else. I'll write a report on the incident and you can file a complaint to the security board if anything's missing or broken. Have a good day, doctor."

He left a whole lot faster than he arrived, probably late for breakfast! There I stood, tired and perplexed, surrounded by my belongings strewn about my feet. Sleep was the most important thing on my mind in spite of the situation. So I negotiated through the debris, locked the door and set my wake-up call for 11 a.m.. I crashed heavily onto the bed; the only sound now was the ever-present hum of the structure as I drifted asleep.

CHAPTER TWO

While Ray Phillips slept, the hotel around him stirred to life. People trickled from their rooms, starting their daily rituals at the restaurants, the pool and gym, even the bars. Life was vacation-like, yet busy. Most would eventually be kept active with some function at the hotel, whether it be recreational or constructive; it was never passive. That was the way they wanted it, that was the way it had to be.

Meanwhile, a large supply shuttle, the Torrus, was making its way towards the Majestik. It was loaded heavy with necessary food, materials, and inevitably, more people. The journey up from Earth was a short one; for most it was a ride they would never forget, a fleeting moment of exhilaration filled with uncertainty and promise. It was unlike the world of memories behind them that could not be forgotten, no matter how hard they tried.

Planet Earth, so long a forgiving mother, had unleashed a power from within that quickly took back most of the lives she grew and nourished for thousands of years. The cataclysms so long predicted had come, but not the way anyone ever thought they would. And most taunting of all was that it came decades after they thought 2012 was the last hurdle for mankind. Humanity was working hard, and successfully, at reviving the weakened Earth. She tried ever so hard to clear her oceans and skies, to grow nutritious food once again, to shelter the inhabitants from the now hostile unrelenting sun. She had almost reached the threshold of rebirth. But then, from deep inside, a still unexplainable slip of the magnetic core sent every inch of soil rumbling apart. Oceans swallowed whole continents while at the same time resurrecting land it had taken long ago.

In just days, the surviving 50 million lives, although fortunate to be alive, found themselves on the surface of a brand new planet, one still shaking from the violent tribulations that had come so quickly. The air was clouded with the foul exhausts of numerous volcanoes. The new land still clawed its way up from shifting swamps and bogs. The prevailing old land; one defiant African continent, sat cautiously waiting. Was this all there was?

So, life had nearly gone, but not the slow passing mankind deserved. The change came as it had at least dozens of times in the past, from within the Earth, not from humans. No one could have stopped it, no one would have imagined. It just came, like a messenger from the Creator, if you still believed in religion. Now, many were more confused about God than ever before. The events allowed some life to survive, but why them? What the survivors now had was a knowledge beyond technology; they had a new sense of wisdom perhaps never before felt by humans. The Earth tempted man once again to try one more time, and that is what people did. That is all they knew. All life tried again, to fulfill a destiny that still lay hidden. But now they knew deep in their souls the future was outward, it was somewhere in space, and yet no one had a clue where.

So doing what humans do, they turned stable land areas into growing communities with new governments. There were also new laws from a novel form of leadership that promised to be different from the past. Ironically, the Earth was quickly appearing overcrowded; the anxious new generation had little useable space to survive. That is why the black reaches of space seemed truly the last hope for humanity. Space was where people wanted to be. What once was a vacation trip had turned into a chance to participate in the greatest of experiments; the human being finally volunteered to be its own guinea pig!

Everyone who wanted to come up was placed on a rotation schedule; one year on the planet matched with one month in the promise of space. To those already in orbit, the feeling was nearly the opposite. From their safe perches above, these people haplessly watched the tragedy unfold below them. Their horror was often deeper than of those on the planet. Yes, most had indeed lost their families and friends, but they were cruelly prevented from dying with them. Being a witness to the end of the world was not to be envied.

So up and down they came. Now, twelve years since the event, people started to lose direction. The situation was constantly stressed by the under-lying fear of further repercussions from the Earth. No one knew what to do up in orbit except to find answers, to just keep going. That is the ever present driving force of all life; just hang in there.

There were some who thought otherwise, who cursed any survival, their prophesies unfulfilled. They sat in the trenches of this new war, the war of waiting. They looked for a sign, anything, so that mankind might be forever released from mortal bondage.

*   *   *

The Torrus closes in on the hotel as its pilot Alicia Martin coolly guides the spacecraft into the Majestik's landing receptacle. She is in command of one of the few remaining space shuttles. The craft is disc-shaped, yet with a slight delta wing flair. It is showing signs of wear, but still it is the best ship of the surviving fleet. Only the ships away from Earth's surface managed to survive intact; the rest were lost with everything else. Replacements had yet to be built, the task too monumental for the recovering society.

The ship nudges ahead until a gentle bump signals the lock of the interface. Numerous color monitors and switches still glow and calculate in the spacious cockpit as the crew works automatically about their tasks of shutting down the computers. The passengers are excitedly crowding into the isles, each with their own hopes and dreams. A small argument breaks out as the tension and stress of the trip finally starts to show among them. Others interject themselves to suppress the unwanted trouble.

Alicia unlatched herself from her seat and removes her headset. She was scheduled to leave again in a mere six hours, and anxiously wanted to stroll about the hotel, but first get some food.

"Care to get some lunch with me while they prepare the ship for our loop back?" Alicia asked her co-pilot Tim.

He quickly replied with obvious excitement in his voice, "A man would be a fool to turn down an offer like that from such a beautiful woman! Ah, begging the captain's pardon." His face now displayed a sheepish boy grin.

She stood up commandingly and gestured him behind her, "Come on, there's a restaurant at this hotel I've been meaning to try. I think it's called the Orion or something like that."

They headed out the gangway, patiently following the last of the passengers. Alicia seemed distant as they crept ahead. Her story was typical of the people living in space at the time of the event. She was the only survivor of her family. A last-minute change in her schedule had her flying between hotels above the earth when it all unleashed. She would never forget the sight below; nightmares woke her all too often.

Today, she thought longingly of her husband and daughter. The little girl was so young to have to die. Could they have survived? The thought never dimmed in her mind. Alicia checked records and questioned people constantly hoping for the impossible, hoping to find them in a sea of new islands and societies. She shook her head and refocused on the moment.

Her lunch guest today was necessary to satisfy her need for male companionship. She greatly appreciated Tim's presence and glanced thankfully at him. Then, for some reason the passenger in front of them turned her attention back away from Tim. The man painfully displayed his nervousness, beads of sweat covered his face. Alicia felt compelled to try and assist him.

She touched his shoulder, "Excuse me, sir." He turned, somewhat startled. She asked him cheerfully, "Have you been in space before?"

"Oh yes. As a matter of fact, this is my second time here at the Majestik!" Then he squinted his face in thought, "No, I think this is my third time here." He quickly turned away, clutching his bulky bag near his chest. Alicia looked back at Tim, forced a feeble smile, then shrugged her shoulders undiscerningly.

The two finally departed the ship and made their way to the restaurants. The hotel was extremely crowded. Extra rooms and facilities were being added daily. The superstructure grew in all directions, like some giant spinning top, rolling slowly on its axis perpendicular to the planet.

There were six similar structures above earth, but the Majestik was the oldest and largest. Majestik Two never was built, but everyone kept the 'one' in the Majestik's name. It was predominantly Russian built. Technology's exponential growth through the turn of the century exploded again once 2012 passed. Space was attacked like the wild west of America was settled. As it turned out, the direction up may have been humanity's salvation, safe in the cold vacuum above the warmth and hold of gravity.

The Majestik lived up to its namesake; it carried a certain nostalgia that made it the favorite place for the earthlings to visit. It had a way of reminding them of happier times. People could forget their troubles up here, at least that was the way it was so far.

*   *   *

Max and Pam stood next to the Orion entrance. Max glanced at his watch and frowned, "He's late, wonder if he's still sleeping?"

Pam sighed, "You know Ray, he probably let himself sleep only a few hours and somehow ended back at the clinic."

"Maybe, I'll call down there and..." Ray suddenly appeared through the crowd, squeezing his way toward his friends.

Nearly breathless, he apologized, "Hope you two haven't been waiting too long, the damnest thing happened to me this morning!" He flashed his ID at the hostess as he guided them through the doorway. "I'll tell you all about it as soon as we get seated."

The three of them made their way to an open table near an external window. The planet below provided a beautiful backdrop, outlining Pam's soft features in a blue glow. Within moments their waiter arrived.

Ray leaned towards the man, "The check goes on my card. We'll skip the cocktails, so give us just a few more minutes to make our choices."

Pam looked up over her menu, eyebrows raised in surprise, "Hey, I wanted a drink, we worked hard for you, Ray Phillips!"

"I'm sorry, I guess I wasn't thinking, I still have last night on my mind."

Pam leaned forward and queried him, "So what happened last night, find a strange girl in your bed who needed an emergency physical?" She stared smiling, her hands now folded on top of her menu.

Ray wanted to laugh but remained serious, "Well, very intuitive young lady, someone *was* in my suite last night and had such a good time they forgot to clean up. But before your twisted minds go off on this, I'll tell you I didn't invite them! As far as I could tell, nothing was missing, but my files were everywhere. That seems to be what they were after."

Max sat forward now expressing concern, "I know that look, you're not joking are you?"

Pam added almost hushed, "Did you call security?"

"Oh yes, and I'm going to have a lot to say about that at our next planning meeting. You'd think I was bothering them or something!"

Max replied mildly, "You'll get your chance sooner than you think. They've called an emergency meeting in just three hours. All I heard is it involves the shuttles."

Ray dropped his head into his palms and groaned, "Of all days, seems these interruptions always come in bunches. How are we ever going to get caught up in the labs!?"

The waiter reappeared and everyone quickly returned to their menus, then politely ordered. Once he finished noting the requests on his electronic pad, Pam added one last thing, "And waiter, bring me a scotch and water, neat." She grinned smugly at Ray, who just leaned back and folded his hands behind his head smiling, letting the soft chair absorb him.

Alicia and Tim arrived at the Orion Room twenty minutes later. By now it was nearly packed as they both scanned the rooms for a table. Alicia spied a couple leaving by the windows and quickly led her co-pilot to it. They reached it at the same time another couple did. Everyone was obviously hungry because a minor disagreement broke out over who arrived first.

Since the table was adjacent to Ray's group, he was compelled as always to offer his assistance. Swiveling his chair around he pointed to Alicia, "I hate to be a busybody, but the captain and her companion were here first. Another table should be available in no time."

Alicia smiled down at him as the other couple compliantly walked away. She reached out and shook Ray's hand, "Thank you very much, that was gallant of you."

Ray stood up, still holding her hand, "I'm Dr. Phillips, these are my associates Pam Aquain and Max Rogers." Tim reached in trying to steal Ray's hand, "I'm Tim Ward, and this is my captain, Alicia Martin." Ray continued to smile, ignoring Tim. Finally he let her hand go and reached toward Tim. He nodded as he quickly shook the man's hand, "Well, you two enjoy your lunch!"

Everybody sat down. Alicia's impressive body showed through her black jumpsuit uniform as her shoulder length blonde hair glistened seductively in the afternoon light.

Ray found himself glancing over at her through the meal, still feeling the command of her firm handshake. She caught his eye finally and politely smiled back, then busied herself with conversation. Ray then looked cautiously at Pam and found her staring at him in obvious disbelief.

He cleared his throat, "Well, ahh.. is everybody finished?"

Max tapped the table as he got up, "I'm full. Thanks for lunch, I'll just be in the lab till the meeting."

Ray stood up too and patted him on the back, "We're down to five now eh pal." They both laughed as Max turned to leave. Ray looked down at Pam who still sat there brooding, playing with the drink straw.

"Come on Pam, I'll buy you another drink in my room, you won't believe the mess!"

She stood and reluctantly followed him, "Honestly Ray, sometimes you are such an ass!" As they walked away Ray snuck one last glance over his shoulder to Alicia, but she was busy looking down at the planet.

*　　*　　*

Pam and I stopped by the clinic on the way to my room, just to see if I had enough staff to handle the workload. She tried to steer me away from the place with logic, but I wouldn't be able to relax until I had a quick look.

Everything was running surprisingly well, unlike most days, so we quickly left. The maid was working on my room when I left for lunch, but I hadn't told Pam this. Once at my suite, the door took its usual sweet time opening but got stuck halfway. After waiting and gently trying to push it, we finally went in anyway. Pam led the way by turning sideways and pulling me in by the hand.

"Well, this doesn't look so bad, just your papers all over the floor. Any ideas who would break in here?"

"No, but since my files appeared to be their target, I plan on being meticulous about refiling them to look for missing pages."

"You weren't planning on sorting through them now were you?"

"No....maybe tonight though. I'd be too curious to let it go too long."

"Good, then we have some time to play before the meeting." She moved close to me and wrapped her arms affectionately around my waist. As she gently kissed my neck, I closed my eyes and tried to relax.

At first I was not sure I wanted her right now, but she had a way of making a man see it her way. I drew her in close to me and became instantly totally involved in her desires. Within seconds our kissing was intense, our mouths exploring each other with hungered intimacy. Soon our clothes fell to the floor as we hurried to enjoy the moment. My mind tried one final shot at distracting me; is the maid still in the room? I quickly found I didn't care as we moved slowly across the room and climbed somewhat gracelessly into my floatation chamber. She smiled slyly as she seductively pushed me all the way in.

This wasn't the first time I had relations with Pam, yet each time became more exciting than before. Inside the cylinder, we set the gravity load for zero and floated effortlessly making love, totally isolated from the harshness of the never-resting hotel. After what seemed like an hour, I finally collapsed from exhaustion.

Pam was much younger than me, and at times like these, I could feel the difference. Age became very unimportant in this new universe. Humans felt their mortality, and many couples of different ages paired; that in the past would have not been predictable. Perhaps this was why she was drawn to me, or perhaps it was something less primal, maybe more convenient. I looked over at her as she drifted off in her mind, eyes half closed. I knew she wanted more, but I had no more to give. Besides, we both knew that meeting at 3:00 demanded that our minds be sharp. We lay there enveloped in each other's arms, quietly floating away the few minutes we had left. The papers on the floor drew my mind again where I didn't want it to go.

CHAPTER THREE

The two of them quietly made their way into the domed committee room. The room was full, which never happens on the Majestik. Many were busy in hushed conversations, while their eyes scanned the room for new faces. The chairman, a balded grunt, looked intensely at the two of them as they sat down. Ray smiled feebly back while helping Pam into her seat. The chairman banged the gavel, "Now that the illustrious Dr. Phillips has arrived, it looks like everyone is finally here, we can begin." He cleared his throat several times as he shuffled papers in front of him. By now the room was stone quiet, eyes focused on his every move.

Ray glanced across at Max, who was trying to suppress his smirk. He looked like a kid with a secret. Ray looked back to Pam who was now busy with her stenographic board, purposely ignoring them both.

The chairman's dark bushy eyebrows drew together when he finally spoke. "This emergency meeting was called because of a sudden development on Earth this morning. It was suppressed from the news media. Somehow, the main shuttle fuel depot on the Lemurian island was destroyed by a series of explosions."

Sudden concerned mumbling filled the room. The chairman continued, "....and the governor suspects foul play, so he has started an immediate investigation!"

Ray pondered loudly enough for everyone to hear. "What reason in hell would someone have to purposely destroy that shuttle fuel? There hasn't been a hint of terrorism on earth since the events!"

The room quieted as the chairman answered, "We don't know yet, but all other earth storage facilities are beefing up their security to level five. What's more, the Majestik and all other space ports are to suspend all shuttle departures until further notice."

With that everyone broke into angered shouts and demands. The chairman banged his gavel repeatedly until he was satisfied he had control again. "That will be enough! I don't expect this to last more than a day or two. Therefore, each of you take the necessary steps to inform your sectors, but in the manner necessary to prevent panic. Dr. Phillips, your group will have a report on my desk tomorrow on the progress of the new synthetic fuel mixtures."

"Now wait a minute! That project had been low prioritized two years ago! You know we haven't done much on it since the shift into food research!"

"I'm painfully aware of that, but just get me an update anyway!" He pulled his pants up as he lifted his chest back at the crowd, "Ladies and gentlemen, that will be all until we hear from the governor. Watch for updates in your secure message centers."

Ray remained seated as everyone else quickly got up to leave. He was obviously very frustrated at this point, yet he forced his mind back to the beautiful sunrise that preceded the day. With his palms flat on the desk he turned calmly to Pam and said, "So where were we anyway on that synthetic fuel project?"

"We? I wouldn't know. I only arrived here a year ago, remember? You must be thinking of another assistant." Her tone had now shifted to a level of frustration that could only have been caught from him. "You'll just have to find that information yourself, big boy," as she gently pinched his chin. She clicked off her board and followed the rest out of the room.

Ray watched in bewilderment as she walked away. Yet he knew he deserved that comment. He tightened his lips trying to remember what he would have been able to do ten years ago. As the doors closed behind Pam, a solitary figure remained at the opposite side of the horseshoe table. Sunlight was streaming in, illuminating a cylinder of particles suspended in the air. Behind the beam Max's silhouette leaned back into a squeaky leather chair.

He finally spoke as Ray stood up to leave, "You know, Ray, most of my life I fostered the desire to go into space and explore the frontiers. As if watching the earth tear apart wasn't enough, now I'm sitting here watching you get saddled with yet another bureaucratic paper chase. I must say I'm having serious second thoughts."

Ray walked over to his friend. He was somewhat surprised by the comment. "What are you talking about? What does *my* insanity have to do with your decision to stay in space?"

"When we became friends back at the university, I admired everything about you. I wouldn't dare tell you that though, God knows you don't need a bigger head! But, in a way, my life was modeled around Ray Phillips. When I lost my wife I barely managed to function, nothing had any purpose..., it seemed like I wouldn't go on." He paused as Ray was now resting his hand warmly on Max's shoulder. "Your support made the difference you know. It kept me alive." He paused another moment, swallowed hard, then continued, "but now, here I am and so what? Is this all worth it? Just what are we accomplishing anyway? What's *my* future; to die alone? To fill out endless piles of paperwork along the way?"

"Wow, that's some deep thinking, what was in that salad you ate?"

Max looked up at him with a slight disbelieving smile.

Ray continued as he plopped into the chair next to him, staring at the persistent beauty of the light beam. "Let me say this. Have patience my friend, you chose a path, and destiny chooses for us sometimes as well. The time will come when it all makes sense, when it becomes worth it. It always takes longer than we'd like, but that's the nature of man: impatience. You forced yourself to survive after her accident because somehow, some part of you hadn't been fulfilled yet. That's why you're here."

Max leaned down and rested his chin on his still folded arms. Ray stood up quickly, much chipper than he felt, and tried one more shot at helping his friend make sense of his dilemma. "Besides, right now I'm wishing I were your age! Maybe I wouldn't be so frustrated as well." He got behind Max's chair, swiveled him from the desk and gently dumped him forward to the door. "Hey, what do you say we get our butts back to the lab and dig up the fuel research files?" Max grunted as the two of them left a quiet dark room behind them. The intense beam of light had disappeared as well.

∗   ∗   ∗

Several hours later at the lab, with piles of paper covering all available workspace, the two men methodically delved through the data. Ray looked around him at the mess and sighed, "I can't believe I end up with so much paper chaos around me in just one day! It usually takes a week to make this much work!"

Max quipped back, somewhat returned to his usual self, "Well, you know the big idea, out of chaos comes order." Ray sighed and made his way to an empty chair to look closer at a paper that had caught his attention. It was an old research thesis done by a subordinate.

"You know, we had some pretty good ideas cooking at the time. This one compound had a weight:burn efficiency of point one! As an earth to space fuel, considering the present levels of volcanic oxide gases, it could pump out cleaner air than it would intake."

Max walked over to take a look at the report. Just then Pam entered the room, surprisingly much more cheery than earlier at the meeting. "Hope I'm not too late to help. I got bored rearranging the dolls in my room."

Max smiled a big grin, "You're a sight for sore eyes. At this rate we were sure it would take all night!"

"Pam, can I get you on this one?" Ray handed the report to her while he searched for the next paper to study. She barely glanced at it as she firmly took hold of his hand, "I'm sorry if I was rude earlier, it's just that..."

"I know, I know. We're all a little tense right now. Everyone will feel better tomorrow. Let's just all do our jobs like professionals right now and get the report ready for his highness. I'll order some food sent up so we won't be distracted by growling stomachs."

Max added one last dig as he winked at Ray, "Make sure you stay away from the salad I had."

Pam stood bewildered with her hands on her hips as the two men laughed.

CHAPTER FOUR

Ray awoke early as the next day raced to life. He wanted to sort through his own papers before breakfast. He hummed to the quiet melodies of synthesized music that seemed to emanate in his own head but were actually carried through the air flow system. It wasn't long until he discovered what was of interest to the intruder yesterday. Actually it was what he couldn't find that gave him the insight. Missing were old research notes he had personally collaborated on regarding the synthetic fuel projects.

He couldn't get the now-apparent coincidence off his mind as he showered and dressed. As he hurried from the room, he stopped in his tracks just past the door. He listened as the door slid closed even slower than before. He shook his head in disgust and headed for the elevator, clutching the finished fuel report the chairman needed.

Once the crescent doors opened to the giant hotel lobby, he made his way across the expanse to his usual first stop at the coffee shop. Not even ten steps in, a sudden powerful explosion rocked the entire floor as a rushing cloud of black smoke burst from the shuttle docking bay atrium. The force of the blast knocked Ray flat on his back like a falling domino.

He lay there motionless, stunned by the impact. He could hear sounds in the distance, a surreal mixture of screams and voices and sirens. He wanted to move, but slipped briefly unconscious the moment he lifted his head up. Once he reopened his eyes, the concerned face of a clerk was peering down at him.

"You OK, mister?"

Ray sat up slowly, holding the back of his head with one hand, the other still grasping the report. "I think so. What the hell happened?"

Before the stranger could answer he dashed away to a nearby person lying motionless on the floor. The montage of sounds now began to refine into frightful clarity as the result of the explosion defined itself all around Ray. He stood up unsteadily, and surveyed the scenario around him. Fortunately, because of the early hour few people were in this area of the lobby. He spied a body on the floor through the smoke near the bay atrium. Slowly he stumbled toward it. He stooped down next to the victim, a female. He squinted trying to clear his still blurry vision. He recognized the woman, it was Alicia Martin!

He gently stroked the blood-matted hair from her face. She was breathing, but needed immediate help. He tore off his shirt, frantically ripping away a strip. Skillfully he made a tourniquet and applied it to her arm, where a large flap of tissue was pulsing out blood. He yelled into the lobby for help.

"Hang in there beautiful, everything's going to be OK." He then noticed another body through the smoke pouring out of the shuttle docking gangway. He rose up and made his way to it, covering his face with the remainder of his shirt in order to breathe.

By now, the entire hotel knew something terrible had happened. The blast had shaken every bolt in the structure. Medical personnel were now swarming in, with them Max and Pam. As the two of them worked in tandem on the injured in the main lobby, Max spotted Ray coming out of the smoke. He immediately ran to his aid and supported the now-coughing doctor. He guided him to a bench and kneeled in front of him. "Are you hurt Ray? What can I do?"

Ray turned his head and pointed, "This lump on my head is a good place to start." He then spied Pam bandaging someone and yelled out, "Pam, can you take care of the captain over there, she's got an arterial wound and needs immediate surgery." He got up and respectfully pushed Max away, "I've got to help these other people!"

Pam stopped Ray on her way to Alicia and looked at his head. She pleaded, "Ray please, go to the clinic, you could have internal injuries!"

"No. No, I'm fine. Have to stay here and help." She shook her head and dashed away into the smoke. Max looked at Ray understandingly and followed after Pam.

Pam was examining Alicia as Max cautiously entered the airlock hall. He approached the damaged primary door, his hand gingerly testing the soft emergency barrier that filled in the missing pieces. "Thank God the sealant membrane worked, the entire lobby could have decompressed!"

He stepped over and looked out the nearby port window and exclaimed in utter disbelief, "Oh my gosh, the shuttle!" He yelled for Pam to come over. Before them was the horrible sight of the Torrus shuttlecraft drifting aflame toward open space. They watched as its burning silhouette quickly dimmed into a distant ember against the eternal darkness. Within moments it was nearly out of sight, and orbit.

As they stood pressed against the window, speechless, Pam cried softly, "I wonder if anyone was aboard her?'

"For their sake, let's hope not." murmured Max as he hurried Pam away from the window. "Let's get the captain out of here, you grab her feet, I'll get her shoulders." As they carried the woman to a waiting stretcher in the now clearing air of the lobby, each had their own thoughts of what the future held now. Fear wanted to have its way with them, but they had a job to do.

*   *   *

Two hours later at the Majestik's clinic an assistant handed Ray an urgent message. Another emergency committee meeting at noon. Ray angrily crumbled the note and exclaimed, "They may fire me for this, but I'm not leaving here until all these people are stabilized!"

He walked over to Alicia's bed and took her hand. With his other held out in front of him, he counted her pulse. At his touch her head turned toward him, her lips struggling to form a sound. Then, as quickly, her face relapsed into the comatose expression it held since the explosion.

Ray snapped his head around to the nearest assistant, "What's keeping her scan findings?"

"Here doctor, just finished," as a report was thrust into his hand by another tech. He scanned the words rapidly and sighed with relief. There was nothing of major concern, just a controllable frontal skull hematoma. It would have to be drained so he called Pam over.

"Good job on her arterial cauterization, but can you assist me while I tap this hematoma?"

"Of course, will she come through this without any brain injury?"

"I hope so, she doesn't deserve this."

Pam quickly added, "None of these people deserve this! I'm scared Ray. What would have caused such a thing to happen?"

"Maybe they'll elucidate that at the committee briefing they just called. Here, Pam, set up the monitor as I inject the nanoprobe enzymes."

The two of them expertly worked on the pilot. Each fought off a barrage of distracting thoughts that kept reviving the morning's horrors. Ray frequently glanced up at Pam, always catching her eyes reflecting back at him. Twenty minutes later the operation was completed and Alicia was cautiously wheeled to recovery.

Several hours elapsed till the last of the injured were stabilized or released. Ray had sent Max and Pam ahead of him to the meeting, not wanting them on the chairman's blacklist.

As he flopped into his desk chair, he grabbed at the head bandage he just buried in his soft headrest. He cringed quietly while he slowly leaned forward. Just then Max returned to the clinic, looking more worried than when Ray forced him to leave. "What's the face for, did you make it to the meeting?"

"Yes, and surprisingly Parker wasn't too upset you weren't present. I guess the report we gave him saved us a little grief. On the other hand, everyone else there were acting like maniacs. He just threw everyone out for a thirty-minute recess to regroup."

"Really? Didn't think he'd ever lose control of a meeting."

Max surveyed the room, "Looks like we have everything under control. How's that pilot doing, Martin isn't it?"

Ray replied, "Poor woman, it's a miracle she survived at all as close to the blast as she was."

"You seemed to pay special attention to her. Do I detect something more than a professional interest?"

Ray got up and led Max to her bed. "I don't know, there's something about her I felt ever since meeting her at lunch yesterday."

Max sighed and said, "Well, let's head over to the meeting. The circus in there ought to really help your headache. It might clear your thoughts about her at least."

As they strolled down the hallways, they were passed by dozens of residents expressing various emotions as they scurried about the hotel. Max commented coolly as he looked at the floor, "I'll tell you something I do know now; Pam seems to be getting a little jealous in her discussions with me about the pilot."

Ray's interest was peaked, "Really, Pam never takes my flirting seriously."

"Oh yeah, from the moment in the restaurant yesterday, she senses something."

"So she's actually talked to you about this?"

"In fact, yes. She's been surprisingly open with me today since the explosion."

They reached their destination and filed in with the other returning committee members. Ray took his regular seat next to Pam and patted her reassuringly on the thigh.

She spoke quietly as she leaned to him, "I'm glad you're finally here. You didn't miss much."

Ray acknowledged, "I know, Max filled me in on everything."

She was now sitting square in her chair. "Everything?"

He looked at her a little embarrassed, "Well, just the meeting you know. This is one day I would prefer to stay in clinic all day."

Soon the chairman was pounding his gavel to resume the meeting. His voice bellowed, "I hope everyone is now ready to contribute something here besides hysteria." He focused his attention on Ray, "Dr. Phillips, would you please elaborate on the condition of the injured."

Ray stood up, "We expect no fatalities. Everyone is now stable, including yours truly." He sat slowly as he lightly touched the dressing on his head again.

"Just one more question, doctor. What will it take to proceed on the project your report cited as the most probable to succeed?"

"That project was the baby of one of my earlier team researchers. His name was Dr. Rashad Ansarid. We think he's at AlphaSeven on Lemuria."

One of the other council members interrupted before he could continue, "So what! What does this have to do with this morning's explosion, we have to do something!"

The room suddenly came alive again, filled with shouts of agreements. Ray stood and uncharacteristically raised his voice to a yell, "I'll tell you what it has to do with! Yesterday my suite was apparently broken into, by person or persons still unknown. This morning I discovered the only stolen items were research papers from the early fuel studies! I don't know about you, but when you consider we just had a fuel depot destroyed, and a shuttle, it all strikes me as damn significant!"

The chairman interjected before the group could respond. "Thank you, doctor, you've been of invaluable help today, and your whole medical staff." He turned to another committeeman and asked, "What's our damage report?"

A short dark man rose. His deep voice and slow speech covered his nervousness. "The shuttle is a complete loss. Ground control reports tracking the wreckage until it left orbit. They said at its present speed it will be past the moon in two days. As for our docking area, it appears to be mostly cosmetic damage, with no apparent major structural faults. We already have crews working outside, with total downtime estimated to be two days."

The woman next to him added, "It appears the blast was centered in the craft itself, and the exit point created a nozzle effect which propelled the craft away from the hotel. If it happened any other way it might have ripped open the hotel like a can opener."

The chairman drew his eyes down in thought a moment, then thanked her as he refocused on the room. "Every other hotel and research station have now increased the security guards at the remaining shuttlecraft. All earth governors have been informed. The only other thing I can tell you is that after this incident, shuttle flights are still suspended."

The same heckler sarcastically mumbled just loud enough for the chairman to hear him, "That shouldn't be too hard for us to do now. How are we going to manage without the Torrus?"

Ray answered him again from his seat, this time calmly. "They'll probably reassign a ship from a research station, at least temporarily. In that event, we'll have to cope with a trimmed-down flight schedule."

Max politely asked if he could add something to the conversation. "To my knowledge there are only 14 remaining transport shuttles of various sizes, none of which are new. Also, most of them are already scheduled at unsafe turnaround rates. If we were to lose another craft or two, serious consequences would develop in food resource management." He then stood up to continue as the room listened intently, "Replacement ships have not been built for years as you all know. And to start such a project even for one ship would take years until completion. It likely could not be done from Earth resources alone. We all know most of our space facilities could never sustain themselves for more than a few weeks without sharing supplies and resources. Therefore it is imperative we lose no more craft."

The room was somber as Max finished, most whispered to each other while the chairman remained unusually silent. Ray looked across at Max and nodded his approval. The chairman grabbed his gavel as if expecting another outburst, but it never came. He lightly tapped it on the desk and finished, "We'll meet again tomorrow and I expect each of you to maintain order in your sectors. Thank you for your attention. Let's be strong, that's why they elected us."

It was after lunch, but Ray sent everyone on to their jobs. He needed to lie down, the pounding in his head was worse than earlier. Once at his room, he crawled into the sleep chamber clothes and all. As he closed his eyes, consciousness quickly slipped away.

Hours later at the clinic, Pam was making her way through the recovery room beds. She arrived at Alicia Martin's station and looked down on the sleeping woman. Gently she reached down and turned off the sleep inducer generator. Within moments Alicia came to life, her eyes open but just slits now from the migration of swelling.

"Do you know your name?"

At first there was no reply, then her hands slowly ascended to her head and explored the bandages. A look of fear started to overtake her expression. Pam quickly consoled her, "You're just fine, they'll be off in no time. My name is Pam, I met you yesterday in the Orion Room. Do you remember?"

Alicia finally spoke, but very softly. "What happened, I was about to board..."

"And boom the lights went out. You were right next to a terrible explosion. We all think it's a miracle you weren't killed."

Alicia closed her eyes and took a few deep breaths. Finally she said, "My name is Alicia, and you're Pamela."

Pam smiled and made an entry in her file. "You need to sleep more to regain your strength. Besides, if you're asleep you won't feel that headache I'm sure is now getting your attention."

Alicia was now looking right at Pam, "My God, was anyone killed?"

"No, and I have to make sure it stays that way. So, I'm going to return you to a deep sleep. We'll wake you tonight for a few follow-up tests, and perhaps security has a few questions for you." With that she clicked on the generator and watched as the woman drifted back to sleep. She remained by her bed a moment just staring down. Confusion clouded her thinking within the compassion she felt. Why did she feel threatened by her? She shook her head to clear her thoughts as she headed to the next bed.

Across the room Max entered from the adjoining lab. He questioned one of the technicians, then walked over to Pam. She watched him approach, "What's the concerned look for?"

"Have you heard from Ray yet? He should have checked in by now?"

"He needed a good rest, I'm sure he's still in his room. Have you called him?"

"Yes, but no reply, not even his message center is on."

"Well, he could be in the sleep chamber, it's pretty hard to hear anything in there."

"Oh is it?" Max smirked.

"Stop it, Max, this is no time to be joking around."

"I'm sorry, it's just that I don't want to see you get hurt."

Pam sighed, "Do you really think I have something to be jealous of with her? I just spoke with her a few minutes ago. She has a powerful aura about her. I don't know whether to keep feeling sorry for her or keep her sleep generator on indefinitely."

"She obviously had to be a strong woman to make it to pilot status. At least you can empathize with Ray a little better now. Did you learn anything talking to her?"

Pam led him back to her bedside, "So far, what you see is all any of us knows right now."

"Well, the investigation team the chairman set up this afternoon will undoubtedly be digging into all the crew's files. As a matter of fact, anyone remotely connected with the shuttles will probably be investigated."

Pam was insulted. "That includes us, most likely! Oh Max, do you really think that's necessary?"

"Nobody knows what to think, we're all grasping at straws. It's just a place for them to start, nothing more."

"I wish this were all just a nightmare. Everything was going so well in my life till yesterday."

Max led her away from Alicia and spoke quietly again, "Pam, why don't we talk later at dinner. Right now, the clinic needs you focused, and I need to get to the communications room. Somehow I must contact Dr. Ansarid on earth. That should be the easy part. The hard part will be getting him back up here to help us with the fuel experiments."

"OK., I'll be by your suite at 7pm. I should be finished by then. And Max, please check the biomonitors in Ray's room when you head to communications."

"Certainly! And please, stay positive. You look so different when you don't smile."

CHAPTER FIVE

A soft, synthetic voice gently prodded Ray from his sleep. "It is now 8:00 p.m., the antigravity field will cease in 60 seconds. Please prepare to leave the chamber or reset the sleep period."

He slowly opened his eyes and peered at the speaker as it began to repeat the message. He realized his headache had greatly subsided, and he could feel a renewed strength in his body. When he pressed the exit sensor, the clear dome swung open. He gave a slight shove and slid effortlessly from the chamber.

After a few minutes in the shower, he called the clinic. A tech appeared on the view screen. Ray's eyes searched behind the man's image on the screen. "Are you looking for someone, Dr. Phillips?"

"Yes, Jerry, is Pam or Max still down there?"

"No Sir, haven't seen either one for several hours. Miss Aquain did leave a message for you, however."

"Oh, can you play it for me?"

"One moment." The man disappeared from the field, revealing a row of beds in the clinic. Ray noticed Alicia's station and fixed his attention on it. His stare was quickly interrupted by Pam's recording. "Hi, hope you slept well. I'm going to dinner with Max. Everyone is still stable down here. You probably will want to wake Alicia Martin for a neurosensory scan, but her cortical functions all seem intact. We'll see you first thing tomorrow. Bye."

Jerry reappeared on the screen, "Anything else I can do for you, doc?"

Ray pursed his lips in contemplation for a moment, then said, "No, that will be all, thank you." As the screen went black he sat down rubbing his forehead. He felt a sense of relief that Max was looking after Pam tonight. He mentally replayed the image of Alicia's bed. What is so compelling about that woman that he can't stop thinking about her?

He took a deep breath and pushed up from the chair. The one window in his room was currently facing deep space. He peered through at the enticing vacuous blackness. As he scanned the sprinkling of stars, he pondered philo-sophically to himself. "Whoever you are that we worship, are you still watching over the humans? If not, does anyone out there care how this story turns out? ....We could use a little help right now."

After humbling himself for several minutes, he turned away and headed for the door. Somehow the sluggish panels didn't annoy him this time, but he passed a technician in the hall and still had to say something. "Hey you, I don't suppose you have some time to look at my door, it's been very erratic lately."

The lanky man stopped and glanced at his workpad, "I've already got a repair order for a door, suite 312B, would that be..."

"Yes, that's mine! How wonderful! Say, aren't you working kind of late?"

"We have to! A lot of the regular crew are busy on the shuttle bay, so this is the only way we'll meet our deadlines. Besides, someone must be taking care of you."

"How's that?"

"Look's like your repair order had been prioritized by someone with clout in the operations committee. Otherwise, this wouldn't have been looked at for another week."

Ray was puzzled, but mildly pleased, "I guess I shouldn't complain then. But, an improperly working door can be a health hazard."

"Yes sir, I imagine it could. We'll have it working in no time."

The two men parted down opposite ends of the hall. Once in the ele-vator, Ray noticed the same cologne he detected in his room the day before. The only problem was there were ten other people in the elevator with him! He looked around suspiciously, but in a moment the doors opened at the main level and everyone was gone before he had observed them enough.

He stood there motionless as new riders filed in. His mind froze, unsure what to do with the clue. The tone of the doors closing jabbed him back to reality, and he thrust his arm out to stop them closing. As he squeezed out he cautiously looked in all directions for anything out of the ordinary. He headed slowly to the clinic but compulsively stopped at the floral stand outside its en-trance. It was closed, but he helped himself to a few roses and left a quick note.

The clinic was very quiet; only two night staff were on duty. They were busy in their cubicles filling out reports. The only real light came from the array of gadgets surrounding the bed stations. He went immediately to Alicia's bed and turned off the sleep generator. Soon she was looking up at Ray and forced a feeble smile. Her eyes were less swollen and poked through enough to twinkle in the dim light. She drew a deep sigh and closed them again.

Ray placed the flowers by her bed and left to fetch a piece of equipment. Minutes later he had several wires sticking to the woman's head, chest and hands. "Alicia, you need to be awake when I run this test. Do you hear me?"

She reopened her eyes and swallowed dryly, "I remember you. You're the nice man who helped us at the restaurant yesterday."

"Here, sip this. It sounds as though you're a little dehydrated yet. Do you remember anything before the blast?" He adjusted the instruments as she thought. She said nothing, but his instrument indicated a rapid increase in her pain level. He reached for the roses and placed them next to her. "These are for you. A pretty woman needs a little color about her in times like this. Besides, they match your face now." He tried his best smile with his attempt at humor.

She lifted the flowers to her nose to enjoy their fragrance. Then, disappointed, withdrew them to her side. "I can't smell the bloody things, what's wrong?"

"You had a frontal hematoma, which probably accounts for the temporary loss of smell."

"I like the word temporary, it's encouraging."

"And I like the way you said 'bloody', where does that come from?"

"It's hard to answer that. I was born in Australia, but there is no Australia any longer, is there?"

Ray looked at his machine again, then turned it off. As he gently removed the electrodes he asked, "Have you any family?"

"I don't know. My husband and little girl were on earth when it happened. I should have been there with them."

Ray's voice saddened as he tried to console her, "There was nothing you could have done anyway."

"I know, but at least we would have been together. This is worse than dying, never knowing what might have been different. ...You can't imagine."

Ray thought a moment, "So there is hope within you that they could still be alive." Alicia turned her head and stared blankly across the row of beds.

"The thought keeps me going. I also concentrate on my job, it has so many responsibilities that it helps me try to forget."

Ray now changed the bandage on her arm and head. He spoke hesitantly, "When I found you lying there in the smoke, my first thought was that you were dead. Your injuries looked a lot worse than they are."

She looked directly at his bandaged head and commented, "I bet they thought the same about you!"

They both laughed but found that emotion painful as they both grabbed at their heads. As Alicia held her temples she said, "It would be a shame for such a handsome man to walk around the rest of his life with a purple egg sticking out of his head."

"Don't you worry about me, I'll be healed a lot faster than you think, and I know many secrets to speed your healing time as well. I'll just have to be creative on getting the necessary ingredients to the clinic. The chef is always a good place to start."

"Really, the kitchen? You really are a versatile one." She stopped smiling and looked thankfully into his eyes. Ray suddenly felt uneasy, not sure why he was chattering this way with a patient.

"I have to check on these other people. I won't put you back under unless you want me to. I think it might help you recall the events of the explosion a lot more clearly if you slept on your own power."

Alicia watched intently as he moved about the room. He returned to her bed with one more thing to add, "You don't want to forget them."

She knew what he meant. Reluctantly she closed her eyes, but flashes of the explosion were coming to life in more detail. It could be a long night.

CHAPTER SIX

On Earth, now two days since the loss of the shuttle at the Majestik, people were going about their daily activities. The constant battle with the weather made it hard for the survivors to care about recent space events, if they knew at all. On most of the lands, the populations were hardened to tragedy. A few new explosions not in their domain barely raised an eyebrow. The explosions did cause great concern amongst the governors, however.

In a large auditorium, a gathering of African delegates met to discuss the monthly business of their province. This meeting's decisions would turn out to be very fateful to the remaining population of Earth.

A nervous Hayden Green was about to give a report to the assembly. He quietly shuffled his papers awaiting his introduction. Two seats to his right sat Otis Payne, the governor, and supreme leader of Africa. Green glanced over at him and saw Payne already casting a suspicious stare his way.

Green's presence on the panel displeased the governor immensely, yet Otis couldn't explain his dislike for the man. Maybe it was simply his mannerisms. Whatever the reason, Otis sat back in his chair to listen to the delegates continue their reports.

The Lemurian island was half a world away, but under geosynchronous orbit of the Majestik. This dictated the governing jurisdiction, which was not Africa. Still, Governor Payne presided over the most populated segment of earth's remaining inhabitants. This made him the most powerful of earth's seven governors. His vote today on whether to continue the shuttle flight ban could be the deciding one. It usually was.

Green began and was probably halfway through the report before Otis finally began to pay real attention to his words. With his fingers folded across his full belly, he listened.

"...and my committee's assessment of all the data so far has failed to provide a link to any political motive for the disasters. Even though we still do not have a sound scientific explanation for the explosions, we feel confident we can rule out sabotage." He cleared his throat and looked up from his papers, "The cost and risk factors of not resuming a flight schedule do not outweigh any apparent risks to the remaining craft. Therefore, we recommend to your honor a vote of resumption of flights effective immediately."

He quickly scurried from the dais as the room remained relatively silent. All eyes were now fixed on Payne as he hoisted himself out of the executive chair. With his six foot frame standing over the rows of men and women, he scanned slowly left to right, making sure he had everyone's attention.

"In the past several days the people of earth and space shared losses of key transport equipment resources. Miraculously no one was killed at either incident. I voted to continue the temporary shuttle ban, which I might add was unanimous. It was a logical vote since the two disasters have such significant consequences to the continued existence of our species. Mr. Green, I'm still bothered by this coincidence, so I cannot in good conscience vote to lift the ban. I'm going against your committee's recommendation with a 'no' vote."

Green sat there holding his notes, but looking down at the table. He tugged at his collar to loosen it as the governor continued. "I want to wait for completion of the security checks at the spacebound hotels and research stations. I have been informed we have about a week before things become subcritical in space, therefore I am prepared to wait that long for this bad feeling in my gut to be squelched with something more palatable."

The room remained respectfully calm as Payne looked briefly to his bodyguards. "Ladies and gentlemen, your input and attention have been appreciated. You will be informed by day's end how the total vote turns out. When we have some decent reports in front of us, we'll call another meeting."

With that, his nod to the crowd signaled adjournment. Turning to the aide at his right side he asked, "What time is the all-governor meeting teleconference?"

The woman replied looking at her watch, "One hour from now. Shall I arrange it from your home?"

"No, I'm staying around here the rest of the day, it's too damn hot to go out. You may go, however."

Payne made his way out of the auditorium, passing Hayden Green at the doors. They glanced briefly at each other as Green forced a timid smile then quickly looked away. The governor headed into his chambers, undoing his now sweat soaked robe with each step. He amused himself thinking of his favorite expression for Green. His smile slowly turned pensive as he arrived at his desk. It was piled high with papers to sift through before the next meeting. He stopped at an envelop marked 'priority' from space station Shepherd. He quickly inserted the attached disc in the monitor. It was a text only message that read, "CONFIDENTIAL: To Governor Payne, from Jaden King. Recent data developments in our climatization procedures defy explanation. We have profound acceleration in ionospheric layering. Attempting to analyze new samples to determine cause. If present readings are correct and remain stable, we are suddenly eight years ahead of schedule! End."

Otis looked up from the screen, a bewildered excitement began to fill him. He swiftly pounded some coordinates into his terminal and sat back staring at the static noise on his screen.

A female operator appeared. "Interspace communications. Your desired party at station Shepherd please."

"I want to speak with Dr. King immediately."

"One moment." The screen went fuzzy again. When it flickered back into focus it displayed a studiously bearded man staring back.

"Otis, how are you, my fat friend?! I assume you got my message?"

"Fat, I'll have you know I'm down to 275 pounds this year! But yes, I hope you're the one who sent it, rather than some hacker."

King rather calmly replied, "Oh yes, it's real. There must be some quantum force we overlooked, perhaps in the planet's changing geophysical spectrum. It's going to take some time to put a finger on it, but we do know our readings are correct. Evidently, the Martian atmosphere will be life-compatible in less than two months!"

Otis could hardly contain his excitement as he stood up and leaned into the monitor, "Jaden, listen to me. Have you reported this to anyone else?"

"No sir. You know this station only reports to your office."

"Good. I want this to stay confidential until I say otherwise. Report to me every 24 hours. Good work!" He turned off the screen and sat back so excitedly into his chair it rolled back about two feet. This was something the other governors should be told, but he began to debate whether this was the right time. It was tempting to rub it in some of their noses, since he cast the deciding vote to restart the Mars terraforming project after the events. His worry over the explosions made the timing bad for such an announcement. Still, the excitement of this information caused him to spring from his chair and march over to his bar. He poured himself a drink to celebrate and calm his elation. Just as he raised the glass to his lips, a knock at the door stopped him.

He lowered the glass to his belly, "Come in."

A tall man quickly entered. He was one of Payne's top council delegates. The man started out apologetically, "Sir, I'm sorry I missed the meeting, but my ride was late. Said he had a flat tire on the way to pick me up."

"I was wondering where the hell you were." He began to sip at his drink. "You didn't miss much though. I'll be voting soon, and it'll be a vote to continue the flight suspensions."

The man breathed a sigh of relief as he sank into one of the chairs facing the desk. "Good, I was worried Green's committee would convince you otherwise. I have only two reports in from space. The rest should be in over the next few days."

Otis laughed as he sat back down, "Trust Green, you've got to be kidding!" He stopped his chuckle and became serious, "Is the Majestik report one of the two you have?'

"No, the big hotels are trudging through the bureaucracy. It must be like looking for the proverbial needle in the haystack."

Otis gestured his drink at the man and asked, "Care for one?"

"No, please, too early for me. Besides, I've got too much on my mind to lose my momentum right now."

"Yes, I know the feeling. For me, this keeps my momentum." He finished with one last quick gulp and had to clear his throat. "I want you to act as a clearinghouse for all the security reports, not just our sector. Find me something in those profiles, anything! Cross check ages, birthplaces, religions, job assignments, favorite foods, get the picture?"

"Our computers could never do all that in time, I need faster machines."

Payne thought a second, "The Majestik has a marvelous set-up. They could help you!"

"Begging your pardon, sir, but as I said, they aren't even through with their own studies, let alone sparing time for us."

He bellowed back belligerently, "They can do both, there's some sharp people up there. Only thing is I'll have to get that crab chairman of theirs to assign the extra manpower. So, just get started, it seems it's time for my meeting. I have a favor coming from Governor Brickman; he can persuade help our way."

As the delegate grabbed the doorknob, he turned, "What do you think we're up against?"

"If you asked me that one hour ago, I would have been fairly sure. Now, I can only guess."

The man looked puzzled, but accepted the answer. He closed the door quietly.

Otis returned to his viewscreen and awaited the start of the teleconference. Soon, everyone was on and Payne promptly started the meeting. As he expected, it was not unanimous this time, but at least he didn't have to be a tiebreaker vote. As other business was quickly dispensed with, Otis endured not mentioning the Shepherd memo. Before long, he adjourned the group and asked the Lemurian governor to stay on the line.

Once the others were locked out of the connection, he asked the perplexed man waiting patiently half a world away, "Jim, I wanted you to stay on line because I need a favor. I have some ideas I need to pursue concerning the security profiling coming in from space. And, I can't do it in time with my own computers. I want to borrow time from the Majestik, can you make it easy for me?"

"That sounds reasonable. Of course, now that we've decided to keep the shuttles grounded, you can't send someone up there." He quickly thought of an alternative, "How about a laser data link? Fast and secure."

"I agree, this has to remain secure."

"Otis, are you as worried as I am?"

"It shows, huh?"

"I didn't want to mention this in front of the others, but our radio observatory has been picking up bizarre signals coming from Mars. We can't make any sense of it, however."

Otis leaned forward excitedly and asked, "Have you tried to contact anyone out there?"

"No, you know I have no authority to do that. Why do you ask?"

"I can't tell you right now, but I assure you, you'll be the first to hear when I know more."

"I'll hold you to that. Stay in touch."

Payne got up to pour himself another drink. He settled on his couch and propped his feet up to enjoy the liquor. His mind wandered to the Martian planet, trying to visualize the sight of humans living there, existing in a new way; in peace and happiness. He shut his eyes and forced himself to relax while trying to still remember the family he once had. Soon, he was napping, his face weathered strong by leadership, but lamenting the deep emptiness inside.

CHAPTER SEVEN

Max sat near Pam in the main computer operations room, each expertly programming information on the old fuel experiments. Suddenly, both their screens went blank then immediately refocused to clarity displaying the glum face of an earthbound announcer. They watched silently as the woman proclaimed the recent decision to extend shuttle flight suspensions. Then, as quickly as she interrupted their work, their screens jumped back to their operations.

They both looked at each other, obvious frustration engraved on their faces. Pam protested as she immediately went back to her touchscreen, "Just great! Who do they think they're protecting keeping us trapped here like rats!"

"Rats, I wouldn't go that far, I still feel pretty human."

She forced a smile as Max added, "Just imagine how the other stations and hotels feel. Most of their people probably think this is strictly a Lemurian problem. They want their lives to return to some sort of normalcy as badly as we do."

"You call this normal? This whole hotel is a joke! Nobody here knows what the hell they're doing!" She started to shove her chair back to storm out of the room when the doors swung open from the hall. Ray Phillips and the chairman walked in side by side.

Ray looked calmingly at Pam as she lowered herself back in the chair. "Pam, Max, how have things been going here so far?"

Max finally looked up at the men as he watched Pam try to ignore them, "They'd be a whole lot easier if we could track down Dr. Ansarid."

Pam snapped boldly, "That's another thing, why hasn't anybody seen this guy since he hit AlphaSeven? He should be doing most of this, it's his damn experiment!"

The chairman responded to her quietly, "Young lady, it sounds as if you don't like this job?"

Ray quickly interjected before she could speak, "Mr. Parker, it doesn't surprise me about Dr. Ansarid's elusiveness; he tended to be a bit frustrating to work around when he was up here. Ms. Aquain is just a bit overworked, that's all. Perhaps your announcement might help ease the tensions."

"Thank you Ray. I've been contacted by Governor Brickman earlier. He wants us to give unique technical aid to the special investigation being conducted by the African team. So, as of now, we are putting the fuel work on hold again. You're to link up by a secure laser channel to these coordinates." He handed Max a piece of scrap paper with multiple numbers and symbols scribbled on it. He added, "Shuttle flights will have to automatically by law resume in no more than seven days. I'm sure the team down there will keep you busy, but perhaps it will be more interesting work."

Ray knew what the chairman was going to tell his team, but he now pondered aloud, "Why the sudden change in priorities? I thought you were in charge up here on what we research?"

The short man remained silent as he walked slowly back toward the door, never looking up from the floor. He stopped and grumbled just loud enough for them to hear over the noise of the machines, "Politics, nothing but politics!" He then quickened his pace as he left the room.

The three of them looked at each other with surprise and yet relief. Ray commented, "Do you think he's getting a little soft in his years?"

Max leaned back and said as he stretched, "Not a chance, it's not allowed as part of the requirements to be chairman."

Ray remained cheery and looked closely at the graph on Pam's screen, "Say Pam, this looks incredible! Could the fuel formula really be that good?"

She stood up and finally stretched, "In theory, yes. This particular projection is basically where you all left off. It's definitely ready to be bench-tested." She and Max glanced at each other like proud parents showing off their creation.

Ray clapped his hands together and beamed, "OK, let's do some recipe testing! So, next step is to transfer this data to our materials lab, and I'll get to work on compounding. We can proceed without Ansarid."

Pam now stood inches from Ray and asked innocently, "There's a new play opening at the theater, can you come with me?"

Ray was caught off guard by her question. "Uh, I don't think we have time right now for fun things like that. I was planning to be in the lab most of the evening running the fuel tests."

She persisted, "Oh come on, you just heard the man telling us to stop the fuel stuff. Start it tomorrow if you insist, but right now we need to relax." She coaxed him to the door by the hand. He looked at Max for help. He was forcing himself to be busy at his terminal as he offered, "I just opened the channel to Africa, but it's apparently bedtime for them now, so essentially we're done here for now."

Ray tried one more excuse, "Well, I suppose I could, but I'll have to make rounds first at the clinic, maybe by then my head will feel a little better. It has..."

"Ray, you're trying to avoid me now, why?" She turned her back to him in the doorway and folded her arms defensively. Ray looked at the floor a moment contemplatively, then started stroking her long braided hair soothingly. He remained quiet almost a minute before saying, "This isn't the place to go into a long discussion about our relationship. It's been terribly confusing for me lately, you'll have to be patient."

She remained still, her lip starting to quiver. He let go of her hair and out of frustration turned to Max, who still tried to be disinterested at his computer. "Talk to her, please! I don't know what else to say right now." Ray left the room and headed for the clinic.

Max obligingly sat her down next to him and patted her thigh. "He's being honest with you at least. Give him some time. You know concussions can affect personalities, maybe that's what's going on. Things will work out." He took a deep breath and added, "Say, I'd sure like to see that play, would you consider taking another friend tonight instead?"

She looked at him as he coerced her to smile and said, "Why not?"

Max's big mustache broadened with a huge grin. "Great, let's shut this link down and get out of here."

Pam remained silent as she watched him save the coordinates, then shred the chairman's note. A tear rolled down her cheek and she turned her head to dab it off with her sleeve, not wanting Max to see it. She looked back to his screen and read aloud, "MEGSIX, is that their computer name or their security system?"

"I assume it's their security program, it displayed the same way when I first linked in." He finished a few more entries and the screen returned to the Majestik's symbol. "There, that should do it."

Pam got up stoically, a determined look on her face. She gestured him from his chair, "Come on, the world goes on, they're not going to hold the curtain just for us, you know."

He had to push to follow her rapid steps, yet finding it hard to resist gazing at her backside as she moved powerfully yet sensually into the corridor. He caught up with her and said, nearly fumbling for words, "I have to go by my room first, change these clothes. Shall I meet you outside the theater in half an hour?"

"That's fine. Max, did you remember to power down the computers?"

"Oh shit!" He thought a few seconds then added, "They're programmed to do that on their own if no one's been using them for two hours. Besides, no one else is going there tonight, and at least the door's locked."

"OK, be lazy, I'll see you soon."

The two of them separated at the elevator as he hurried down the hall. Back in the darkened computer room, the blue glow of the displays light the room. Suddenly the computer pattern changed back to the MEGSIX logo.

Several sentences typed themselves across the query line. The screen color turned to red as a reply flashed back: 'Welcome to MEGSIX D.O.V.E. How can I help you?'

In seconds the unit turned itself off, leaving the room pitch black.

CHAPTER EIGHT

Most of the injured had been discharged from the Majestik's clinic even though it had only been three days earlier when they were hastily packed in. Alicia Martin remained, relaxing on a reclining chair in the clinic's atrium. The healing beams of the sun totally enveloped her, warming her to the point of perspiration. Ray pulled up a chair next to her, a cool tea in his hand.

"Care for something cold?"

She looked at him and smiled, "No thank you, the IV they gave me earlier is still doing its job."

"Your wounds have mended beautifully. Today I will start some manipulative therapy on your neck area, and soon you'll be able to see a plastic surgeon in one of the other hotels."

Alicia replied softly, nothing like her powerful self Ray remembered from their first meeting. "You've done so much for me, how am I ever going to repay you and everyone here at the clinic?"

"Repay? Last time I checked socialized medicine was alive and well! Just consider this a worker's compensation issue if you ever get a bill."

She smiled and replied with a little more energy in her voice, "You know what I mean silly."

Ray felt uneasy as she gazed thoughtfully at him. He looked away out the window, suddenly self conscious. Alicia asked cautiously, "Do you have a wife, I don't see a ring?"

He wanted to say his answer the right way, but let it just come out, "No, never married. Always too busy with work I guess. Long hours make it hard on relationships."

"Your assistant Pam is quite beautiful."

He knew what she was getting at and tried to look at her honestly. "Yes, she is. We date on occasion. ...No, that's a lie, we sleep together and call it dating." He relaxed back into his chair, "I never really thought about asking

Pam to... you know, marry. She's always been there for me since she came aboard last year. We share a lot of the same interests and work hours."

Alicia discerningly replied, "Sounds like a good friendship, very convenient. But you don't love her, do you?"

Ray now felt embarrassed by the subject, but compelled to answer. She continued to look deeply at him, her stare somehow now easing his defenses. "I don't know if I even know what love is. I've always been so calculating and mechanical, love seems like a subject I failed to sign up for in school."

Alicia reached over and touched his hand, conveying an understanding that she knew he needed. "I think your lives have been full of love."

He looked perplexed by the comment, but before he could ask, Jerry, the lab assistant, interrupted. "Dr. Phillips, they want you down at the computer operations room."

"Thanks Jerry, tell them I'm on my way." He turned to Alicia as he stood, "It was nice talking with you this morning. I should be back by afternoon. Please continue to just rest, but don't overheat in the sun."

She had to ask before he left, "Ray, have they discovered any clues yet?"

"I'm not sure. Say, that reminds me. Someone is due to talk with you today about the explosion. I told the team your full memory should be nearly recoverable by now."

Alicia sighed, "I'll do my best, but I don't know what help I can be."

"Just tell them everything that comes to mind, you never know what might be relevant. If that doesn't satisfy them, fall back on rank and serial number!"

*　　*　　*

Ray breezed through the computer room doors. There were six people stationed about the room. He saw Max and headed over to him.

"How's it going? Did you need me?"

Max finished an entry and then leaned back. "Not really. Nothing exciting about personal files, makes me think fuel research wasn't so bad after all. This delegate on Africa is a go-getter, however. I can see why they needed our computers. Their security program MEGSIX makes it way too slow to mine the databases."

Ray's interest was perked, "What is he looking for with all this?"

Max replied coldly, "A conspiracy." He then looked up at Ray and asked, "Why don't you sit down, now that you're here. I want to show you something I discovered earlier, but don't know what to make of it." He continued once Ray was next to him, "I believe someone else is tapping into our data link with MEGSIX."

Ray looked puzzled as he asked, "How can you tell?"

"Well, last night after you left, Pam decided to go to the play with me instead. Oh, by the way, she's at the lab now, she said to send you over when you arrived." Ray interrupted, "You two have a good time?"

He thought a moment, "Yes we did, and I was a perfect gentleman the whole evening!"

Ray smiled quietly, then asked as he rubbed his chin, "So... you didn't call me to come down here just now did you?"

Max looked puzzled, "No, should I have?"

"No, just curious. So you were saying about the link..."

"Yes, yes. We were in a hurry to leave here last night and I forgot to shut down the system fully. Now that's no big deal, since they shut down after two hours dead time." He continued as he loaded a page on the monitor, "When you bring the system back on after an auto shutdown, the programs are supposed to show the last work or screen display. And this is what I was wondering about. Look at this."

Ray looked intently at the word D.O.V.E. embedded in red on the screen. "What does that mean? Is that someone or some group?"

"I've already run a check, but I can't find it recorded anywhere."

Ray turned to leave and hurriedly ordered Max, "No one is to know of this except your man in Africa. Maybe he has some answers. I've got to get to the lab and see what Pam is doing with the fuel. Don't want any explosions."

Max watched him leave and shook his head with disbelief.

As Ray made his way through the hotel for the laboratory, a barrage of images occupied his thoughts. He of course worried about Pam, but the piles of work on his desk got plenty of thought as well. The closer he got to the lab, the conversation with Alicia started to replay. By the time he reached the special elevator to the lab, he realized he was nearly jogging.

Once the chamber stopped at the top level he took a deep breath to calm his pulse as the door opened. He stepped out into a darkened lab. Why were the lights out? He immediately got a little panicky thinking of his room experience earlier in the week. He took one step and asked, "Pam?"

There was no response. The glassoptic roof let in the little ambient light the stars gave off. The light sensor refused to illuminate but one group of lights near the storage bins. He tried but couldn't see anyone in the quiet lab with the available light. Then he noticed a small desk light on in his personal office. Now, concern over Pam's safety overwhelmed him and he rushed to that door. It was still locked, so he quickly pulled his passcard out and scanned it.

Once the door opened he moved cautiously in a few steps, "Is anyone here? Pam?"

"Behind you."

He spun to see her on his couch that was in the shadows from the desk lamp. She was lying seductively on her side, completely naked. "Hello Ray, I thought you'd never come to work, it's been getting a bit chilly in here."

He now stood next to her looking down, "Pam, it's you! And you're naked."

She sat up and sensually stroked her hair behind her shoulders, uncovering her breasts as the dim light now highlighted every detail. "Of course it's me, were you expecting someone else?"

"Why uh, no. It's just that I didn't expect to find the lab deserted now, and I certainly didn't expect to find you this way!"

"You're an excellent diagnostician, doctor. You see, I discovered this worrisome blemish on my body. It needs a proper exam. It's in a place that normally requires the patient to disrobe to examine it accurately."

She stood up slowly while gliding her hands up the sides of his body. Then she extended her chin back enticing him to be drawn near her neck. He looked excitedly back into the lab, "Honey, this is not a good idea, someone could come in."

"Relax, I told the other assistants the lab was closed till this evening due to a gas leak. And you know how busy everyone else is, either at the clinic or the operations room." She tightened her grip on his sides and asked tantalizingly, "Wouldn't it be exciting to do it here in the lab, Ray?"

By now all he could do was stare up and down her body, his breathing quickened in a way he hadn't felt in a long time. He fumbled for words, trying one last feeble attempt to stop her, "I've got some concerning news from our security work, I should follow up on that quickly."

She persisted unfazed, "Don't you want to get wild when I want you this way?" She drew herself closer, her fingers discretely undoing his shirt. She eased her breasts against his bare chest and looked into his eyes with a determined naughty giggle.

By now, his willpower was disappearing with each breath. She took his arms and placed them around her. He gazed deeply at her as he slowly lowered his hands to her firm cheeks. She smiled dreamlike as he drew her in tightly. He kissed her gently on the forehead, then her nose.

"There now, isn't this going to be much more fun than those boring experiments? I'll make sure we get everything done today we have to, but right now, you're mine, Ray Phillips."

He guided her down to the couch, their lips locked in a deep passionate kiss. They fought the soft cushions as she removed the rest of his clothes. He had one more silly comment to make, feeling quite youthful, "This gives new meaning to health research here at the Majestik!"

Pam giggled some more as she settled into the cushion, "Just shut up, Ray, and make love to me."

The near-dark outer lab continued to let the starlight in, but the universe seemed like a far away entity to the two bodies embraced in the office next door. Their moans seemed boldly out of place in such a hardened room of chemicals and machines. Eventually, the room was quiet once more.

CHAPTER NINE

Jaden King preened his long gray hair back as he squinted at the display of tiny numbers dancing across his computer. He sat back perplexed once again, then stared out at the Martian planet above him. The image through the observatory bubble was kaleidoscopic, as atmospheric gasses collided and blended in a cosmic show unlike any he had ever witnessed. He nearly shouted at his faceless adversary, "Why is this happening, dammit?!"

A voice from below startled him. "Anyone up there?"

Jaden turned from the planet and yelled back through the stair conduit, "Me, Pete."

His coworker continued on an intercom, "I've been looking for you. You won't believe this new data that just came in!"

King started to climb down the narrow hatchway from his deck, "I'm pulling my hair out trying to keep up with what I'm recording and now you have more for me?" He jumped down the last few steps and cast a weary eye at his excited associate.

The man waved a portable data screen, "Jaden, get this, inner O2 and O3 ratios have just balanced. Also, we're at 75% saturation in the tropospheric layer! Do you know what this means!"

"Oh yes, it means I'll have to come up with some reason for it all when I contact Earth with my report tonight. I'll just act like a brilliant scientist, stay calm, and pretend this is all quite natural."

It was obvious his friend didn't feel the same frustration, so Jaden patted him on the shoulder as he led him to the main deck. "I'm sorry I can't be as excited as you, Pete, but it's my job to worry when things like this happen."

"Hey, that's the cosmos for you, just like a woman sometimes!" The man then walked over to a workstation wearing a big smile, anxious to get back to his measurements.

King stood there a moment, then peered back up through a porthole at the now mysterious red planet, that wasn't so red anymore, "Whatever, or whoever is doing this to you...don't stop now. You've gone too far already, so don't stop now." He dropped his head back down and focused on a communication monitor. A single touch and the screen jumped to life with a fuzzy, erratic picture. A moment later the distorted image of a woman wearing a helmeted spacesuit appeared. "Lensa, how is everybody feeling down there?"

"Sir, I have to tell you we're all a bit edgy, maybe it's just the strong electrical fields sweeping over us constantly. It has our hair standing up, and that's hard to feel wearing these helmets!"

Jaden smiled but remained serious, "Do you think they're down there?"

She knew what he meant, "I almost wish they were, it might help explain."

"Well, everything still looks relatively safe from up here. Listen, don't let anything slip by your analyzers, no matter how insignificant, it all helps. Check back in with me in eight hours. Remember, you all are part of one of the most profound astronomical events ever witnessed by humans."

"Yes sir, we'll try to keep that in mind. Over."

Jaden drew his lip in tight as he switched off the screen. He yearned to be down there with his people, but he knew he was more help in the orbit station. He tucked in his shirt, trying to feel organized, and strode to Pete's station.

*   *   *

Ray lay on his back, eyes closed, motionless. Moonlight traced the flowing lines of his and Pam's bodies onto the floor below them. Their minds drifted yet remained aware, each wanted to say something, but words continued to escape them. Ray grew uneasy by the long silence and spoke first. "That was incredible, I felt like I was a teenager again."

Pam immediately added, "See what being bad can do for a love life."

Minutes more elapsed, an eternity in the darkness for Ray; he had to continue, "So why don't I feel like a kid in love right now?"

She didn't want to say anything, but she too felt what he was talking about. "Something is different, isn't it?"

Ray got a sick feeling in his stomach, yet he knew he had to continue to explore his feelings. "Pam, don't you think we're just too convenient for each other?"

"Convenient?" She sat up and leaned forward, elbows on her knees, her voice now tight with emotion. "I always wanted us to become something special, more than just convenience. You never got that message Ray, no matter how hard I tried."

"It has to be more than physical, and you get an A for trying in that part. It's me, it has to be. I think I'm afraid to love someone for fear of having to lose them in this knife's-edge existence where we're all trapped. I've seen so much grief when people lose the ones they love, I ...I don't think I can bear to go through that. I'm not built for that."

She turned to look back down on him, "Wow, I think I actually hear emotion coming out of your mouth. So, you can't express love to me because you're afraid of losing me?"

He thought about that a minute, then said, "No, I think I'm saying that true love has to happen without trying. It should be like a nuclear reaction, something so powerful and uncontrollable that it goes beyond logic and fear." He thought a moment about what he said, then quickly added, "Well, that may not be a great metaphor, but what do you expect from a scientist?"

She smiled knowingly at him as she stood up and started to dress. "I don't know if I'll stop trying to be convenient for you, but I am beginning to understand why you're so different lately. It's Alicia Martin isn't it?"

"There's nothing between us, if that's what you mean, I still hardly know her. No, she just somehow makes me stop and think about things, to feel again. I kind of like listening to my feelings, and they seem so illogical now." He was staring at her as she slipped her uniform up over her hips. "Your body will always get any man excited, part of me doesn't want to stop doing this kind of thing."

"Well don't stop. Meanwhile, until you're ready again, you can just torture yourself imaging me through my clothes every day when we work." As she closed the final flap near her neck, she turned on the room's lights. He grabbed a cushion and covered himself, "Hey, no fair! A man gets a little shy in moments like this."

She tossed his pants to him and quipped with a fresh cheerful innocence, "You know Ray, there's this guy with a big mustache that seems to be paying an awful lot of attention to me lately!"

"Ol' Max really does care for you, he just has a hard time expressing it, like me I guess." He continued as she stood, arms folded, watching him get dressed. "It's probably harder for him to have a relationship again since he lost his wife. I'm glad I don't have to carry that burden around with me."

"What makes you think losing his wife makes it hard for him to express emotion? I think he expresses himself quite deeply."

"Max? Really? Humph."

By now he was dressed and Pam turned to leave, saying one last comment while eyeing some of the lab equipment. "I think I'll go back to my room first, freshen up a bit, then I'll be right back like I promised to help with the day's experiments." Once at the elevator she added, "I'll check in on Max at the computer operations before I come back, just in case he needs me down there for something *more* important."

"That a girl, go with the flow!" He stood there watching her disappear into the elevator. He buttoned one last cuff, straightened the couch cushions, then went into the lab. As he busied himself with one of the food experiments, he noticed he was whistling. Surprised, he stopped and looked blankly ahead.

Deep inside him, for the first time in his life, he felt sure about something that involved his emotions. He knew what he wanted.

He finished bringing the lab to life. After he was satisfied everything was warmed up and ready, he called Max at operations.

"Max, anything yet on D.O.V.E.?"

Max peered back intently, "Say, you look like you just woke up."

Ray smiled back in his prudent grin, "In a way, you might say that, yes! But anyhow, what about our alleged hacker?"

"It has to be somebody from earth, nothing in space connects with it."

Ray glared back at him rubbing his chin in thought, "Well, then your man on Africa is all we've got left. He can help you go through all earth-to-space records from yesterday to see where the breach came from."

Max leaned in close to the screen, his voice drained, "First, I'm going to get some chow. Second, in case you forgot, you're supposed to be helping us here, not doing experiments!"

Ray looked slightly indignant by the response and stuttered back, "Pam found a gas leak here in the lab, I helped her find it. It could have been disastrous."

"I'll bet. So, no one got hurt I assume by the ordeal?"

"I don't think so. By the way, Pam will be stopping by shortly to check on your progress. So, why don't you wait for her, and when she gets there, take her to eat with you, my treat!"

"Well, I'd much rather work with her than you, she's prettier than you."

"She thinks you're not so bad yourself, must be that colorful mustache! Anyway, I really need to stay here, so keep her with you as long as you need the rest of the day. Bye."

Max immediately accessed the security trackers and found Pam's location. He saw her ID marker traveling down the corridor just outside the door. He closed the screen, spun his chair to the doorway and placed his hands behind his head as he leaned back awaiting her arrival.

One hour later, Ray finished final preparations on the day's fuel tests. As he reviewed the graphs one last time, he couldn't help but think of Dr. Ansarid. His tour in space was generally uneventful, he did just what was required of him, nothing more, nothing less. That always frustrated Ray, as he felt incredible potential in the man, but never could coax it out of him. Ansarid always preferred to be by himself while on a project. Ray now thought aloud, "Damn this fuel looks good. How could we have let it slip through the cracks? Why didn't I see these reports before?"

He turned, startled, as the lab doors sprung open. It was Pam, accompanied by another woman. He asked surprised, "Back so soon?"

"What did you expect, we have work to do!"

Ray looked at the other woman, "I see you brought some help, I don't think we've met before."

Pam chided him, "I'm surprised you don't remember. Sarah helped Dr. Ansarid occasionally, although that was before I arrived. She stayed on here for another tour, but on the other side of the hotel. I found her name when we initiated our search for Rashad, figured she might help speed things along."

Ray smiled and nodded his head, feigning remembrance, then cleared his throat, "Nice to see you again, Sarah. So why don't I get you busy right away with that magnatron chamber. Set it up to the screen parameters and we'll run today's burn in there." He then led Pam a few feet toward the door as the other woman busied herself. "Listen, I certainly appreciate your coming back to help, but did you get to check on Max yet?"

She smiled modestly, "Oh yeah, he was very insistent I eat with him today and then help him finish a backlog of entries he was working on."

"And...so..."

"And so I took one look at his screen, saw that he was basically done, and told him he was not very clever."

"Really, what did he say?"

"He said I was not very clever either by creating a fake lab emergency. So, in the name of compromise we agreed on lunch tomorrow, on your nickel of course." She smiled as she walked over to Sarah, getting one last comment, "Honestly Ray, sometimes you act more like a high school troublemaker than a world class scientist."

He stood there a second, thinking about the comment, "Well, that's good, I think. I'm making progress!"

CHAPTER TEN

Alicia stared back across the conference table at the two men and one woman. Three hours of questioning had tired her physically and emotionally. Frustrated, she leaned forward and demanded, "Look, you've asked me the same things over and over again, do we need to go on much longer?"

The committeewoman looked over at her two assistants, then said stiffly, "I believe that's all I can think of, gentlemen, do either of you have any other questions?"

One of the men stood up and stretched, "I'm satisfied." The other shuffled his papers, looking for minutia in his scribbled notes, then replied, "Just one more from me. That man you described, the nervous one with the brief-case, what part of the ship was he seated in?"

Alicia rubbed her forehead while she thought, "I don't know, I never left the cockpit once the last passenger came through the door. Maybe..., maybe if I recognized his face in the photopass records, you could determine his seat number." She stood up, albeit slowly, looking eye to eye with the man still standing. "Do you think he planted the explosives?"

He seemed to ignore the question as he commented to his aides, "One of you accompany Captain Martin to the computer records room so she can look at the Torrus' passenger manifest." He looked back respectfully at Alicia, "We can't thank you enough for your cooperation. We may need to talk with you again, but I know this has been difficult for you." He extended his hand, and she reciprocated with an attempt at her once firm grip. The other two got up to leave, each remaining very businesslike. She followed them to the doorway.

Once in the hall, an armed guard joined them as they proceeded to the records room. Alicia asked the committeeman, who led the way, "Is the gun really necessary? I almost feel like the accused here!"

He turned to her, never losing stride, "Captain, this is for your protection, not ours."

*　　*　　*

As Alicia entered the small records room, a man sitting at one of the terminals looked up and burst into a big smile. She immediately exclaimed, "Tim, I haven't seen you since the day we arrived here! I see they're putting you through the same torture as me."

He remained seated as she approached, "Yeah, I think it's a waste of time, I don't even know what I'm supposed to be looking for any more."

She sat next to him in the only other chair in the room, then leaned back and sighed, pulling her hair behind her ears. "How long have you been in this awful little room?"

"This is my second day, I'm going over all the system maintenance records for the Torrus." He paused a moment as he looked at her injuries. "Say, you must be a quick healer, I expected you to look a whole lot more banged up. That shaved area on your head really adds to your character."

She glared back at him unamused and somewhat baffled. His grin faded as he realized his attempt at humor was flopping. She rotated her chair to the terminal where the committeeman had logged in the manifest for her. After a brief silence scanning the faces, she asked softly, "How come you didn't visit me at the clinic?"

He defended himself quickly, "Shit, I didn't even know you were injured till yesterday, and that was when they came for me to start all this stuff! I wanted to come by, but I wasn't sure you'd be up for visitors late at night when I finally got done."

She started to scan the pages again, thinking about his response. Then she had to ask a question that was building inside her for days. "Where were you when the ship blew up? Usually you're there ahead of me to run the morning status logs."

He dropped his head remorsefully, "I overslept that day. I knew we were grounded and completely forgot we still had to run those flight checks. It's so hard to remember so many different sets of procedures from every one of these space ports, they're all different! And I can't remember the last time we were grounded this long."

She felt more satisfied by his answer than she expected. He sat there a moment looking at her, waiting for her to say something. When she didn't, he added, "Hey, if I was where I was supposed to be, I'd be freeze-dried in deep space right now."

Alicia finally relented, "I suppose you're right. Why don't you stop what you're doing and help me look at these photopasses. Do you remember what that nervous man looked like that I spoke to while we were disembarking?"

He smiled, "No, but let's go at it anyway, has to be more fun than what I've got to look at."

They were about fifteen minutes into the scans before Tim became bored with it as well. He looked nervously at her and suddenly said, "Stop on this man."

She immediately complied and said, "Is that him, I don't think he was that fat?"

"No, it's just that I wanted to say something else." He noticed the guard at the door was intently watching them both. He whispered, "I actually knew you were injured the next day after the blast. The truth is, I was afraid to come and see you. I heard you were so close to the blast, I didn't think I wanted to see what had happened to your body. I just didn't think I would be brave enough to look at you all disfigured."

She looked at him intently, her lips rolled in, fighting back emotion. He waited again for her to say something. Finally she sighed a deep breath in and out, "Well, you can see I'm still quite myself, and Dr. Phillips says my arm can be made completely scar-free." Then she restarted the scan screen and simply said, "Let's get this done, I've had a long day."

In minutes, the man they both remembered flashed on the screen. Alicia pounded her finger down on the stop key as she exclaimed, "That's him, isn't it? I'm sure that's him!" Tim leaned toward the screen, half squinting, "Hmm, I guess you're right, now what? What do we do with Mr.......Victor Seeb?"

"I'll tell you what we do with him." She commanded the computer to download the man's flight data to a portable crystal. Then she took it to the guard at the door. "Here's what you wanted. Give this to the committee people."

The guard took the device and walked over to Tim and peered over his shoulder at the picture. "Do you agree this is the man Captain Martin and you encountered leaving the shuttle?"

Tim replied, "If that's what the captain said, that's the man." He looked over at Alicia who was now starting out the door. "Can I go now, too? I don't think I can be of any more help today."

The guard looked at the time and said authoritatively, "You may leave also, but you must return tomorrow to finish your assignment."

Tim bounded from his chair, yelling into the hallway, "Alicia, wait for me!" His momentum slid him through the doorway several feet into the hallway. He quickly looked both directions down the empty corridors. She was gone. He swung his fist and muttered, "Damn!"

CHAPTER ELEVEN

"Good morning Dr. Phillips. It's 6:00 a.m.. Good morning, Dr. Ph———"
Ray's hand landed hard on the shut-off pad, squelching the mechanical voice.
He squinted hard as the room automatically illuminated. Slowly, he opened
his eyes again, staring at the ceiling in thought. He tried to clear the night's
dreams first. He shifted his thoughts from the late night at the lab to Max.
Somehow, intuitively he felt Max had discovered more about the D.O.V.E.
mystery. He wanted to call his room right away, but restrained himself.

He sat up, rubbing his face, feeling the sore back muscles from bending
over the lab counters too long. He went to his computer monitor and commanded, "Today's schedule, please." Even without the schedule, his first duty
every day was to make clinic rounds. Today looked uneventful. He began
dressing, and his thoughts shifted to Alicia. The reconstructive work required
on her arm needed to be done soon. As the uncertainty grew over shuttle priorities and reassignments, he worried she might have to wait too long to avoid
scarring.

After dressing, he went back to the screen and rang Pam's room. She answered immediately and turned on her viewer. He commented on her appearance, "How do you manage to look so good this early in the day?"

She smiled slyly and answered, "That's a secret. Now what do you want
so early, Ray?"

"Last night at the lab, when we burned the final fuel sample...I've been
starting to worry about the results. There's too much thermal output spectral
shifting coming from our sample size. I don't know where to go from here.
Bottom line is I need to talk with Dr. Ansarid. I need you to try again today
to find..."

"Ray, I've tried every trick in the book to find him. Maybe he doesn't want
to be found."

"Pam, please, this is too dangerous to mess with on our own. It's important to me, to all of us in space."

She looked away from the screen in weakness, then said, "Well, at least you said please. Perhaps I can ask our go-getter on Africa for some help. After all, turnaround's fair play."

Ray smiled thankfully, "Great, I hope that guy down there doesn't mind all the extra work we're giving him."

"What do you mean?"

"Well, I have Max looking for something down there also. I'll let him tell you about it."

Pam asked bluntly, "Are you seeing Alicia Martin right away?"

He got slightly offended, "Yes, I'm going to the clinic first just like any other morning."

Pam sighed, "I'm sorry Ray, she's been on my mind a lot. Of course you need to go to the clinic. I'll get right down to the operations room. Max and I obviously have a long day ahead of us."

"Apology accepted. I'll talk to you later at lunch. Oh, that's right, you're having lunch with Max!"

She smiled dryly, "Goodbye, Ray, and try to remember to get yourself some breakfast. I know you too well Mr. Ph.D. Good nutrition is important for everyone but you!"

"All right, I promise; goodbye." He switched off the monitor and hastily left the room. He stopped about three steps from the door and turned to watch it quickly slide shut. What pleasure it gave him to have such a simple thing working again! He automatically headed for the clinic, but in the elevator he remembered Pam's last remarks and smiled to himself as he pushed the button for the restaurant level.

*   *   *

Hayden Green sat at the back of the dark, crowded room, shifting in his chair. It was hard to see the speaker. Rows of heads blocked his view of the man standing purposely behind the single beam of light illuminating the podium. The clandestine gathering met in an abandoned building on the outskirts of City Newburg in Africa. The speaker continued talking in endless excited phrases as Green turned to the person next to him and whispered, "Things are going rather smoothly so far."

The man was uninterested and simply nodded, still looking up front. Green spoke again to the man, "Our leader has thought this out well. What assignment did you have?"

By now the man appeared perturbed and said in a gruff but quiet voice, "You know better than to ask." Green sank back a little in his chair and redirected his attention to the podium. The speaker raised his pitch and volume as he finished his motivational address, "Our astral guides have told me where we must strike again to battle the evil Vor Empire! You must not question their guidance and wisdom, no matter if your hearts tell you otherwise! Fulfill your assignments tomorrow and maintain the secrecy demanded battling the Vor. There is no higher authority you will answer to on this operation than me! Tomorrow, we meet again, after our latest victory!"

The man stepped behind the black curtain hanging five feet in back of him. The room remained eerily silent. Then idle chatter and planning commenced among the crowd, so Green turned once again to the man next to him, but the chair was empty.

He stood up and got in line. Once at the assignment box, he reached in blindly and grabbed a sealed envelope, stuffed it in his shirt pocket and made his way out of the building. He nervously looked about him as he got into his vehicle for the long drive back.

*   *   *

Station Shepherd was very quiet; nearly all available personnel were on the Martian surface. Jaden King had just awakened and was heading for the showers. As he walked down the dimly lit corridor, past the computer data centers, he detoured into the main conference room. He was greeted by a view of the planet below through the room's giant observation window. The reflected surface lit the room almost ablaze in orange, contrasting with piles of unstored equipment, spacesuits and food paraphernalia. He stepped cautiously through the obstacles and grabbed a microphone, addressing the whole station, "Pete, where are you?"

There was no answer, so he tried again a little louder, "Pete, you up yet?"

A tired voice came back over the speaker, "I'm in the dome, be right there."

A minute later Pete arrived in the doorway. Jaden took one look at him and declared, "You look like you didn't sleep at all last night."

"And *you're* still in your underwear. Should we both be worried?"

King laughed as he looked down at himself, "And I see I forgot my towel, damnit."

"Hey, I stumbled onto something late last night, and I couldn't let it go. I want your opinion on it; I can't take this any further." He walked past King and turned on a screen, displaying a histograph. Once the data loaded, Pete transferred his extrapolation plots. Jaden walked to his side and stared down at the lines materializing on the green background.

Pete spoke slowly but excitement welled in his voice. "I've scanned through all the upper frequencies from these electromagnetic storms and found a common denominator. Once I discovered the specific band, it was easy to plot all of our seemingly random readings. If my guess is right, they all triangulate to only three distinct areas on the planet."

They watched as the last of the lines drew itself. "There, look at that; I knew it had something to do with them!"

Jaden leaned closer, "Of course, the monument pyramids! The only unnatural things we've found on the planet. But how? We excavated them years ago; there was nothing but rock! How in the hell are they creating this much energy?"

"I don't know, but it seems logical to check them out again. However, we'd better move soon, because at the rate the gauss readings are going up, it won't be safe for our people in another day or so."

Jaden quickly walked over to the surface com-screen and waited for his crew to respond. "Lensa, listen to me, take six people from your group over to the pyramid south of you. Use the large six wheeler, not the small rovers. We have limited time. Once you get there, I want full electromagnetic probes run inside and out. Also, see if anything looks different in the gross structural integrity."

The woman looked perplexed, "What do you mean 'structural integrity'?"

"I'm not sure myself, but those things have to be humming down there, and we know what vibration can do. If your instruments give you any specific hot spots, focus there."

"You guys finally on to something?"

"Maybe, but we won't know until your close-range readings get up here. It should take you about four hours to get there, and that only gives you two hours on site to make it back in daylight."

"I was thinking more like you send a shuttle down and get us from the site. It will give us more time to collect data and it's just too many hours moving on the surface to drive back."

He thought a minute. "OK, I can pilot down, you guys have been down there long enough to get back on mother."

"We're on our way sir, over."

Jaden took a deep breath and made one last comment, "Also, tell your people to proceed with caution when you go back inside the structure. Over."

Pete looked at Jaden as the screen darkened. "What are you worried about? There's no one down there but our crews and a dead planet."

"Wrong, Pete, it *was* a dead planet!"

CHAPTER TWELVE

Max got up from his table, walked over to the service counter, and poured himself another cup of coffee. He stared thoughtfully at the swirling powdered synthetic cream he had just added. A cordial woman's voice broke his concentration, "Care for a little sweetness in that concoction?"

"Pam, I was wondering what happened to you! You said you'd only be at the library about an hour."

"I'm sorry, I got carried away apparently. I'm not too late am I?"

"No, no, I was just tanking up to hold my appetite, but let's get in line for food. We can talk while we move through the line." He lightly guided her by the arm into the snaking line. "So what did you find at the library that we don't have in our computer databases?"

Pam grabbed a tray and handed one to Max. "Well, Ray really needs to find Ansarid, and I thought I might get some answers from our contact on Africa. When I saw how much work you had piled up with him this morning, I thought I'd follow a hunch on another route."

Max held a wrapped sandwich up in front of him and inspected it before placing it on his tray. "Did Ray tell you what he has me looking for down there?"

She licked her finger after tasting a nondescript glob she had plopped on her plate, "Well, no, he said you would tell me."

"Yes, he called me before you arrived this morning and told me to fill you in sometime today on our 'D.O.V.E.' secret."

"Dove? What's that supposed to mean?"

Max paid at the end of the bar, then waited until they sat down before continuing his explanation. "Well, I really haven't gotten much further on the thing since talking with Ray yesterday. Our man on Earth is looking into it, he thought the acronym sounded familiar but had to do some checking.

Anyway, the term showed up on the computer screen as a hack after we left the lab two nights ago."

Pam ate selectively from her tray, intently sniffing a piece of synthetic meat. She put it down and said, "Well, as for me, I think my information is much more exciting. I was doing my usual morning inspirational reading, from a real book of all things, when I got the idea to use book records for Dr. Ansarid. I knew the library was collecting genealogical records from whatever people brought up to space from earth. And, the library personnel have been building a sort of computer family tree of the survivors. So the rest, as they say, is history. No pun intended."

Max stopped eating as his interest grew. "Well, don't leave me hanging! Did you come up with something, Madam Sherlock?"

She grabbed his arm, "I think so; listen to this! The Ansarid family tree is very interesting. Put very simply, there isn't one."

"What? That's impossible. That name is not that uncommon among the survivors, is it?"

"Well, it is. So, the next logical thing to do was have the computer cross-check spelling variations and similarities, and it found a surname tree of Ancerid, with an 'E'. That's pretty damn close in pronunciation as well, so I ran through that tree and found someone with the same first name: Rashad!" By now her nails were almost digging in his arm.

Max pounded his hand down triumphantly in excitement at her finding, but also to loosen the painful grip she had, "Great going, that must be him. Did you try to make contact with him?"

Pam picked up her fork again after disposing of the food clinging to it. She used it as a pointer, "Yes and no. The man was on Africa up to six months ago but disappeared during a homicide investigation."

"Murder? Good God, that doesn't seem possible! He didn't seem like the type capable of such a thing."

"Well, they don't think so either, but he was a suspect in the disappearance or murder of one of their propulsion scientists."

Max took another bite of food, then stopped chewing as his face lit up with recognition. "Hey wait a minute! I've seen that last name Ancerid recently! But it wasn't Rashad Ancerid. I remember, it was in one of the security checks we ran on spacebound facilities. Let me think....was it on a hotel or research station? ....Got it! The name was listed at station Shepherd out at Mars. It was, ummm, Peter Ancerid!"

Pam looked puzzled, "Are you sure? If he was there, they would have found him immediately. Station Shepherd is under Africa's jurisdiction!"

Max grinned, "Sounds like a good mystery to me; maybe they didn't want him found."

"Max, we have to get in touch with the station immediately." Before he could finish another bite of food, she was pushing out of her chair. He took one last discerning look at his sandwich and tossed it onto the tray as he followed her.

*　　*　　*

Pam looked over Max's shoulder as he entered coordinates for the Martian research center. They both silently waited for the reply after basic security passwords were entered. The response didn't begin to show verification for several minutes. Finally Pam exclaimed, "Why is it taking so long, our laser transmission is not that slow!"

"Strange, isn't it. It's as if their computers are bogged down with something big. If that's the case, we'll just have to be patient for our turn."

Pam straightened and sighed, then started to pace the room anxiously. Max continued staring at the screen while he tried to relax her by changing the subject. "Why don't you get on that other screen and see if there is currently a shuttle at station Shepherd."

She quickly grabbed a chair and got to work, "That's an interesting point, Max; let's see." She waited a moment while the shuttle log rolled out. "Nope. One was scheduled to leave Earth yesterday for them, but obviously it didn't with the suspensions."

He rolled over to her screen, "See if it was due to carry any new passengers to or from the station."

"What do you mean by new?"

"People who are not on the research team roster or maintenance support personnel."

She wrote a quick program to sift the list and sat back to watch the results. Quickly, the long list shrank to a few names. "There are only eight names that are new to the station, all listed as crew rotation specialists."

"That could be nothing, they do rotate about that many people every six months out there." Just then his screen lit up with the information he asked for. He smiled and proclaimed, "Take a look at what I found."

Pam was elated as she read the name Peter Ancerid, "Oh Max, you're a genius! Do you really think that's our guy?"

"Well, we won't know for sure till we see his picture, but it seems those files are restricted. We'll need direct permission from Governor Payne's office for that."

She started for the door, "Well, you've got the connection, go for it. I wouldn't know what he looks like anyway. I'm going to find Ray and tell him personally. He should be delighted."

Max turned his chair to watch her leave. He yelled after her as the door was about to close, "Tell him not to call me until tonight, I have a feeling this won't be quick!"

*　　*　　*

Otis Payne sat quietly as he read the latest report from his first delegate. With each word his face grew with disappointment and anger. He slammed down the paper and growled at the man sitting across his desk. "Two days of research on the fastest computers in what's left of civilization and we still have nothing! Also, why isn't the Shepherd's security study completed? They're the only ones left out there not finished with the basic profiling."

"Your Honor, the Shepherd's computers are all tied up, I've never seen anything like it in their systems. We know they're running, we just can't get them to respond! What do you know about them that you're not telling me?"

Payne appeared somewhat surprised by the question. "Hmmmm, Tom, seems you know me too well. Let me assure you I'll get you up to speed as soon as I know what the hell's going on. Tell you what, let Shepherd go for now, I'll handle them personally from this point on. Meanwhile, tell me some good news that's not in your report."

The man got up and walked over to the window, gazing outside at the yellow haze. "Well, Max Rogers, one of their top research people up there has been asking some very interesting questions of me."

Payne leaned toward the man with interest, "Oh, like what?"

"First of all, he wanted to know if I knew what D.O.V.E. stood for."

Otis interrupted him, "Dove? Why is he interested in them?"

"I don't know, but begging your pardon sir, what does it mean?"

Payne sat back deep in his chair again as he answered, "Oh, some nut group that sprang up in the last few years. They think everything inexplicable is due to an evil race of aliens. They call them the Vor."

"So where does D.O.V.E. come in?"

"Divine Opposition to the Vor Empire! Can you believe it?"

Ivory tinted the window slightly and walked back to the front of Otis' desk. "Do YOU believe it?"

"I believe in our friends, whoever or whatever they are, but so far nothing has convinced me of anything else out there, especially anything like this Vor."

The man spread his arms wide and looked around him, "What about the whole mess the planet's in, what about these recent explosions? Blaming it all on some bastard aliens would make a whole lot more sense to a lot of people."

Payne stood up and went to his bar, "All this, I'm convinced is due to what it usually comes down to; human error." He took a quick swallow of his favorite drink and continued, "And, I'm determined to find them,... to show them the error of their ways. Now, we have just five days left before we let those ships fly again. So get back to work and I'll contact station Shepherd and get some answers."

The delegate got up and cleared his throat cautiously, "I need to mention the other thing Max Rogers asked of me. He wanted to know what we knew about a man named Peter Ancerid on station Shepherd. He wants to see his picture."

Otis walked directly up to him, inches from his face. "You tell Dr. Rogers he is in classified personnel files and is to immediately discontinue that line of research. Do I make myself perfectly clear?"

The man stepped back a few inches and quietly replied, "Yes, sir. But he did say it was imperative to the fuel research they were doing."

Otis pointed to the door, "I said discontinued Mr. Ivory! Goodday!"

As soon as the man left, Payne went to his communication screen and logged directly into station Shepherd. Jaden King's image appeared and Otis snapped at him before he could even say hello. "Jaden, why the hell haven't your people replied to our security requests?"

"Well, good to see you too, Otis. In a word, no time. I've got all my researchers on the planet except myself and Pete. That leaves six other support staff here to hold it all together. We're running almost nonstop."

"Make time, dammit. This information we need is as important as anything Mars is doing!"

Jaden smiled slyly, "Oh yeah, I guess you don't want to know what we finally pieced together today."

Payne's attitude softened by the prospects. He sighed back, "All right, what have you got that you didn't know yesterday?"

"We have localized a triangular configuration that seems to somehow focus magnetic vortices from the three ancient pyramids on the planet. The response from the planet's core is even more exciting. It's responding with unique particles that are activating the bacterial gene codes to replicate at an exponential...."

"Jaden, speak slower and in plain English for the mere mortal here."

"Sorry, let me start over, in my classroom mode. As you know, when we came here to terraform the planet, we decided to create an atmosphere first and not worry about the nearly nonexistent magnetic field. The thought was our sun should be stable enough over the next century that we didn't need the magnetic field to shield the planet. So, away we went using microbial seeding of the soil. The species were genetically engineered to reproduce under present conditions and make various gasses, especially carbon dioxide. Then, after decades, the planet would warm up by trapped sunlight; the water would melt out of the soil and poles, and in theory we could grow green things that would make oxygen. It all seemed very simple, and was supposed to work relatively fast compared to the usual hundreds of thousands of years. Follow me so far?"

"Amazingly, yes. Go on."

"OK, so what we see happening is going to sound a little spooky. The pyramid ruins told us nothing when we first explored them. Now, the three that we know of are either creating or focusing a specific frequency of energy. They seem to act as a single unit and are in essence sending a stimulating signal to the Martian core. Whatever mineral elements the planet harbors down there are coming to life. It's like a nuclear reactor kicking in, and exotic particles are spewing out to the surface in all directions. And they're riding out in magnetic waves!"

"Are you saying the planet's magnetic field is returning? I thought it was permanently dead?"

"Our theories told us the field died out long ago due to the smaller size of the planet when compared to earth. Our field on earth is still fluxing, but it now has dozens of norths and souths. As we all know, that was disastrous for the crust stability. In theory earth's field will eventually die out completely as well, but not for another half billion years or so."

"I wonder how many scientists still think it has that long to go?"

"Well, that discussion is for another day and good cognac. But back here, these particle waves are bringing our little bacterial friends to life in ways we didn't imagine. It reminds me of the old earth legend of the incredible hulk. The only difference is the microbes are not getting *bigger*, they're just reproducing faster than we can even watch with the naked eye. As a result, atmospheric carbon dioxide levels have reached a degree of saturation that we didn't expect to see for 30 to 50 years."

"So is that making it warm on the surface yet?"

"Not enough to write home about, a few degrees perhaps. The rise we need to bring out all the water will take years even at this rate, but some ice is melting. However, the atmospheric gasses are doing something extraordinary. The particles emanating from the core are also creating reactions high up. We are seeing layering. We are seeing oxygen and nitrogen being manufactured without help from plant life."

Otis leaned close to the screen, "Are you saying the planet is making oxygen?"

"Yes, governor, oxygen, and lots of it!"

"What are you projecting?"

"Well, right now we're worried the surface of the planet is getting unsafe for our crews due to the high energy levels in the triangle, so we're getting everyone up very soon. But, if those particle waves settle down, the air might be breathable in just a few more weeks."

Otis tried to remain scientific and not get excited by what he just heard. "Back to the pyramids. You're sure you have no idea how they're doing it?"

"Not yet, but I have a team going in one again very soon for some deeper readings."

Otis held his cheeks in excited thought, then returned to his concerned expression, "Jaden, please complete the security profiles. If I don't come up with some answers down here, everything happening out there might be for nothing."

Jaden jumped away from the screen, "For nothing! How can you say that! We nearly have a whole new world here ready to be occupied! What could possibly screw it up?"

Otis hesitated, then replied as he stroked his forehead back, "What if nobody could get there?"

Jaden returned to his monitor and continued to listen, his excitement deflating from him. "Jaden, you're no doubt aware of the explosions we suffered on Lemuria and the Majestik. Most people think they're not related and are accidents. I think someone's behind them both. I know your people have little in common right now with all this, but you have to wonder at the timing of everything. I need those security questions addressed. Has anyone been displaying unusual behavior in the past few weeks, especially Peter?"

"Pete? He's my best man up here, what does this have to do with him?"

"Is your end secure right now in our conversation, is anyone within earshot of us?"

"Secure as can be, we're alone."

"I know Pete's a good man, I sent him there, but that's not important now. I need to know if he's behaving himself."

"I trust him like a brother. Is that good enough?"

Otis smiled approvingly, "That's good enough for me. But tonight, finish the profiles on the others and transmit them directly to me, not Mr. Ivory. I'll still expect to get another update from you tomorrow on our miracle planet. Good-bye."

*   *   *

Pam excitedly completed her story of Dr. Ancerid on the Shepherd outpost while Ray sat quietly listening. "Well, what do you think?"

"If he is there, that won't help us one bit, it would take too long to get him here. By the way, is there a shuttle out there?"

"No, but one was supposed to be on its way there now."

Ray sighed and walked over to a row of glass beakers. He held up one and swirled its contents, "Maybe if we altered the hydrogen catalyst ratios a bit more alkaline, it would stabilize better."

Pam grabbed his arm and guided the beaker down to the support. "Ray, are you listening? I thought you wanted his help!"

"Yes I do, but I'm trying to be practical. He's not here and this is what we have to work with!"

"What's real right now is the same old Ray Phillips! Always practical and inflexible, playing by the rules. What happened to listening to your instincts?"

Ray pulled his lip in and leaned onto the counter, his head hanging slightly between his shoulders. "Perhaps you're right, he would fit right in at Mars. That was quite an elite team they put together out there. All right, I'll tell you what my instincts tell me. They tell me Max is going to get no deeper than he already has. They tell me I'll have to go down to Earth and personally pry the information out of Governor Payne. If he acknowledges he's out there, then I'll insist he let me talk with him over his direct link." He grabbed the beaker again and looked at it intently, "I should also stay down there and use their labs to complete the fuel tests. That way, if the lab blows up, I won't take the whole hotel with me!"

Pam placed her hand on top of his and said, "I'll go with you."

"No way! With me gone, Parker would never let you go down there at the same time."

She stood there, folding her arms, but managed a slight proud smile for him. "Well, at least you made up your mind! OK, fine, but until anybody can fly again, you're stuck here. So why don't we call it a day. I'm tired."

"You go on. I want to talk with Max later, then I promise to cash in early tonight."

Pam said goodbye with a peck on his cheek and left reluctantly. Ray started into some calculations on his notescreen, but stopped after a few minutes. He rubbed his hands together as he walked over to his viewscreen. He rang Max's room and waited. Max didn't respond, so he tried the operations center. Max popped right up, "Hey, big guy. Pam told me all about your discovery today; anything new since then?"

"What do you want to know?"

"First, what about the D.O.V.E acronym?"

"Divine Opposition to the Vor Empire."

He nodded in remembrance, "I've heard rumors of such a group, so do they exist?"

"Best I can tell, info's straight from the governor's office."

"I bet they didn't help you any more on Peter Ancerid."

"You know Payne better than I do, I guess. But Mr. Ivory gave me some background on the Vor. Over the last few decades a growing number of people began to suspect something behind many negative or catastrophic events, so the legend grew of this race of aliens known as the Vor."

"I can understand blaming someone on what the planet did, but since then what else are they blaming on the Vor?"

"Missing persons and livestock, disease, just to name a few."

Ray rubbed his eyes deeply, then yawned, "Wow, you know what; I'm just too tired to deal with this stuff now. Let's sleep on it and maybe we can make some sense of it tomorrow. I'll tell you more then about my decision to go down to earth and do a little elbow bending at the governors."

"I'm calling it a day as well, but don't expect me to have any better ideas on the Dove group."

Ray sat there a moment after the screen went black and rubbed his lesion, then finally locked up the lab. He nearly made it to his room before the urge to stop at the clinic one last time overtook him. Once there he looked for Alicia and found her sitting by a window gazing at the stars. He pulled a chair up next to her. She turned toward him, pleasantly surprised. He pondered, "Stars tell you anything interesting tonight?"

"I never get tired of their beauty, I guess that's why I became a pilot."

"Did the committee talk with you any more today?"

"No, it's been a quiet day, I've been resting, thinking. You know, the usual things we bored patients worry about. I'm trying not to fuss about this scar."

Ray took her hand and looked into her eyes, "I promise you, we'll get you to the right doctor soon enough. Are you in pain anywhere?"

She smiled halfway and replied, "Can I get a hotel room tomorrow, I need to start feeling like a person again and not a patient."

"I'll see what I can arrange. You look great otherwise, I can almost feel your optimism."

She prophesized, "It's determined the remainder of us will all survive, I feel it. I know it."

"How do you know it?"

"Because you believe it, Ray. I feel that the most."

Ray sat there fascinated by the riddle once again. He smiled as he finally got the courage to ask, "When you get fully recovered, I'd like to have lunch with you sometime."

Without hesitation she replied, "I'd like that, Ray Phillips, I'd like that very much."

CHAPTER THIRTEEN

It was near midnight, the moon shone brightly on the brush and trees, illuminating the three figures crouching near the fence. Their breaths steamed in the cold air, adding to the eye-stinging mist that materialized every night. Hayden Green sniffed quietly, then rubbed his nose on his sleeve. He turned excitedly to one of his accomplices, "Do you think we'll accomplish our mission tonight?"

The man ignored him by focusing intently downward to the weapon he held. He pushed a test button and the surge indicator on his laser lit up. It emitted an eerie red glow as the needle swung over to the 'kill' range. He finally looked at Green and gave a deranged grin as he patted the weapon, "I'm confident, we're ready."

Green looked down at the old iron shooter he brought along, stroking its long cold barrel. The gun was given to him as a youngster by his father; he cherished the piece; it was one of the few things he had left to remind him of his parents. He turned his attention back to the expanse of runways and fields looming before them through the fences.

His other cohort tapped him on the shoulder, "I think I hear something!"

Everyone froze motionless, nearly holding their breaths as they strained to hear anything. Thirty seconds past and Hayden impatiently stood slowly, trying to see better above the mist.

"Green, get down you idiot, do you want to get killed?"

He quickly stooped low and complained, "There's hardly any guards on this side of the facility, what are you so worried about?"

"I'm not worried about the guards!"

"Oh, do you know something I don't?"

Just then a massive energy bolt arced from high in the sky and hit the main runway, showering debris and sparks like a blossoming night flower. The particles landed hundreds of meters across in all directions. An immediate second, smaller flash hit near it, and Green could see several figures running toward the impact points. The men next to him jumped up with exhilaration and started climbing the fence. One yelled back to him, "Let's go, buddy, yee-haaaaah, this is it!"

He followed their lead to the top of the fencing, struggling to maintain his grip on the heavy gun as he jumped down on the other side. He ran frantically toward the runway, his gun pointed straight ahead as he looked for something to shoot at. Around him, laser blasts were being fired into the sky in the vicinity of where the lightning came from. The shouts and hoots of nearly a dozen men sounded like Indians attacking a fort in the 1800s. Suddenly another bolt struck behind him as the heated blast of air knocked him forward. As he fell the gun flew from his grip. He lay stunnned on his belly, now only aware of the warm runway surface against his face and hands. He rolled onto his back and felt a severe burning between his shoulders from a wound. He cried out in pain, "Daddy, help me!" but within seconds he passed out in shock.

*   *   *

Ray lay motionless, deep in sleep in his room. The sudden buzz of his viewphone startled him to consciousness. He sat up slowly while the buzzing became more persistent. "All right already, I'm coming!"

He shuffled across the room and sat down in front of the screen. He used only the audio, "Yeah, what is it?"

"Ray, this is Parker. I need to talk to you immediately."

"You've got my undivided attention, I can assure you." He yawned again as he sat back to listen, "Go ahead, sir."

"Ray, last night we had more trouble on Earth. Africa's main shuttle runway was badly damaged. All hell seemed to break loose down there."

Ray's stomach tightened, "Shit, how could that happen? Didn't they have extra security teams all over the place?"

"Apparently not enough. I don't know all the details, the report simply stated the time of the attack, and it said they had a prisoner!"

Ray was definitely awake now and he turned on the camera. "A prisoner? That means there were people behind all this!"

The chairman looked puzzled, "Who or what else did you think was involved?"

"Oh, never mind, just something Max and I tossed around."

"Well, I wanted to talk with you right away, before you heard it on the morning news. I don't know how this is going to affect the start-up of shuttle flights in four days. After all, Payne's vote was to continue the suspensions. I bet he's steaming mad right now."

"Vote or no vote, in four days things have to fly. All our space facilities need supplies. I hope they learn something from the man they captured. That is, if it's a man."

"There you go again talking weird, what's that supposed to mean?"

"Quite simple, we don't know if they captured a man or a woman."

"Very good, Dr. Phillips, we must never jump to any premature conclusions."

"Mr. Parker, I have to get my morning going here. Let me know later what else you learn." With that he switched off the screen and sat there a moment thinking. He flashed back to his conversation with Max before going to bed and was anxious to talk with him about this latest development.

He quickly dressed and headed out the door. As it opened, he stopped dead in his tracks, nearly running into the person standing outside his suite. He reached out to stop himself as Alicia lunged back in surprise. Her expression immediately refocused as she anxiously grabbed his hands. "Ray, something's wrong, we have to talk."

"Alicia, what are you doing here? Are you OK?"

"Of course I'm OK, it's you I'm worried about."

He looked up and down the hallway, then led her back into his room. "Here, have a seat. Tell me what this is about."

She took a slow, deep breath and folded her hands on her lap. "Last night, something happened, something evil. Ray, I feel it may change everything, even your life. You must understand before you leave."

"I was just going to the clinic, what could be so important about..."

"Before you go back to Earth."

He stood in shocked silence staring at her, then slowly backed away to the still-open door and signaled it to close. Uncharacteristically, he pulled out a bottle of alcohol from a cabinet and poured himself a shot. She sat quietly observing him as he gulped it down. He leaned on a counter, his back to her. He then asked in a quiet, interrogative voice, "How did you know about last night and my going back to Earth?"

She walked up to him and gently turned him around. "I heard about the runway attack on the early news this morning. It's all they're talking about. As for your impending trip back down to earth, I dreamed it last night. Was I right?"

His eyes probed hers, just inches away. Then, a sense of peace filled his body as he reached out to touch her shoulders. "Yes. So, what do I have to fear on Earth?"

"You are up against forces that are very determined, very strong."

With total trust in her, he decided to ask an unusual question. "Who are the Vor?"

"They are not your concern now."

Somehow not surprised by her answer he replied, "So they exist?"

"They exist because people want them to."

"That's wild, but I don't understand."

"You will, but for now please proceed with caution, you are a very important person in all this. This trip to Earth cannot be taken lightly." She backed away from him and went to his window. He followed her over. "Tell me, were you always this way, I mean before the explosion?"

"If you mean have I always cared about people, the answer is yes, I love all life."

"No, I mean this intuition of yours. It's scary."

"I have nothing more than everyone else possesses." He thought for a moment, then walked to the door, motioning to her, "Come on, let's go find you a real room. It's on my morning 'to do' list."

She remained at the window in thought. Then she turned and gave him a satisfied smile, projecting again the dominant aura he remembered from their first meeting.

As they walked down the corridor, he glanced at her frequently. She seemed oblivious to him, her mind busy with things he could only wonder about. At the elevator, she took the lead and pushed the door button. She stepped right in to an empty car, but he remained outside, hesitating.

She asked intrigued, "Aren't you coming?"

He stepped in slowly, his arms now folded behind his back inquisitively, "Yes, of course. It's just this sudden flash of memory I had. The other day I thought I would solve who broke into my room in this very car."

"How's that?"

"Oh, just by smell." He smiled at her as the doors closed. He felt for once she didn't seem to have a clue what he was talking about. He reached out to push the floor level they needed.

She replied with a coy smile, "Nice cologne you're wearing, doctor."

*   *   *

Otis Payne sat quietly in the back of his chauffeured vehicle, the melodic hum of the motor entranced his thoughts as he stared out the window. His first assistant, Ivory, was driving. "Should only be a few more minutes till we get to the hospital, Governor."

Otis turned his head to him and simply nodded, then returned his gaze to the expanse of makeshift camps littering the tundra. Soon the vehicle rolled up the long path toward the hospital emergency entrance. Once stopped the driver jumped out and ran around the vehicle to open the door for Payne. It was a cold, rainy morning, and they both glanced up at the orange-grey sky framed by dark undulating clouds looming on the horizon.

"I'm glad we got here before that hits, sir. Certainly would have been treacherous driving on these roads."

Otis nodded again but remained silent as he walked commandingly into the hospital. Two guards joined him at the door, one ahead and one behind as they escorted him up the sloping corridor. They rounded the corner and approached a room where two more armed guards jumped to attention when they saw the approaching entourage. The three stopped at the door. Payne looked at each man's frozen posture as he removed his overcoat. His face was now tense with anger as he handed the wet coat to Ivory. He opened the door and told all the men to remain where they were.

A doctor stood next to the single bed in the room, reading a chart. He glanced up to see who had come in, then returned to his notes without speaking. Otis approached the bed and looked down at the sleeping man in it.

"When will this vermin be conscious?"

The doctor put the chart down on the bed and adjusted one of the monitors, then folded his arms. "This man has suffered a severe spinal injury, I should hope you change your tone of voice before you question him!"

Payne looked at the doctor standing defiantly next to his patient. He drew a slow, deep breath in as he stroked his palm down his face, "Very well, doctor, is he able to speak with me today?"

"As soon as I bring him out; it should take just a few minutes once I change the medication." Payne walked over to the man's pile of clothing and held up the tattered shirt covered with mud and sticky blood. He dropped it in exchange for something more intriguing. He slowly raised up the long barrel of the steel rifle and sighted it at the bed. Sudden moans from the bedridden man made him lower the gun to see what was happening. He walked back to the bed, holding the gun in front of him like a trophy. He bent down to the man, "Green, can you hear me?"

Both men watched as the patient stirred to consciousness. Minutes later, once he was fully awake, his eyes started to inspect the room. He recognized Payne standing over him and immediately pulled the sheets up over his head.

Otis grabbed them and yanked them back down, exposing the cringing face of the man. "I always suspected you were no good, you son-of-a-bitch..." The doctor immediately interrupted, "Governor, please, I asked you..."

"You're right, I was getting ahead of myself, I'm sorry doctor." He took another deep breath and walked the gun back to the shelf. He returned composed to the bedside.

"Mr. Green, I would like you to tell me, in as few words as you are capable of, what you were doing last night at the shuttle runways?"

Hayden seemed to ignore the question as he squirmed under the sheet. Then a sudden look of horror shot across his face. "Doctor, my legs! I can't move my legs!" Otis looked on emotionless as the doctor took Hayden's hand in comfort.

"I know young man, you've suffered an unusual spinal cord trauma. There was a piece of flying debris that apparently hit you very hard in the upper lower back. It micro-fractured a vertebra, creating swelling on the cord."

Still filled with panic, he asked, "Am I going to be this way forever?"

"No, I don't think so, we can't detect any sort of permanent damage, but normal motor function will only return when the swelling has substantially subsided."

Payne interjected, "There you see, you got away with another thing. Now stop blubbering and answer my question!"

The man sighed and looked timidly up at Otis, "What did you ask?"

"Jesus, Doctor, has his brain been paralyzed too?" He leaned in closer as he tried again through nearly clenched teeth, "Why were you at the space shuttle runway?"

The man lay there staring at the ceiling, then looked out the window. Finally he replied, "You could never understand."

Payne lost his temper again and spun away from the bed. "I'll tell you what I understand. I understand my runways were severely damaged last night by a group of militant scums, you apparently being one of them. I understand your people somehow got past all the extra security I thought we had in place. I understand you were stupid enough to get hurt by your own people and get yourself caught. And finally, I understand you will be shot for treason if you don't tell me what I want to know!"

"I can't tell you why they're doing it."

"Mr. Green, I think I'll have you shot anyway, my life will be so much more peaceful." By now he was right over the bed, inches from Hayden's face.

He sunk away into the pillow, clutching the sheet. "All right, I'll tell you, but if they find out I could be killed."

Otis straightened up, finally satisfied by his answer and replied, "No one gets to kill you but me, so tell me everything if you want to live."

Hayden looked directly at Payne and said very seriously, "Please ask the doctor to leave the room." Otis motioned him to the door. Once they were alone Hayden began to explain. "I belong to an organization called D.O.V.E."

Otis interrupted him, "I should have known."

"You know about us? How?"

"How do you think I got to be governor? Go on!"

"Well then, this shouldn't be too hard for you to comprehend." His courage was returning and he pulled himself up higher on his pillows. "We were stationed there to counter a possible Vor attack."

Otis put his hands on his hips in frustration, "For Christ's sake, Green, I thought you were going to tell me the truth! Not some whimsy bullshit alien story!"

Green struggled to prop himself up even higher, "Bullshit? The Vor are very real, and they were there last night!"

"Did you see them?"

"Well no, they never left their ships. With that kind of weaponry, they didn't have to."

"You expect me to believe that story, and not that your gang deliberately planted explosives at that base to disrupt shuttle flights?"

"Governor, think for a moment, what would we have to gain by doing that?"

"Oh I could think of many things, how about ruining my Mars project for starters."

"No, no, we support that! Listen, have the crater debris scanned for evidence of explosives, you won't find any. I tell you the Vor were there!"

"If they exist, and they were there, what did you and your puny gun expect to do against them?"

"Actually we weren't expecting the actual aliens to be there. Our leader had only anticipated their human supporters being there."

"Oh wonderful, now the plot really thickens! You know, I'm thinking back now to three days ago when your committee recommended I re-establish the shuttle flights. That would have suited your people just fine, so the ships would be right there; nice and vulnerable."

Green tried to roll away on his side, but was unsuccessful as he grunted back, "You still don't understand." He closed his eyes and sighed, "We needed to draw them out, our forces were finally strong enough to counter-attack them at that shuttleport."

Otis had heard enough and walked away to the door. He bellowed back over his shoulder, "There will be 24-hour guards around this room and hospital. They're out there for two reasons. One, to make sure you don't go anywhere, and secondly, to protect you from your own people."

Once in the hall he grabbed his coat from Ivory as he marched toward the exit. His aide strained to keep pace with him as they approached the vehicle. "Your honor, may I ask what went on in there?"

"No, but you may drive us to the shuttleport and have one of their military forensics investigators meet us there. And drive fast, that storm will be chasing us all the way there."

CHAPTER FOURTEEN

Alicia sat in the clinic's family area, watching Ray make his rounds of the few remaining patients. He wrote the discharge order on the last of the shuttle victims and surveyed the nearly empty rows of beds before him. He turned back to Alicia and raised his hands in the air in a silent triumph, displaying a rare smile of satisfaction. She got up, feeling the contagiousness of his smile and reached out to hug him in congratulations.

Of course, Pam walked into the room the moment he wrapped his arms around the woman's back. She stopped in her tracks when she recognized it was Ray and Alicia. He immediately let go, as if caught stealing a cookie. Alicia turned to see what had interrupted them. She immediately walked over to Pam, who just looked at Ray expressionless.

"Good morning, Pamela, I was just congratulating Ray on the wonderful job he's done for the explosion victims. The last one was just released."

"If that's so, why are *you* still here?"

Alicia was about to answer her when Pam looked right through her to Ray,

"Doctor, have you talked with Max yet this morning?"

Ray raised his eyebrows as he walked around Alicia to Pam, "Alicia is technically still a patient until she is officially released to the plastic surgeon. We're getting her in a regular room, however, this very day."

"I asked if you've talked with Max yet. I didn't know if you heard the news from Earth." She looked back wearily at Alicia's eyes as she waited for his response.

"Yes, the chairman informed me bright and early. But again, it's really out of our hands. So, why don't we get down to the computer operations room and see what they need from the Majestik."

Pam grabbed Ray's hand and pulled him toward the door, "Well, let's go, I have lots of questions today."

Ray looked back at Alicia as he was led away, "You don't really need my help getting a good room here, why don't you stop down at the operations room after you settle in?"

Alicia scurried a few quick steps to catch them, "I'd rather come with you two, I might be of some help."

Pam looked at Ray unapprovingly, "I don't think that's a good idea, this is pretty high security stuff."

Alicia gently scorned back, "I'm a shuttle captain, I have top security clearance already!"

Ray jumped right in, "I think she could be of tremendous help! Pam, you won't believe this woman's sense of intuition."

Pam mumbled to herself as the three of them left the clinic, "I probably won't."

*   *   *

Victor Seeb received a knock on his suite door. He cautiously got up from his chair parked in front of the satellite viewscreen and leaned close to the intercom. "Who is it?" A deep voice boomed back, "Hotel security, open the doors or they will be opened by our override."

He sighed angrily as he touched the button. Two men immediately rushed into the room, both brandishing weapons. They grabbed him and plowed him up against the wall. One body- searched him while the other applied wrist restraints.

He screamed in obvious discomfort, "What the hell is this about?"

"You are Victor Seeb?"

"So what?"

"You are being detained for questioning." As they led him from the room, he demanded, "Questioning about what? You have no right to do this to me!"

In no time he found himself shoved into a hard chair in another location. His head was spinning from the adrenaline and the tight extension of his shoulders onto the chair. He looked up around him, trying to focus through beads of sweat stinging his eyes. Three people were sitting behind a small table at the far end of the room. They were the same three who had questioned Alicia Martin. The woman spoke first.

"Relax, Mr. Seeb, we will not harm you."

He struggled against the restraints, "Oh yeah, then prove it and release my hands, I can't feel them!"

One of the three motioned to a guard who immediately worked behind him to free his hands.

"There, you see, we mean you no harm, as long as you cooperate."

"I don't know who the hell you people think you are, but I have rights..."

The woman jumped up, "You have no rights up here, Mr. Seeb, especially when you are a suspect in the loss of a five billion dollar piece of government equipment!"

"Oh, so that's what this is all about! Well, I had nothing to do with it other than the fact I arrived here on it."

One of the two men stood up, "According to our passport records, this is your third time here at the Majestik."

"So?"

"Third time within a year! That's not allowed under the rotation system. Now, just how did you accomplish three trips here in one year, Victor?"

"Everybody breaks the rules. If you want to be in space bad enough, there's always someone willing to sell a seat at the right price."

"And so you forged the passport dates?"

"Maybe, hey listen; I want some counsel before I say any more."

The woman replied, "Mr. Seeb, I told you already, you will cooperate if you want to stay healthy. Now, why are you up here now?"

"For a vacation."

"And you like it here so much you didn't want to leave. Is that why you destroyed the shuttle?"

"You people are nuts, I'm getting out of here." He stood up, but before he could take a step, one of the guards bludgeoned him on the jaw so hard he fell back into the chair and crashed backwards onto the floor. He lay there stunned, fear now started back with a vengeance. He painfully crawled back up the chair, a trickle of blood oozing from his mouth. He sat holding his jaw, then began to speak, his throat tightening with emotion. "OK, this isn't worth getting killed over."

The woman smiled and gestured for the guards to wait outside. "Mr. Seeb, we searched your room, but couldn't find the small case you brought to the hotel."

"When did you search my room?"

"Mr. Seeb, does it really matter? Where is that case?"

"I gave it to a contact here at the hotel."

"Who? And what was in the case?"

"I don't know who, it was dropped at a predetermined location." He reached in his pocket nervously and took out a cloth to wipe his mouth. "All it had in it were a handful of lasers."

One of the men questioned, "Lasers? No explosives?"

"Explosives? You know they'd never get past the sensors. Say, you people really think I blew up that ship! Well, I'll say it again, you're nuts. I'm here to try and save this place."

"And who are you trying to save us from?"

"I can't tell you that."

"Then tell me who or what group you work for!"

Seeb stood up slowly, this time looking behind him first. He cleared his throat and proudly stuck his chest out, "I'm a member of the Dove."

The three of them sat there quietly, looking at their prisoner. The woman whispered to the others, "I think we should get the chairman down here."

They nodded in agreement as she spoke to Seeb, "Sit down, sir, we are going to take a short break."

*   *   *

It was late in the day by the time Governor Payne's vehicle rolled up to the shuttleport security gate. One of the sentries leaned over his weapon to look at the driver. Ivory ignored him and lowered the rear glass as Payne wasted no time to bark out a command. "Where's the adviser I asked for?"

"Sir, he's waiting for you at the damage site. Have your driver proceed to the main taxiway; my men will escort you from there."

"That won't be necessary; I imagine after last night there is plenty of security here now."

"As you wish." The man backed away and snapped to attention as the gates swung open. The drive into the facility took several minutes to reach the still-smoldering runway. Several uniformed people were walking about the area, busy examining the evidence with expensive instruments or just simple measuring tape. Otis tapped Ivory on the shoulder, pointing to the right, "Stop over there, that must be him."

Payne was out the door before his driver could even come to a complete stop. As he walked over to a man in a safari hat, he put his hand out to sample the tiny raindrops dampening his day. "Are you in charge of this investigation?"

"I am as of a few hours ago when you put the request in for forensics." He reached out his hand to shake the governor's hand, "Oh, by the way, I'm Captain..."

Otis waved his hand away, "I don't care. Tell me what you think happened here last night."

"It's starting to piece together. Our soldiers on duty last night didn't see a thing until all the commotion started here at the runway. We had basically all our guards covering the perimeters and shuttle hangers."

Payne interrupted, "Do you think that was a very smart way to guard this facility? The hangers were empty, why would you put so much emphasis on them and not the runways?"

"Sir, you're asking the wrong man those questions, I'm more of a scientist. You need to talk with the base commander, he's right..."

"You're right. So, what is your opinion on what left this big hole I'm standing next to?"

The captain pulled a single sheet of paper from a small bag draped over his shoulder. As he looked over the data, he spoke thoughtfully, "Our instruments cannot detect any known explosive residues in the samples we obtained. That's why we're still here; trying to find something we missed."

"Tell your crew to pack it up. Thank you for your opinion, but I doubt you are going to find residues."

"Excuse me for questioning, but how can you be sure?"

"It appears we have a reliable informant. Anyway, I need this runway open in four days, so I have to go motivate someone right now." With that Otis headed back to his car, his pace quickened by the increasing rainfall and thunder rumbles. Once safely out of the weather he got on the voicecom. "Get me the shuttleport base commander." As he waited he calmly said to Ivory, "Go over to the tower, we have one more person to see."

As they drove the short distance, Otis made sure the man he needed to see was where he expected to meet him. They pulled up to a 150 foot tall control tower and parked under a long overhang. Within moments, the door to Otis' right swung open and a tall, lanky, uniformed man jumped in next to him.

"I'm Commander Matouba, it's nice to finally meet you, Governor."

Otis shook his hand as he shifted his weight to his right leg to better face the man. "Did your air surveillance systems pick up anything when this place lit up?"

"I can't tell you. Our entire system suffered a snow-out at the exact time of the attack. We figure the saboteurs jammed it."

"You figure the saboteurs jammed it? What the hell does that mean?"

The man tightened his lip before he spoke, "There was no damage we could find to any of the surveillance hardware. So, we 'figured' they had some sort of electromagnetic jamming technology that our computers were unable to compensate for."

"Why is that, commander?"

"Sir, it was like something we've never seen before. It's as if the signal came out of the sky, because to create that powerful a frequency, the equipment would be too heavy for those on foot last night."

Otis turned straight in his seat again, then looked intently out his window. The sky was nearly dark; the runways reflected back an eerie orange-green hue. He took a deep breath as he peered up at a hole in the clouds. "Commander Matouba, the runways must be in perfect condition in four days, no excuses. Second, keep the security intensity where it is, with additional men in vehicles every 500 feet along each runway. Lastly, I want a back-up plan for air surveillance. I don't care if you have to use tin foil. Apparently our enemy, whoever they are, came at us from the sky. The ground attack may have been an elaborate diversion."

Matouba nodded understandingly, "Is that all sir?"

"No, one more question. How is it you only managed to capture one prisoner, and an unconscious one at that?"

The man started to slowly open his door, "I'm not sure myself. The field reports all state no one was out there when our men rushed to the runways. It's as if they all disappeared into thin air."

Payne looked curiously at Matouba, "Mr. Ivory, take us home. Good day, Commander."

They drove off in what was now a heavy downfall. Tom Ivory held both hands tightly on the wheel as they sped out the base gates. "Those were some pretty weird looking holes in the ground. They'd make for quite a bad landing if you hit one."

Otis slumped back in his seat and closed his eyes with his hands folded on his belly, "Yes, Tom, those were indeed some holes."

* * *

As the security doors opened into the Majestik's operations room, Max looked over his shoulder to see Ray, Pam and Alicia parade in. He immediately shoved out of his uncomfortably short chair and slid it aside.

"Well, Captain Martin, you're looking very well today. What can we do for you here, deep in the bowels of our humble hotel?"

"Thank you for the compliment, Maxwell, or should I call you Max?"

"Yes, call me Max, my parents never liked it." They both laughed as Ray and Pam went over to the small pile of reports that had been produced that day. Max immediately joined them, "Our African connection, Ivory's his name, hasn't been in communication today, but I've been busy running some of his search algorithms. You won't believe the interesting characters we came up with."

Ray started reading the first paper on the stack. "Max, what is all this? Have you managed to draw some conclusions?"

"Oh yes indeed! These pages show names of people stationed or visiting various hotels, research stations, shuttleports, and earth-based government compounds over the last year. The search strings create degrees of separation by six orders of magnitude. In other words, it finds common threads in relationships. So, what you end up with is a list that started out with thousands of names, but gets reduced to just a few hundred." He pulled the bottom report out and handed it to Ray.

Ray looked intensely at the report for over a minute, then handed it to Pam, "Here, they're just names to me, I try not to memorize many names, it just gets too overwhelming with all the clinic patients I see."

She stared at it for several minutes as they all watched quietly. Finally she spoke, "Well, some of these people are here now, some are back on Lemuria, but I'm sorry, we'll have to see what Mr. Ivory can do with it. Alicia interjected, "May I see the list?"

Pam gave it to her reluctantly and folded her arms as she waited. Alicia's eyes went over each line slowly. The further she got down the page, the more she started to close her eyes after each name. By the end of the list, she was trembling and beads of sweat were forming on her forehead. Ray grabbed her arm gently, "Are you feeling OK, do you want to sit down?" She nearly threw the report at Pam as she reached out for Max's chair. They all stood around her trying to understand what was happening. Pam rolled her eyes as she watched Alicia and then began taking a second look at the information in her hands.

Finally Alicia spoke, focusing her eyes directly at Ray. "Those people are becoming part of a very dangerous game. The more they unite, the more hardship they will endure."

Pam cleared her throat and said, "Excuse me, I must have missed this the first time, but I see your name on here, Alicia." Max grabbed the report and scanned it quickly, "You're right; I didn't see that earlier, I wonder how I missed it too."

Ray knelt down in front of Alicia and calmly asked, "Is that what upset you, seeing your name on the list?"

"No, it's hard to explain, as usual. All I can feel is that there are those among us who are not what they appear."

Ray stood back up, "What are you saying? Are you incriminating yourself somehow in the shuttle explosion?"

"The list brings together people who are players in this game. There will always be sides to choose from, or be chosen for you. You have to believe me when I tell you with all my heart; I would never do something to hurt other people."

Max interjected, "Alicia, what else about these names, what links them now to the 'sides' you speak of?"

Ray got an idea while she pondered his question, "Do they belong to an organization called D.O.V.E.?"

She turned her head slowly up to him, "Some of them, yes."

He persisted, "What about the rest, why are they on there?"

"They are why Dove exists."

Pam asked suspiciously, "How could you know all this unless you were somehow involved with them?"

"I cannot tell you, Pam, but you deserve an answer." She stood back up, having regained her composure. "My gift of intuition came from my parents, or it came from God. At the very least my parents taught me how to utilize that gift. You can find it, Pam, if you believe. For now, please trust me. I'm on your side." She gently extended her hand onto Pam's shoulder.

Ray shifted the moment with a quick comment to Max, "Why don't we ring up Ivory again? Maybe he'll offer some insight."

They all crowded over Max's shoulders as the viewcom displayed the security codes he entered. Soon the screen revealed Ivory, who seemed a bit road-weary. He looked into the screen as he yawned, "Hey there Majestik, what's the word?"

"Have you a copy of what we ran up here today on your search algorithms?"

"Yes I do, very impressive. The governor will be very pleased."

Max replied, "When you told me what Dove stood for, did you know if any of your local people were in the group?"

"No, I told you I had to ask Governor Payne what it even meant."

"Well, as you can see, some of the people on that final list are employed in the government compounds. We think they may be Dove members."

"Is that so? How very interesting. And how did you come to that conclusion? I don't have a search thread for Dove in the program."

Max smiled slyly, "Remember, you asked us for help, that's what you get when you contract with space-bound scientists. And as scientists, we feel you're still withholding data."

"Dr. Rogers, I assure you I'm cooperating fully. We want this thing solved as quickly as anyone else."

Ray leaned down into the view, "I'm Dr. Phillips, the research director up here. What can you tell us about the prisoner you have?"

"We have an injured man who happened to be a council member. I wasn't in on his interrogation so I don't know any more than that."

"What's his name?"

"I suppose that should be no secret. It's Hayden Green."

Max joined back in, "His name was on that list, Ivory!"

"Very observant, Dr. Rogers. That's why I'm so impressed with the report."

Max asked one final question, "Are you sure you can't tell me anything else about Peter Ancerid?"

"I told you before; I have very strict orders from the governor not to release anything on Dr. Ancerid. Besides, I personally don't know a thing about him. Now, if that's all, I've had a long day and would like to get some rest."

Max disconnected the man and looked up at his friends, "Well, that wasn't much help."

Ray added contemplatively, "On the contrary, he may have told us more than he realizes." He pulled up a chair next to Max, "Tell me, how would this MEGSIX secure line be tapped into, how could Dove do such a thing?"

Max thought a moment, "Hmmmm, either they have a high intensity laser probe and a very sophisticated computer to reconstruct the transmission, or..."

"Or, they used a terminal from the MEGSIX base station itself!" Pam stood back proudly after her contribution.

Max broke into a huge grin, "That's my girl, thinking like a detective again! It makes perfect sense; someone down at the African Parliament compound is a Dove member who is very good at computer code."

Alicia added, "I'm not sure it's this Hayden Green character, however; I can't see him being that technically sophisticated."

Ray put an arm around Pam and Alicia in a celebratory manner, "What say we all play detective over some dinner? I think we've gone as far as we can today on the computers."

Max jumped up to join them as Ray led them away from the machines, then stopped in his tracks. "Oh wait a minute, let me get these things properly shut down." As he busied himself, Ray released the two women and folded his arms watching Max. Pam looked at him and Alicia, then said sarcastically, "Ray, this is so unlike you to think about others at a time like this."

"What do you mean? I'm just getting better at listening to my inner voice. Right now it was yelling for food. It would be rude not to invite good company."

Alicia started again toward the door on her own, "You three enjoy yourselves, I've got a room to book and some packing to do. Besides, I'm not very hungry at the moment."

Pam watched her walk away and felt compelled to yell after her, "Good night."

CHAPTER FIFTEEN

The day had barely started, but Jaden King was busy at the monitors watching his crew on the planet. Pete came up behind him holding a recent spectrograph. Jaden looked over the numbers as he asked his friend the same question he had asked two times already that day. "How much longer do they have?"

"I'm afraid this is it. They have to get out of there now, the fields are just too unstable."

"Damn, nearly two days of crawling over that thing and we still have no clue how they're doing it! What the hell are we overlooking, Pete?"

"Jaden, just get them out of there; we can regroup when they're back up on mother."

"You're right. We think better when all of our heads are together in one room anyway." He sat down in front of another monitor and got Lensa on the screen.

"Lensa, do you hear me? The upstream picture is terrible."

He tried several more times until finally she barely came through. "Yes sir, we think we've come up with.................we're going..........it out and take a..........., Over."

Jaden slapped his hand down on the table, "Dammit, we're not getting through the electromagnetic fluxes! Lensa, listen to me, get your team out of there. Your suits won't hold back any more at this point!"

They both looked intensely at the screen, nearly transfixed by the colorful visual noise dancing across the viewer. Pete suddenly turned his attention to a blinking red light at the far end of the table. He quickly went over to attend it and yelled back, "Jaden, our surface seismographs are all going crazy! The planet's crust on this side is starting to move!"

Jaden grabbed at the microphone and yelled, "Lensa, get out of the structure, get into the shuttlepod now!"

Pete stood over his instrument cluster, "Good Gods, Jaden, this thing is shaking at 9's and 10's everywhere on Richter. I hope that old pyramid is solid enough to take it!"

King slammed his fist down and bounded over to a telescope monitor. He quickly aimed it at the surface location his crew was at. It took tortuously long for it to focus in on the planet from their perch 400 kilometers up. Finally he could see the site clearly. Pete asked excitedly, "Can you see anyone outside it yet?"

"No, where the hell are they? Wait! Yes, I see someone, now two. They're getting out, they're getting out!" The microphone cracked to life again, "This......Lensa.......walls are cracking.........we..... ....see......lar.....metal that......sticking out fro.....may be.......of....focusing th......"

Jaden ran back to his microphone, "No, Lensa, get out with the rest, the quake is too powerful, get out!"

Pete now was manning the telescope screen. "Jaden, the pyramid is getting obscured in dust, I think it's collapsing!"

Jaden screamed at the mike while he strained to look over at the telescope screen. "Nooo! You've got to make it. Run Lensa, run now!!!!"

Suddenly the communication monitor went completely dead. The two of them stood side by side watching the telescope picture. When the dust started to clear, nearly five minutes of quake activity finally came to an end. Pete walked back to his seismographs and saw the shaking had completely flatlined as if it never occurred. He printed out the entire event on an arm's length graph and brought it to Jaden. King reached for it but never took his eyes off the screen and the billowing dust clouds.

"Jaden, look at the graph. It flatlined like a switch was thrown off. I bet there won't be aftershocks." He put his hand on his friend's back, "I hope she made it out, she wouldn't try to be a hero."

Jaden seemed to ignore Pete as he moved in inches from the screen. "I think the surface is starting to be visible again, please help me look, I need to see all of them."

Together they searched the site meticulously, trying different resolutions to the lens. As each minute passed, their hopes grew dimmer. Suddenly Pete jabbed his finger at the upper corner of the picture. "There, that looks like them!"

As the image grew clearer, a small group of human figures took shape. They both were breathless as they counted over and over again. Pete spoke first, his voice low and shaky, "I see four, we're missing two, Jaden. I don't think they got out in time."

Jaden pressed his head against the screen in sorrow, tears running down his face. "Maybe they're alive in the rubble."

Pete hesitated to speak, but he knew it had to be said, "If they were in that pile, we have no equipment out here to dig them out. We need the survivors to get in the shuttle and get up here immediately."

Jaden rubbed the tears from his face as he sat back in his chair. "I killed them, I should have known better. They should have stayed up here today, it wasn't safe. I.."

"Stop it, nobody in hell could have forecast a crust shift like this! Nobody! You get paid to make the tough decisions up here, and I would have done the same thing. We all know what the risks are out here. Lensa was in command down there, she didn't need you to tell her to get out."

"What do you think she was saying in her last transmission?"

"We should replay the message and study it, but let's get in contact with the survivors first."

King walked over to a laser transmitter and turned it on. "We might get through with this."

He then sat back down at the viewscreen, "Mars, this is mother Shepherd, do you read?"

A line of static crackled from the speakers, then a voice came through, "Shepherd, this is Markson, do you read?"

"Barely, but good enough. We see four of you, where are the other two?"

"Lensa and Stanson never got out. The whole pyramid came down on them."

Jaden sighed deeply before he spoke, "Is the bioscanner still working?"

"Let me see.......Yes, give me a minute to look for life signs."

Five minutes later the voice of Markson came back, "I'm sorry, Jaden, but no signs of life. What do you want us to do?"

Jaden replied back with an air of defeat in his voice rarely heard by anyone, "Retreat back to mother. Repeat, retreat to mother immediately."

*   *   *

The lights to the committee chamber clicked on the moment the doors snapped open. Two guards entered first, followed by Victor Seeb, his three interrogators, Chairman Parker, then Ray Phillips. Seven of them took designated places in high-backed leather chairs around a horseshoe table, while Seeb was placed in a hard chair in its center, facing them.

The chairman nodded to the guards, who locked the doors behind them. Parker glanced through some file notes in front of him, then handed duplicates to the rest of the table. He spoke in a confident manner, "What we have here is an interesting situation, Mr. Seeb. Yesterday you were detained for routine questioning. You managed to give us more questions than answers. You also refused to talk with me yesterday, Victor. I was not very pleased. So, today we start fresh, now that you've had a comfortable night's sleep."

"Sleep! You think I could sleep with these two thugs in my room!"

Ray finished reviewing the file and spoke next, "I was asked here today, Mr. Seeb, because of the connection to our fuel research program and your group, I believe you called it Dove."

"That's right, and as I said, I'm not ashamed of my beliefs."

"While I admire a person standing up for what they believe in, we're still not sure what you believe in. We can't decide what to do with you unless we know what type of involvement you have in this group, and we must know what the group's objectives are."

Seeb folded his arms, then crossed his legs, "You're all supposedly intelligent people, you can't possibly be that ignorant! Don't you know there are aliens everywhere?"

Ray continued, his expression unchanged, "What kind of aliens?"

"I'm not talking about the dozens of races that have come and gone over the lifetime of the planet. We're concerned with only one species right now, the Vor!"

Parker interrupted, "Mr. Seeb, I told you yesterday you would have to do better today. I'm disappointed so far. Why do you insist on this alien hunting story? Is that your cover?"

"We only operate undercover around nonbelievers and supporters of the Vor. They have human help you know; people who will follow their every command, even kill!"

Ray asked politely, "If they can convince humans to kill for them, what do they use to motivate such behavior?"

"Mind control of some sort; we're not sure what turns certain people."

"Did you come to the Majestik to stop a specific human from harming people on this hotel?"

"Hey, Doc, now you're gettin' it! Where were you yesterday?"

Ray continued while the rest of the table sat quietly, "What did the Vor want to do to the Majestik?"

"Oh it's not just this hotel, it's much much more! They want the whole race gone, every last one of us!"

"You're not answering my question."

"You're not listening!"

The committeewoman slapped her hands down in frustration, "Mr. Chairman, this is going nowhere again! If he continues with this line of fantasy, we'll never get to the bottom of the explosion!"

Parker leaned over and looked at Ray, "What do you think, doctor, do you want to hear more alien stories?"

"Yes I would. Thank you for indulging me. Mr. Seeb, can you tell us who you were supposed to stop up here?"

"No, I told you I was just a delivery person this time around."

"Who else on the hotel right now belongs to Dove?"

"Can't tell you, don't know. But maybe I can tell you who is working for the Vor."

Ray got up and walked around the table to the man's side. He handed him a list of names, the same list he reviewed the prior day from Max's work. "Look at these names, Victor; who are with the Vor?"

The man at first glanced quickly over the names, but began to read deeper as his eyes jumped from one name to the next. He looked up in amazement, "How did you get this? Who's the snitch?"

"Mr. Seeb, you see more than just Vor names on here don't you? You see names of Dove members."

"Well even if I did, all I offered was the Vor supporters."

The chairman stood up, his interest now very peaked, "Dr. Phillips, may I see that list." Ray pulled it away from Seeb and walked back to his seat. He passed it over to the chairman.

Parker's dark eyebrows moved up and down as he read the names, his balding head now shining with tiny beads of sweat. "Doctor, did we generate this list or did you get it from earth?"

"Max was running the African programs, as you ordered, and he generated this. They're all linked through a complex algorithm of circumstances. Several of us brainstormed its implications last night, and I decided to test a theory on our friendly guest here."

"Well, it certainly looks like we have some serious work cut out for us now. Your group is to be commended for their work and insights." He placed the paper gently down in front of him. "Mr. Seeb, you will be released after you do two things for me. One, circle names on here that are with this Vor group. Two, answer this question. Where did you leave the supposed bag of lasers?"

The man folded his arms again, "It won't do you any good now, but in a flower stand outside the hotel clinic." Ray's eyebrows raised in surprise.

The chairman stood up and had one of the guards bring the list back to Seeb. He watched intently as he circled a small number of names. "I changed my mind. These are our Dove people. We haven't committed any crimes. That's all I feel I can safely tell you right now."

Parker looked over his work and had to be satisfied, "Guards, take him to his room, but put a tracker on him. Mr. Seeb, I hope I don't have to talk with you again soon. I want you off this structure as soon as ships start flying. We'll be keeping an eye on you till you get a trial on earth. Now get out."

He watched as the man took one last look back at him as he was escorted out the doors. Parker then sat down and picked up the list. "Ms. Najib, will you take your aides to the flower station and see what you can find? Also, is there anyone else you need to interview yet based on all our security reports?"

"Yes there is. Tim Ward, the shuttle's copilot."

"Very well, please do so now and report to me at 8 p.m." He waited for the three of them to leave before speaking to Ray.

"Ray, this alien thing is obviously a touchy subject any time it comes up in public. Most of us in government are still aware of the visit earth received years before the turmoil. Although as I think back, it all seems so unreal right now."

"I remember it well Sir, the Andromedians came in peace to Russia, of all places. The world has a lot to be thankful for because of them, our technology was advanced by decades."

"Yes, yes it was, but they also disappeared as quickly and mysteriously as they came. Since they were so humanoid, they fit right in to the populace, no one knew if you met one on the street they weren't one of us." Ray grinned slightly as he looked directly into Parker's face, "And what do you think, did they really leave?"

"It's nice to believe they're still here, protecting us, policing us. God knows we need all the help we can get nowadays."

"Even so, what are we going to do with this mess that came out of nowhere? Do you really believe there could be a hostile race that would dare come here knowing the Andromedians had helped us?"

"Sure is a frightening thought. With all the worries the human race has now, that rumor could spread and push everything into chaos again."

"Mr. Chairman, I..."

"Ray, please call me Bernie, but only in private you understand."

Ray smiled comfortably, "Bernie? OK, Bernie, I need to go to Africa as soon as we get a shuttle over here. I have some things to take care of regarding the fuel projects. I also might be able to shed more light on our mysterious Vor friends."

"Oh, holding back on me?"

"No not really, sir, uh Bern. But I think someone else is, that's why I need to go." He stood up to depart, "Anything else you need to talk with me about?"

"No, just be careful, for God's sake. I don't know how many more nuts like Seeb are up here, or on Earth for that matter. And those lasers, I've got to... never mind, just have a good night, doctor."

Ray reached down and looked over the list of names, focusing on the few that Seeb had circled. He smiled as he slid it back in front of Parker. "Good night, Bernie."

CHAPTER SIXTEEN

Alicia stood outside the room suite and checked the room number once again against the number she held in her hand. She took a deep breath, then touched the bell. The doors opened instantly, startling her head back.

The occupant marveled, "Captain Martin, what a surprise, come in!"

She cautiously surveyed the room first, then casually walked in. "Tim, I know it was three days ago, but I wanted to come by and apologize for being rude to you. I was just feeling sorry for myself. I had confusing thoughts when we last met. It seemed you were not the man I had been flying with this last year. But, I feel I wasn't myself that day either."

He sat down in the largest chair in the room, then noticed his empty glass on the stand next to him. He shifted away from it as he hit the mute button on the telescreen that was blaring rock music. He motioned her to the couch, "Please, have a seat."

She nodded and sat at one end of the couch.

"Tell me, Alicia, you don't mind that I call you that now, do you? After all, we are off duty."

"That's fine."

"So how are you? The injuries have continued to heal magnificently!"

"I had a good doctor; he has the magic touch, I guess."

"Well he mus have sumthin, he sure has seen you quite a bit 'dis last week." She looked at him surprised, then slyly smiled back, "How would you know, have you been spying on me?"

"Oh no, no! I jus saw da two of you once or twice together the last few days, that's all. Affer all, 'dis hotel isn't that big, you know!" He jumped up and fiddled with something behind the viewscreen. In moments he pulled out a bottle of Scotch. "Hey, join me in a ....celebration drink. A toast to your recovery an us flying again soon."

"No thank you, it seems you've had a few toasts without me already."

He walked back next to her, "What else are we suppos' to do while we sit around waiting fur the bureaucrats?"

"Anything but stay drunk all day. You know it's against the rules."

He sat down right next to her as he poured from the bottle.

"You and your rules! I guess that's why I'm not a captin, too many rules fur me."

She stood up, uncomfortable with him so close to her. He gulped down the tall drink as he watched her walk over to the desk. He slammed down the glass on the small table in front of him, "Wha's the matter, you look nervous. Why are you really here?"

"I'm sorry Tim, this probably wasn't a good time to come by, I think I'd better come back another time." Just as she started for the door he grabbed the remote and aimed it at the door control panel, activating the lock. She turned back just as he shoved the control in his pant pocket.

"Come on, Tim, stop playing bloody games. Open the door and I'll call you tomorrow."

He sat back down on the couch, his hands stroking the cushions on each side.

"Not until yooou have a drink."

"I told you I didn't want one!"

"Well, why not?"

She folded her arms defiantly, "My doctor said no alcohol yet."

"You and your precious white knight doctor. I can show you a bettr' time than he can, I'm mucsh yunger. Hey,..let's get nekked!"

"Don't be absurd, certainly not with you in this state! If you want to know the truth, I really came to ask you one more important question." She walked right up to him and put her hands on her hips, "Why didn't your name make the list?"

"What list?"

"You're working for the Vor, don't deny it! I've wrestled with these thoughts for three days and I can't stop the feeling, you're with them!"

He reached for the bottle again but she swiped it away before he could touch it. "You've had enough, why don't you come with me to the clinic."

"I'm not goin' annnywhere with you until you gif me my bottle!" He lunged up at her as she immediately stepped back, raising the bottle high over her head. He clawed upward for it, his one arm wrapped over her shoulder pushing it down. She resisted him while trying desperately to get the remote from his pocket. He babbled out, "See, you can't wait to have me."

They fell backwards onto the rug, Tim landing on top of her. His face was now inches from hers as she clenched her teeth trying to push him off.

"Get off of me you bastard!"

Losing interest in his bottle, he now held her arms down as his face filled with an aroused grin.

"Dis' is what you came for!" He drove his mouth against hers as he forced a kiss on her tightly drawn lips. He released one of her arms as he reached in to unzip her suit. At that moment she crashed the bottle over his head as hard as she could. He barely whimpered as his eyes rolled up into his head, and he collapsed onto her.

Still frantic, she pushed him over and pulled the remote from his pocket. Once the door opened she threw it down and ran from the room. Stumbling in near hysterics, she went to the end of the hall emergency phone.

"Operator, please get me Dr. Phillips. This is an emergency!"

Panting heavily she turned her gaze to Tim's open door at the opposite end of the hall.

"Come on Ray, please answer the call!"

Suddenly his voice enveloped her from the phone, "This is Dr. Phillips." She swiped her hand across her forehead, then held her head comfortingly as she cried, "Thank goodness you answered! Ray, this is Alicia, I need help."

"Calm down, where are you?"

"Level 7, in corridor 6a. Ray, I think I killed someone, I think I killed Tim!" By now tears were flowing down her cheeks as she stared back at his room.

"Stay where you are, someone will be there in less than a minute. Alicia, I'm on my way too. It will take a few minutes, just stay on the line with me."

"Ray hurry, I'm scared!"

*　　*　　*

Soon the hall and suite were crowded with official personnel. The medics worked on the man as he lay motionless on his back. Alicia stood in the doorway, her arms folded tightly as she looked down at her copilot. Suddenly he groaned as one of the medics injected him. One of the other men at his side stood up and walked over to Alicia, "Looks like a simple concussion and laceration, complicated by inebriation. He should come out of it OK by tomorrow, although he's gonna' have a huge headache. We'll take him to the clinic now."

She mumbled softly to herself, "That's where I wanted him to go."

Just then Ray's firm hands took hold of her shoulders. She looked back at him relieved and proclaimed, "He's going to be OK."

"Alicia, what happened?"

"I'm not sure, it happened so fast. I came here to talk with Tim, he was drinking, at least it seemed he had indulged a few. And then he attacked me. It's so unlike him. I knew he had an occasional drink, but I never dreamed he would behave like this."

"Come on, let's get to the clinic, I want to check you out before he gets there." He led her out the door but was stopped by the arrival of the security investigation team.

The lead woman spoke to Ray as her eyes examined Alicia, "Doctor, what's going on here?"

"Ms. Najib, there's been an accident. Tim Ward is being taken to the clinic for observation and testing." He started to step past her when she touched his chest firmly with her palm.

"We came here to interrogate Mr. Ward. This is a bad coincidence. When can we speak with him?"

"I'll tell you as soon as I look him over properly. Now, if you please, I need to get past, the captain here is in need of medical attention."

The woman stood there, hands on hips watching the two of them leave. She turned to one of the two men, "Come on, let's check out this suite, we may not get another opportunity."

*   *   *

The large doors swooped open into the clinic atrium as the gurney carrying Tim Ward rolled through. Pam was waiting with Jerry by an empty exam table. Ray was busy running a test on Alicia in the next room. As soon as he saw Tim, he yelled out instructions to the two of them.

"I want all three basic scans run, and keep him quiet. That shouldn't be too hard since he'll likely still be intoxicated."

He returned to Alicia as she sat up. "This is going to be sore for a few days," as he touched her cheekbone. He continued, "I guess things could have gotten really ugly in there." Alicia remained pensive as she watched them roll Tim into the large scanner.

She shook her head sadly, "I know there's something not right with Tim, they've done something to him."

Ray looked at her curiously, but not surprised, "What do you feel is wrong with Tim?"

She winced a little as she stood up from the table, "Ray, I accused him of aiding the Vor, and he went wild. I didn't expect him to hurt me; as a matter of fact I was hoping he would deny it. I guess I went there because the man I fly with seemed to disappear the day of the explosion. I thought I could find him."

"Do you think he destroyed the Torrus?"

Alicia thought as she fixated on the scanner's lights, "I don't know now. I hate it when I can't get a clear read on someone. It's very hard to bond with a mind that has already been changed."

Jerry called in to Ray, "Doctor, I think you better have a look at this."

Ray walked over to a screen displaying a rotating three dimensional view of Tim's brain. Alicia was right behind him as he approached the image. Pam made some adjustments to tunnel in to an area near his lower frontal cortex. She froze the image when Jerry exclaimed, "There, stop at that spot!" He pointed to a small density, "Look at this three millimeter cube just next to the Thalamus, its crazy!"

Alicia leaned in, "Did I do that when I hit him?"

Ray quickly answered, "Oh no, it's way too unnatural to be from a trauma, unless you teletransported the object into his brain."

She looked at him unamused, "Is that an implant then? It almost looks like it has intelligence."

Pam came over for a closer look, "Good God, Ray, how did it get in there? I didn't see any scars big enough to accommodate it surgically."

Ray went to the console and moved the picture around a bit while everyone watched intently. He tried to be objective as he thought aloud, "Since we still can't teletransport, if human intelligence is behind it, they could possibly grow it in there with nanotechnology."

Alicia backed away with arms folded on her abdomen, "Ray, you have to get it out!"

"I agree, but I'll need to study it some more to find a way to get at it."

She continued, "If you need to do surgery, I expect you'll need Tim's permission to do the operation. I wonder if he would consent."

Ray chuckled, "You should know the answer to that! You folks are government property, your health and his are solely my call up here."

She sat down on the nearest chair, "Wonderful, I'll try to remember that next time I need brain surgery."

He looked over to her, "You didn't do too badly now with the care we gave you this last week. The system works pretty well." He got up from the console, "Pam, let's do a microfiberoptic probe. I want to start as soon as his blood alcohol is low enough. As a matter of fact, Jerry, why don't you shoot him up with some glutathione to speed things up a bit."

Ray went and sat next to her as soon as Pam left the room. "Alicia, this is all getting too unreal, too cloak and dagger. The situation seems to boil down to two possibilities. One, the explosions and related incidents are being perpetrated by humans in some sort of mad game or outright lunacy. Or two, the situation is due to metaphysical-like things. You know, aliens if you will."

She looked at him somberly, "Or three, you have both."

Ray sighed as he leaned back on the rear legs of the chair, "Why is it I think you're right?" Jerry interrupted, asking for help getting Tim from the scanner. As Ray got up he asked her quietly, "Would tonight be too soon for a little dinner, I have a lot of questions yet?" She smiled and simply asked what time as he started to help pull Tim up from the bed.

CHAPTER SEVENTEEN

The Martian day was waning as Jaden King finished suiting up for his trip to the surface. Pete stood opposite him, helping check the details on all the closures. The two worked together silently.

"Jaden, once you get down there, remember: no heroics. I still don't understand why you have to go down alone now. Everyone that got out made it up here in one piece. And besides, the place could quake again."

King smiled, "I remember you earlier predicted we wouldn't see another big one." His face was now expressionless as he put his helmet on. "Just make sure I land as close to the site as possible."

"Don't worry about that, I've got you programmed all the way in, just sit back and trust the computers."

King gave a salute-like gesture as he turned to enter the craft. Once inside, the airlocks hissed as the curved hatch sealed itself. Pete stepped from the airlock umbilical and sealed it behind him. He made his way to a port window and joined all of the remaining crew as they watched Jaden's departure from the mother station. Then, the main drive kicked in and the craft shot away in a blur toward the planet. The now-dense Martian atmosphere was reacting with the ship, leaving a glowing blue streak in its trail.

Pete walked away to an instrument cluster to monitor the ship's trajectory. He hoped their atmospheric readings were accurate, as the shuttle's descent was programmed from the day's measurements. If he got it wrong, his friend would burn up in an agonizing free-fall to the surface. He picked up the radio transmitter, "Jaden, how's it feeling?"

The man's voice came back loud and clear, "Smooth as can be. Sure is getting warm. Nothing like my last descent a month ago into the thinner atmosphere."

"Stay cool, buddy, you're almost in. Shouldn't get much hotter." Soon the glowing streak faded from view as the ship slowed and began a long arched turn. Pete spoke once again, "Jaden, you should be a minute away from the site. You're now one kilometer up. I've programmed a vertical landing one hundred meters south of the pile. Remember, stay off the wings, they'll be too hot for you to walk on. Just jump down from the hatch."

"I'm glad gravity is still the same, otherwise that might hurt a bit. OK, I'm hovering from final descent; so far everything's running perfectly. Looks like I'll beat sundown by a few minutes like I'd hoped."

By now several crew were at the telescope watching the ship land. Pete went over and joined them. He wondered aloud, "I don't know what he expects to find down there in the dark." One of the surface crew replied somberly, "He's going to find peace."

*   *   *

Jaden sat back in his seat and closed his eyes. He took a deep breath and let it flow out slowly through his lips. He watched yet again the cloud of dust envelop his two lost crew. He heard himself screaming into the microphone. A sharp beep from the instruments broke his trance as he opened his eyes. In front of him lay the ruins of what was once a mighty pyramid-like edifice. He glanced at the digital timer by his side counting down his expedition. He quickly unbuckled the restraints and verified his helmet airseal. Before opening the ship's hatch he communicated with mother, "I'm exiting the lander, I'll check in again as soon as I'm in the ruins."

Pete responded flippantly, "If you get hurt you know the governor is going to blame me for this."

"Of course he will, but he'd be even madder at me if I let *you* do something this irrational. Over." He maneuvered himself to the hatch and waited for decompressioning. It amazed him that his ship's atmospheric pressure wasn't much different than outside. The hatch opened in just seconds. He stuck his head out and looked down to the surface. The jump would be about two meters, so without hesitation he shoved himself out the hatchway. He landed with a forward roll to his side and ended up on his back. He lay there motionless, instantly mesmerized by the color of the twilight stars above. Unfortunately he had no time to enjoy the earthen nature of the planet's sky.

He rolled to his side in the soft dust and pushed up to his hands and knees. There he glanced at the instrument readings on his forearm. The air was 22°C and nearly breathable. At first he thought the instrument had been damaged by the jump. He hit a reset button and watched as the same readings flashed again on the small screen. Either the air was like this all over the planet and they didn't detect it from the space station, or this was a freak atmospheric pocket somehow associated with the proximity of the ruins.

As he stood up, he again thought of the crew he had lost. They came so close to being able to take a real breath of Martian air! He shook off the thought and gathered a few instruments from a storage panel in the ship's belly, then began a brisk walk to the ruins.

Within minutes he was face to face with an ominous pile of rock. From space, its original shape challenged the imaginations of many who looked down on it. Now all he saw was a grave. He stood motionless, hands hanging at his sides. Then, something inside him let go. It let go in an explosion of pure insanity: all of his logic, his pride, his fears, and his helmet. He ripped it off and threw it down. Without hesitation he drew in a huge breath and screamed it out in a primal yell that reached all the way to his soul. The sound bounced several times around him off the surrounding hills. As the last millimeter of air left his lungs he stooped forward and dropped his hands onto his slightly bent knees and hung his head.

At first he was almost afraid to breathe again, but the craving for oxygen was too powerful. So through his nostrils he drew another breath, this time slowly and analytically. At first the dusty brew stung slightly as it coursed into his sinuses. It inflated his lungs, but did not satisfy his brain, so he quickly drew another breath, this time faster. After several breaths, he began to feel stable. The air was breathable, the planet, or at least this place, was alive with oxygen!

He would have to breathe at a slightly faster rate than was normal, but he was determined not to put his helmet back on again. It would be easier to work without it. So he started onto the pile, this time purposely replaying Lensa's last transmission in his head. He was still trying to grasp what she was trying to say. What did she see that she was willing to give her life for?

He stopped after stepping over the first few rocks. He reached down and picked up one of the smaller red blocks. It was surprisingly light for its size. He held it in one hand as he reached behind him into his pack for an instrument. He waved a small device over the rock several times to calibrate its meters. Once he was satisfied, he dropped the rock and proceeded to climb upward on the pile.

It was hard not to marvel at what these stones had once been. He suddenly mourned the many pyramids on Earth that had been destroyed by the cataclysms. Until now their destruction was almost inconsequential compared to the billions of human lives that were lost. Yet now, this loss resonated in him all the way back to Earth. This structure had existed for perhaps hundreds of thousands of years. Now it too was gone, its true meaning never discovered. He couldn't accept that fact, because if he did it would mean Lensa and Stanson died for nothing.

By now he was 25 meters up and breathing desperately hard and fast. This would have to do, he could go no further. He started to scan for any minerals and metals that were not in the smaller rock he calibrated against. He waited as the scans were calculated. He was sure Lensa was saying the word metal when he lost communication with her. Then as he glanced back down at the instrument screen, he opened his eyes wide at the reading that was flashing in the near blackness surrounding him. It showed there was gold below him!

He quickly slid out of the heavy pack on his back and retrieved a portable light. Within minutes the rocks were lit in a harsh white beam. He stood back and nearly squinted from the reflections. Then he saw it, a shiny reflection calling out to him from beneath the spaces of the debris. He dropped to his knees and threw several pieces aside to reach what caught his eye. There it was, a shiny, thick strand of pure golden color woven through a rock the size of his arm. The strand was nearly as thick as his little finger. As he compared it to his anatomy, he touched it with that finger. The metal was so soft it was nearly gel-like. He snapped his hand back and looked closer at the material, then stood up, grabbed the light and started to walk down the pile, scanning for reflections. Sure enough, several more shiny strands screamed out to him with their vibrance. He went back to his backpack, removing the remainder of its contents by simply dumping it onto the rocks. He then quickly collected several manageable pieces with the gold strands and shoved them in the bag.

With light in hand and a heavy load of rocks on his back, he cautiously made his way down the pile. Sweat was pouring off his body, yet the chilling night air rapidly cooled his head. He was slightly nauseous by now, but too excited to worry about it. He reached the spot his helmet lay on the ground and gratefully snapped it back on his suit. The purified air from the helmet smelled almost sweet as he sat on his heels breathing, waiting to feel the strength to make the walk back to the lander.

Finally he was ready. He stood and looked up at the billions of stars blanketing the heavens above him. He then looked at the strobe light his ship was now flashing in the distance. One last glance at the pile behind him and he was off. As he walked he realized his heart was still pounding hard, but his breathing was back to a normal rate. He was excited, and in a manner he hadn't felt since the planet began its transformation, and certainly not since the recent loss of his crew. A smile enveloped his face the entire duration of his walk back to the lander.

As he climbed up the now cool wing ladder and hopped through the hatch, he quickly glanced at the timer. It had just finished counting down to zero the moment he focused it in. He quickly called the mother ship. "Pete, this is Jaden, do you read?"

A voice immediately sprung back, "Thank God, why the hell haven't you been in contact!"

"I couldn't, I forgot my helmet."

"What! Don't mess with me, commander! Are you in the lander?"

"Yes yes! I'm about to seal the hatch. I'm ready to ascend any time you're ready."

"Did you find anything? Did you find any bodies?"

Jaden hesitated a moment, then replied, "No bodies. I did find what Lensa found. I think I know what she was trying to say to us. I'll fill you in when I'm back on mother, over."

"OK, as soon as I see you're buckled in, I'll get you airborne."

"Looking forward to seeing everyone again, seems like I've been gone a long time."

*   *   *

Alicia checked the time once more. She sighed as she flopped back into the soft couch in her room, resting her head against her hand. The room was quiet; the only light came from the lamp suspended above her. She reached for the viewscreen control and was about to push the 'on' button, when the door signal interrupted the silence. She calmly placed the controller back on the table, and then walked to the door.

The door jumped open as she touched the control; Ray was standing with his back to her. He turned quickly, revealing a handful of flowers. He smiled as he extended them to her, "Sure is convenient having a flower stand outside the clinic."

"Oh, Ray, they're beautiful!" She took them and nearly buried her face in the petals. "Wow, I can smell every morsel of their sweetness! I didn't think they were real!"

"Oh yeah, we mastered growing them up here a few years ago. I'm happy you've recovered your olfactory senses so completely. It proves they were real flowers I gave you before."

"Funny you would feel that, Ray; I never doubted they were real. I just wasn't sure if you were a flower guy or not."

"Well, am I?"

"You have excellent taste. I almost forgot about not being able to smell. It came back so subtly!"

"That's just human nature; we don't notice things about our health when we're feeling good, just when components of it are not working." He stood next to her rocking nervously back and forth on his heels. He glanced at his wrist and then apologized, "I'm sorry for being so late, the surgery on Tim took a little longer than we expected."

"So you got it out?" She grabbed his hand and led him to the couch, "Let's sit down a moment, I want to hear all about what you found in him."

"Well, there's not much to say at this point. The implant was living tissue, which is why it took so long to untangle it. The borders were completely blended in with the brain tissue. We tried several useless methods to separate the tissue away. It was just dumb luck how we got it out."

"Really, how's that?"

"The visual probe apparently generates enough of an electrical field to irritate the implant tissue. Normally that frequency is harmless to human brain tissue, but this thing hated it. It pulled in its tendrils before our eyes! Once it let go, I just sucked it out."

"Just like that?"

"Just like that, vomp!"

"So what's Tim's prognosis?"

"We don't foresee any complications. There were no major blood vessels involved. It appears the implant got its nutrition from intracellular diffusion and may have excreted neurotransmitter-like chemicals to influence his personality."

"What type of substances do you think it was making?"

"That may take as long to figure out as the new shuttle fuel experiments. Max and I will start running studies on the little thing tomorrow. We'll eventually dissect it for microscopic analysis, but for now we'll leave it in one piece."

"I'd like to throw it on the floor and step on it!"

Ray looked at her with a surprised smile on his face, "Really, Captain, no interest in discovering how new life forms work?"

"I've seen enough of it in Tim, that's all I need to study!" She then reached for her purse.

"I'm glad Maxwell can help you study it, he'll welcome the change of pace. Is he done with the African delegate studies yet?"

Ray stood up to head for the restaurant, "Max just finished their work today as a matter of fact, but somehow I think you knew that."

"Dr. Phillips, I guess I'll take that as a compliment." She followed him as he gestured her to the door.

"How else would you take it?" By now they were in the hallway.

"Oh, I suppose you could still be thinking I was a spy or something."

"A spy, wow, that never occurred to me. Do you think anyone on the investigative committee would accuse you of that?"

"Only if you gave them a reason to."

The elevator doors closed and they descended to the restaurant level. All the while Ray chewed his lips in thought. Once the doors opened he led her out, "After you, Captain." He hesitantly put his hand on her lower back as the two of them made their way through the noisy lobby.

*   *   *

They arrived at a small restaurant in the corner of the Majestik's huge lobby. A uniformed hostess greeted them as they entered the darkened dining room. Soft candles flickered on the tables as quiet conversations from the patrons blended with harp music playing near the end of the bar. The woman guided them to a secluded table adjacent the tall floor-to-ceiling windows. The current view displayed the rest of the hotel magnificently against the blue Earth below.

As they settled into their chairs, a waiter was instantly there filling their water glasses with the refiltered and endlessly recycled water so few people actually drank. He politely folded his hands behind his back and tilted his head. "Would madam care for a cocktail?"

Alicia looked at Ray and smiled, "No thank you, I'm still under orders to avoid alcohol. Something fruity and fun would be nice, though."

He turned to Ray, "And you, sir?"

"I'm going to surprise you, young man, and actually drink this water."

The waiter pulled his chin in and said, "Very well, I'll be back in a few minutes for your order. Since it's late, I must tell you the kitchen will be closing in 30 minutes." Alicia fiddled with her utensils a little while looking out the window. "This is really a beautiful view. I've never been in this part of the hotel before."

"Well, I don't come here often, just when I need a little mood change. Say, I didn't tell you how pretty you look tonight. That hair ornament completely covers the wound scar while at the same time making you look more like royalty than military."

"Less military? Now that's really a compliment! I haven't worn my flight uniform since the day I arrived. I kind of miss it. Somehow I felt stronger wearing it."

"I must say you definitely gave a strong impression. A tall, beautiful blonde in a captain's uniform can be quite enthralling."

"Enthralling? Is that another male word for a sexual comment?"

He decided he better think about this answer before blurting it out. "Sexual? Me? I'm not like most men, I only think about sex 80% of the time."

They both laughed as Ray reached for his glass of water. After a long slow sip, he commented, "I can't believe it's only been a week since I first met you in the Orion restaurant. I feel so at ease around you now, it's as if I've known you my whole life."

She reached for his hands and touched them lightly, "That's what being a human is all about. When we let our defensive self relax, all we have for each other is simply love."

Ray swallowed another large sip loudly, "Love?"

"I mean all humans are bonded ultimately not by genetics, but by love. It's a vibrational thing."

"We've all heard that message before, seems no one knows how to believe it or what it really means."

"Oh Ray, it is just a matter of what to believe in! My father was a great man; he brought the Earth so much. He met my mother at a time in her life when she was confused like you were. In a way he really saved her life."

He looked down at his empty plate, then back into Alicia's eyes. "I don't feel my life needs to be saved, if that's what you're implying. But I think I know what you mean. So...who was your father, Alicia?"

"He worked at the ASA from its inception in 2012."

"The Australian Space Authority, wow, that' quite a feather! What did he do for them?"

"He worked in the secret division studying Andromedian propulsion systems."

Ray reached across and squeezed her hands tightly in excitement, "You're kidding! He would have had regular contact with the Andromedians! There were so few that actually were allowed to interact with them!"

She looked intently into his eyes and lowered her voice, "Ray, no one has ever known this before except my mother, me and a few ASA diplomats. You are at a point in your life where you must know also. My father *was* Andromedian."

He sat there in stunned silence, eyes nearly bulging out of their sockets. Then, a look of fear seemed to overcome him as he loosened his grip on her hands. He gently retracted his hands to his lap and leaned back in his chair. Just then the waiter reappeared with her drink. "Are we ready to order yet?"

Ray ignored the man as he continued to stare at Alicia. She smiled politely at their server as she picked up her menu, "I'm sorry; we haven't even looked at our menus yet." The man bowed and diplomatically pointed to his watch. He then walked away while subtly talking to himself with his hands.

"Oh Ray stop staring, you look so immature right now I can't stand it."

He almost whispered in his disbelief, "You're an alien!"

She set her menu down hard and leaned forward, trying to restrain her voice, "I am not! First of all, only one of my parents was. And secondly, doctor, you should know the genetic crossbreeding possibilities would be impossible if his gene pattern wasn't of the same basic characteristics of the rest of the human race."

"Now I'm confused again. If the genes were compatible enough to allow interbreeding,...that could mean the Andromedians were our ancestors!"

She looked at him frustrated, "There you go again jumping to conclusions. Did it occur to you that we could be their ancestors? Or, perhaps different planetary life systems began under the same basic program?"

"Program?"

"Boy, for a man as smart as you, I don't think you get out very much."

He was now leaning intently toward her, "Are you talking about a program as in the concept of a computer program?"

She looked at her menu and pretended to ignore him, "Is the algae salad tasty here?"

"I don't know; never brave enough to try it. Did your father believe in God?"

She sighed and lowered her menu, "My father said they believed in a supreme creator. However, like us, God never officially revealed himself to them. How about the mushroom soup?"

Ray looked at his menu in frustration, "I'll tell you what, call the waiter back before he decides to put something we didn't order in our food. Let's both have a go at the tasting menu, five samples of the best they've got. So, please tell me more."

As she waved for the waiter she added, "Once their technology was advanced enough, they set out into the universe in search of answers, much like the human race is doing now."

The waiter arrived and took their order. As soon as he left Ray scooted his chair around next to Alicia. "This is so profound; I really don't know what to say. It seems so unbelievable. So, of all places, the Andromedians end up on Earth!"

"Oh, it's more than Earth, they've been to thousands of planets, but they've made Earth a special project." He was speechless, and could only stare at the tabletop contemplating the information and his next question.

"Do you believe me, Ray?"

"Oh yes, of course I believe you, but will anyone believe me!?"

She grabbed his hand very intently, "Ray, you cannot tell this to anyone! I told you, and you only, do you understand?"

He looked at her a little surprised by her forcefulness, but somehow made himself appreciate the situation. He nodded reluctantly and turned to look out the window.

She took a huge sip of her drink, "Ray, you must feel I know a lot about you, but I don't. So, it's my turn to ask a question. Who is Ray Phillips?"

"Oh, that guy is not really as smart as people think. Sure he can mix up a mean rocket fuel or probe inside your brain, but don't get into deep philosophy with him."

She giggled but made him continue. "What was your childhood like?"

"My childhood, are you kidding? That could take all night!"

She smiled coyly at him, "Well, I don't think I've got too many other plans for the rest of the evening, if you know what I mean. I'm a good listener."

Ray chuckled shyly, "All right, Captain Martin, I was born..."

CHAPTER EIGHTEEN

Hayden Green awoke to a nurse prodding a sharp instrument at his legs, "Ouch, that hurts!" He excitedly pulled himself up in the bed and looked down at his feet, then immediately at the woman, "My legs! I can feel my legs!"

"Yes you can Mr. Green, how about that!"

He pulled the remainder of the sheets away and rubbed his hands lovingly up and down their lengths. "Oh how wonderful to feel them. I want to try and walk!"

"That is not advisable right now sir. We'll bring a therapist in later today to begin the rehabilitation process. Right now, I want you to stay in bed and simply work on moving your toes and ankles. Also practice bending and straightening your knees."

He flopped back disappointed, and folded his hands behind his head. "I guess you'll have to tell the doctor about this, who will in turn tell Governor Payne."

She looked at him puzzled, "Of course I have to tell the doctor. Why wouldn't you want them to know you got your legs back?"

"Oh, you wouldn't understand. It's just that my life is safer the longer I can stay in here."

She folded her arms in slight disagreement, "If you're referring to those guards out there, I think we would all relax a lot more if they weren't here every second of the day."

He pulled up the sheets frustrated, "I see what you're implying. Never mind, nobody understands, you're all fools waiting for destruction!"

"The doctor will be around shortly to check on you. Please try and do what I asked." With that she left the room shaking her head in disbelief.

He lay there focused on the ceiling, thinking about the runway attack three days earlier. He stewed over the insensitive way Payne threatened him when he visited. Ultimately his emotions battled with logic, which led to more anxiety and frustration. He wanted to scream out in anger, but instead settled back to reality, and began to wiggle his toes.

*   *   *

Governor Payne's personal secretary entered his office. "Sir, there are two urgent messages coming in for you. One is from Interspace communications, and the other is from the hospital where Mr. Green is still located."

He lowered the papers in front of him, "Well, this could be an enlightening morning. Very good, I'll handle them both on my own. You may go."

He turned to his viewscreen and accessed the space transmission first. The usual static preceded the picture. Then Jaden King's face appeared.

"Jaden, you look terrible, what's going on?"

"I'm sorry; Pete and I were up all night examining some surface samples. But first, I must report some bad news." He paused and looked away for nearly ten seconds, then composed himself. "We had a severe, unexpected quake under the Sarovian plate yesterday. We lost two surface crew members; Lensa and Stanson."

Payne sunk back into his chair and rubbed his face once then immediately sat back up, his face stiffened with concern, "What happened, how come no one saw it coming with all that fancy equipment we have out there?"

"We had a crew on and inside the southernmost tetrahedron. The quake came out of nowhere. We tried to get them all out, but Lensa was either out of communication or disobeyed the command to evacuate."

"So, you're telling me that on the one hand we have a planet terraforming at lightning speed, but now it's buckling like what happened here on earth?"

"Oh no, nothing that bad. We actually think this was a good thing so far, that is, for the planet's sake!"

"When the hell is an earthqu..uh...marsquake a good thing?"

"It means the core is starting to churn, perhaps spin. That in turn will raise the magnetic field."

Now Otis was beginning to feel excited again, "So not only are we getting a planet with a good atmosphere, but we might get her shields up as well?"

"Yes, and I think what Lensa saw in the structure before it went down has a key role in the core reaction we are now seeing."

Payne reminisced about his crew choices, "Lensa was always a smart and yet stubborn go-getter. I wouldn't think of Stanson that way."

"We think he went in after her, and obviously he gave his life for hers."

"What did she find, doctor? Is that what you were examining all night?"

"Yes, I went down and personally retrieved various samples from the ruins. I'll try and have a better explanation tonight. Right now, I can tell you we have a metallic substance that is predominantly gold, but in the form of a viscous aerogel. It was fixed throughout the inner monument in some pattern. We're running simulations to try and recreate what that configuration was. Also, when the pyramid was intact, it was effectively shielding our probes from this substance. Now however, it is easily detectable, even from up here. We think we can accurately estimate the quantity of the substance in the pile. So, we're excited, but we still have a lot of new pieces to weave together."

Payne was nodding as he followed the story. "Jaden, are you sure there was no outside influence on what happened to the planet?"

"Absolutely! I know where you're going with this, but we haven't seen any ET's or UFO's. Now, if you wouldn't mind, I'll have to get back to work. We're having a little service here shortly for our lost crew."

"Fine. Please give my condolences to the rest of your staff and crew. We'll handle notification of any kin from down here. It's the least I can do." He switched off the screen and sat back thoughtfully in his chair. After a few minutes of stressful quiet, he contacted the hospital.

"I was told there was a message for me."

"Yes sir, let me put the doctor on." Soon the face of Green's doctor appeared wide-eyed and smiling.

"Good news, Governor, Mr. Green has nerve function restored to his legs!"

Payne sat there unemotional in thought, and then replied, "Marvelous; I never doubted your skills for a moment, doctor. Now tell me, when can he be moved?"

"Moved? Where do you want him moved to?"

"The small clinic at the shuttleport complex."

The doctor glared back at him, his face now a mixture of confusion and anger. "That is probably the worst place I could think of putting this man right now! The facility there has only minimal medical staff and no form of rehabilitation department."

"Doctor, you said the man has no permanent injuries; what's the problem?"

"I know what I said, but there is always a remote chance something could complicate things, such as a surprise infection, blood clot thrombi, to name just a few! If he had such an emergency we might have to transport him all the way back here."

"I'm willing to risk that. I am dealing with a situation much more complex than one man's legs. Now, can he be moved tomorrow?"

The doctor sat back with folded arms, "I suppose, but I'm going on record as opposed to this!"

Otis reached for the screen to shut it off, "Good day, doctor." He grumbled to himself as he quickly heaved upward from his chair. He walked over to the door and poked his head through, "Find Mr. Ivory for me, he should be somewhere in the building." The woman immediately stopped what she was doing and paged Tom Ivory. Less than two minutes later the delegate promptly appeared in the inner office.

"Yes sir, what can I do for you this morning?"

"Ivory, I thought I was going to have a good day today, but now I need some cheering up."

"And....you want me to cheer you up?"

"Oh relax; it's just a figure of speech. Sit down, Tom. I want to summarize the last of your data from the other day." Otis shuffled the piles of computer reports in front of him. "There's something you're not getting across to me here. Let's see, so far you've said that most of the names on this homology profile fit an old Central Security watch list of Dove supporters. What about the rest on the list? Are they not members of something? Maybe the data was mined from too many old sources to be accurate."

"Your Honor, when I gave that to you yesterday, I told you the Majestik people came up with the Dove conclusion part, I simply confirmed it. Actually, I was quite surprised myself. The list simply tells you why those people were likely to join a group such as Dove, nothing else."

"Well, I hope they're not all like Green, for God's sake! By the way, the chairman at the Majestik informed me today they've been holding someone for two days who claims to be a Dove member also. I've already confirmed his name is on this list."

"Did they get any information out of him?"

"Yes, but not what they had hoped for. He basically said he was up there to help stop a group of Vor supporters." Ivory sat down while maintaining his focus on Otis, "Here we go with the Vor again."

"Yes, here we go. Now, let's suppose for a moment the Vor are real, after all, I am open-minded." Tom almost bit his lip while he continued to listen, "Why would they need humans to do their dirty work?"

The man thought a moment, "Because they don't want to be discovered?"

"I don't know. If on the one hand they want to destroy us, why wouldn't they just do it all at once, instead of this pissy cloak and dagger stuff? Besides, what could they possibly be afraid of from humans; we're no match for an alien culture, certainly not now!"

"Maybe it's not humans they're afraid of."

Otis sat up quickly in his chair and gleamed wide-eyed back at him, his face full of wonderment. "Of course, that must be it!"

"What's it? What did I say?"

"Tom, I could hug you, but my stomach's too big for that. All these years since the visits by the Andromedians I never believed hostile aliens existed! We all were left feeling the universe was full of benevolence! But they never did share much about other races, and we were too busy picking their brains to really push the matter. Yet *somebody* had to ask the question about other threats. I'll bet that information exists and never made the light of day."

"Well, it won't be easy to ask one now, it's been years since the Andromedian's visits. However, if they knew of threats to our species, don't you think they would still be warning us now?"

"I don't have an answer for you. What makes this so frustrating is the fact that this Dove group formed years before the Andromedians ever showed up. I can't believe a bunch of everyday people could have the insight into something this profound."

"Maybe they did have some help." Ivory leaned forward and pulled the list toward him, "Your Honor, all I gave you was the final results of the Majestik's analysis. The hundreds of variables in the profiling are overwhelming for our minds to organize, so the computer programs do it effortlessly. The only thing is, the computer can be looking right at something we consider important, and not flag it unless we ask. So, I ran this list into our database asking for some new commonalities."

"I'm listening, but not sure where you're going with this."

"Everyone on the list, and I mean everyone, have all had various levels of UFO sightings or contacts in their lives."

Payne rubbed his chin with his head looking up. He closed his eyes as he continued to think. "Mr. Ivory, can we now assume that if someone on that list is not a Dove sympathizer, is it likely they are a Vor supporter?"

"I think that's a valid hypothesis. The only trouble is, we still have no way to see which side they're on. And, there likely are many more people on each side of this problem who are not in our computers and therefore not on this list."

"It appears we don't know as much as we thought we did Tom. But I know someone who can help sort things out a bit."

Ivory stood up in anticipation of running the errand, "Who's that, sir?"

"Sit down, man, you'll never find him down here. He's not on Earth now."

"Ah, one of the stations. We could fly him back in just two more days you know."

"I doubt that's possible. He's at Mars."

*   *   *

Pam stood over Tim Ward as he lay in the recovery room. She adjusted his head wrappings and made one last entry in his record. The man was still deep in modulated sleep, but his body behaved as if he was only in alpha state. His face twitched in various emotions as he struggled through dream upon dream. She took his hand and squeezed it gently. He seemed to respond as the tension began to melt from his brow. She noticed the brain wave monitor also displayed a calmer wave pattern. She smiled softly and made her way across the clinic to the bench where Max and Ray were busy experimenting.

"How's it going here, all ye mad scientists?"

Neither of them looked up from their microscopes, but Ray finally did answer her when he felt her presence burning into his focus. "It's my guess this thing was implanted the same way we got it out, through the optic foramen. We discovered traces of optic nerve cells in it."

"How do you know we didn't contaminate the specimen during the extraction?" Ray looked up from his scope at her, "Quite simple, the implant had them entwined throughout the inner mass, which could only have been introduced before this thing started to grow."

Pam leaned back against the table, "You know, Ray, there are not too many places in the world where that type of brain surgery can be done. We know his medical records show no history of anything like this. Who could have done such a thing?"

Max broke his concentration to contribute, "You remember who taught our surgeons to do this technique?"

Ray looked at him amazed, "The Andromedians!"

Pam stood up abruptly, as if she had just been bitten, "Hey, you guys are talking aliens! Were they really here?"

Ray smiled as he leaned back on his stool, "You were just a youngster when they went public. They shared all kinds of technological information, then left as mysteriously as they came."

"Why don't you ever talk about them, Ray?"

"I guess after the events on Earth, people lost a lot of faith in the 'wonders' of the universe. Before that, I imagine most people were afraid to."

"Afraid of what?"

"Afraid of ridicule. The whole thing never got too much media attention. That's the way the governments wanted it, just like they did for nearly a century before. Always the secrecy."

Pam gritted her teeth lightly in anger, "Here we go with the government again. What would they accomplish by hiding intelligent visitors? Were they afraid of losing some sort of control?"

"Actually you may have hit the proverbial nail on the head. The biggest thing that alien life challenges is our oneness, our uniqueness in the universe. All concepts of religion have to change. The second threat is to the basic principles of commerce. Humans work for the most part because we have to, not so much because we want to. Advances in technology that aliens brought here were so mind boggling that the potential for total economic collapse was always just around the corner."

Max interjected, "So the governments simply try and let these changes trickle into civilization, waiting for us to become mature and virtuous enough to handle it."

"But who in politics is smart enough to know that?"

Ray smiled at her increasing insight, "Ah, now you're starting to get to the biggest part of the debate. We think the aliens decided for us when it was time. They made the first move on *their* agenda. If you remember long ago when the first etchings appeared in crop fields, you could say that is what started the dialogue."

Pam pondered, "Stonehenge. I read they went on for decades, increasing in complexity and beauty every year. But the history books say we never found out what they said or who was making them."

"Oh, but they did find out! And that's where it all started."

Max was busy at his microscope again, "Ray, I think we've gleaned all we can from the physical studies. Why don't we run some DNA probes now?"

"Sounds good, and while we're doing that, Pam would you please go get a skin DNA profile run on our Mr. Ward over there. Let's see if anything matches up."

*   *   *

Chairman Parker was finishing his lunch when his secretary found him and delivered a message.

"Excuse me sir, Governor Brickman is on the line. Do you want to take it here or shall I tell him you'll call him when you get back to your office?"

He looked around him at the small cafe crowd and decided, "Give me the call here, I don't want to make him wait." He wiped his face with a napkin and then turned on the handheld viewscreen.

"Yes, Governor, what can I do for you?"

"Thanks for taking the call, Bernie; I hear you were eating lunch."

"No problem, just finishing. What's on your mind?"

"Well, I appreciate all the good updates you've been sending me, but quite frankly, I'm getting worried. For just a simple hotel and research center, you seem to have more going on than I'm comfortable with. You've got this Victor Seeb character, the co-pilot's attack on his captain, Dr. Phillips suite burglary, and now this list emerges of conspirators."

"When you put it all in one breath like that it does sound like a soap opera up here."

"I'd be happy if it was all fiction, but I have no confidence things are going to get any easier very soon. Do you have any plans or direction of action yet?"

"Not yet, but I am confident we'll connect the dots real soon."

"Bernie, I'm calling Governor Payne right after our conversation. Do you have any suggestions for me?"

"Besides the usual on how to get through his pig skull? I'll bet he knows more about all this than both of us."

Brickman pursed his lips slightly then smiled, "Thanks anyway, I'll try to get him to open up."

"Nice talking to you, Jim, say hi to the wife." With that Parker calmly placed his handset on the table, and then started to chew a fingernail as he contemplated nervously.

*   *   *

As soon as Otis Payne's face came in clearly enough, Governor Brickman spoke, "Otis, we haven't talked since you asked me the favor of getting into the Majestik's computers. I know that went well for your team, but we have some catching up to do."

Otis shifted uncomfortably in his chair, "I suppose you deserve an update."

"Good, why don't we start with what's going on at Mars. The readings we were picking up have continued to baffle us. What can you share?"

"I guess now is as good as ever. Five days ago my research crew reported an unusual series of events occurring in the Martian atmosphere. They were so profound and yet so confusing, that Dr. King informed me right away."

"What type of things?"

"Quite simply, the long term terraforming project suddenly got a mysterious shot in the arm. I imagine by now some of the air is stable enough to sustain human life without breathing apparatus."

"Good lord, that was supposed to take a century!"

"No, you're forgetting the changes we made in the process about five years ago. You see, the original idea simply consisted of melting the ice caps to free up water, thus starting an atmospheric cycle. Then Dr. King made some discoveries on one of Mars' moons that allowed a more rapid acceleration. They first found a microbe capable of generating a large amount of heat in its daily cycles. They introduced it onto the polar regions. As you can guess, the caps started melting dramatically faster. Then they seeded the thin Martian atmosphere with some sort of mineral dust they collected on the surface. That in turn stepped up the chemical reactions in the atmosphere."

"You make it sound so simple. How could such a small crew do all that?"

"I put lots of money into it, plain and simple."

"It seems to me they are playing with fire out there, who is authorizing all this?"

"You know I don't have to get any approval for their ops outside of my own council. Do you want to hear more, or do you want to bitch some more?"

Brickman sighed, "Go on."

"They believe the moon Phobos was formed originally from Mars, not a capture. Therefore, they didn't feel concern introducing that heat microbe onto the caps. It shouldn't have been a foreign organism. And secondly, when Earth went to hell, I felt we should do more out there to speed up the terraforming. I was beginning to feel the surviving humans might need another planet real fast."

"You broke every rule in the book, Otis! How did you get your entire council to keep all this quiet?"

"Here on Africa, we've had centuries of the rest of the world telling us how to live our lives, or exploit our resources. Everyone here feels Africa was made the main surviving continent for a reason. That planet out there is our Africa, do you understand?"

"Wow, I guess I should stop being surprised by anything anymore. Don't you feel you're playing with those people's lives at Shepherd?"

"They know the risk, and they also know what a tiny thread the human race hangs on right now."

"Otis, I think the human race is doing just fine considering our circumstances."

"You don't believe that for a minute, so cut the political crap. This is me you're talking to, not the press! Now, are you ready for me to finish?"

Brickman was silent a moment, "All right, so what caused the recent activity jump we've been watching?"

"We don't know exactly. My people are close, I can assure you. They're all more determined than ever since the loss of the two personnel yesterday."

"What do you mean loss?"

"Dead, killed in a surprise earthquake. I should call it a Mars quake."

"Goddammit Otis, that's what I was just talking about! I..."

"Jim, we're all saddened by this, so please spare me the tongue-lashing. Jaden tells me they found something so profound that it cost them their lives trying to extract it. He's contacting me tonight with an update."

"I don't want to hear anymore, this is your problem! So what about *our* problem, you remember, the shuttle flight suspension? We're all waiting for your update."

"I plan on allowing the ships to fly again in two days, in accordance with the suspension mandates."

"So you do occasionally follow the law after all?"

"Very funny. I would love a few more weeks. You see, in the beginning of this mess, I simply suspected a group of terrorists, even though popular opinion was leaning toward equipment decay. Then, our runway attack dispelled all those happy thoughts. Next, we thought we had it pinned on this nut group called D.O.V.E., who I'm sure you're familiar with. However, with all the loose ends still taunting me, quite frankly I'm starting to believe the Dove people, and that scares me!"

"That means you think the Vor might exist, and are here now?"

"I just don't know! Something's out there, there has to be some different paradigm to all this."

"If they're here, do you think they could be out at Mars?"

"Good Lord, I don't even want to think about that!"

Brickman thought quietly a moment as he stared away from the screen. He then looked back intently at the viewer, "Otis, you must realize you're basically running the whole damn show. Are you relying on outside advice, or are you going to continue to act like a dictator?"

"Both actually. For now it seems we're simply in a waiting game until the shuttles fly again. We have no choice but to try and get back to a normal routine and hope to draw some of the responsible people, or things, out in the open."

"Otis, if there is a hostile alien force out there, we probably won't stand a chance."

"I'm not so sure Jim. But first, I'm going to have a talk with the leader of the Dove organization."

"Really? How do you intend to find him?"

Otis smiled, "Simple, my friend, I'm going to make him very mad."

CHAPTER NINETEEN

Max and Pam sat in front of the sloping viewbox as the computers compared thousands of chromosomes. The tiny information fragments almost danced with their twisted shapes as each piece was superimposed in various ways, not unlike the process of tackling a jigsaw puzzle. Max refined the process every minute or so as possible matches were parked in unique subgroups. Just as the last pieces were analyzed, Ray made his way into the darkened room.

"Well, how do they look?"

Max answered cautiously, "So far, I've only got one segment, about 920 nucleic acids long, that is foreign to his DNA. The clip occurs in the nerve system architecture framework. I'd like to run that segment against the rest of our population databanks. With such a specific target, it should only take about thirty minutes to check them all."

He tapped in a few quick commands, then sat back to watch the whirlwind of numbers zip by in various directions. There were millions of people in this database, millions of humans. Finally the process stopped, right back where it started. There were no matches. Max looked up at Ray, who had watched the entire scan, "Looks like we're dealing with either a non-human sample, or one designer-made for this application."

Ray leaned over the interface and commanded another run. "Let's see how it compares to all known artificial DNA clips, and if there are no hits there, run it against all other lower life forms."

Pam was confused by that one, "You mean this thing could have come from a microbe?"

He stood back holding his chin, "Oh, I'm open to anything. Who knows, a fish maybe."

She shook her head, "Very funny, why not a bird?"

"Let's see what the program finds before our imagination gets too wild."

In moments, the same results. No matches. Ray drew a deep breath, "OK, I guess it's reasonable to assume we have an unregistered piece of designer DNA or truly an alien source."

Pam leaned forward, hugging her arms between her legs, "How will we find out?"

Ray started from the room, "I'm going to ask Tim Ward."

*   *   *

Phillips leaned over Tim's bed, accompanied by Max and Pam at each side. He lifted one of Tim's eyelids, "OK, Pam, bring him out of it."

Soon the man came to consciousness and promptly started to moan as he reached for his head. Ray spoke firmly over his pain, "Mr. Ward, your head hurts for at least three reasons. One, you were very drunk yesterday. Two, you received a nasty but well deserved blow to your head by your liquor bottle. And three, we did minor brain surgery on you yesterday to remove a foreign piece of tissue from the middle of your skull. Do you remember anything from yesterday?"

The man slowly opened his eyes and looked at Ray, "If all that happened to me in one day, I'm glad I don't remember it."

"So you don't recall Captain Martin coming to your room?"

He smiled, "She did? Did we have a good time?"

The three of them stared down at him unsympathetically as he searched for a smile back. "I guess we didn't. Hit on the head by a bottle you say?"

"Yes, you were very aggressive. Mr. Ward, if I say the word Vor to you, what can you tell me?"

"What's Vor? Never heard of the word."

Ray turned to Max, "I was afraid he wouldn't remember. Let's induce a hypnotic state to see what his subconscious can tell us."

Max promptly left to retrieve the proper equipment. Tim looked up at Pam and grinned, "Boy, first I get to fly with a knockout as my captain, now I get another as my doctor. I must be dreaming."

Pam blushed shyly and reached down to adjust up his bed. "Mr. Ward, first of all I'm not a medical doctor, but thank you for the compliment. But honestly, I'm afraid you're just too much man for me."

He looked surprised and confused by the comment, but Pam coyly reached down and gently lifted his sheet, nodding her head for him to look down. He tucked his chin, peering down to see his naked body. He glanced defensively up at her holding back a laugh. "Oh that's not fair, this table is cold!"

Ray stood by watching Pam have fun with the man, then interrupted his embarrassment, "OK, Tim, this machine we're hooking up to you will quickly and electronically set your brain wave patterns to the hypnotic state. You'll feel full control of yourself, just very relaxed. In a few minutes we'll be able to get important answers from your subconscious."

"Now wait a minute doc. How do I know you're not going to brainwash me or something."

"Mr. Ward, if I wanted to damage your brain, I would have done it yesterday when I was literally inside your head. The information I think you know will help us understand who or what put the implant in your head. More importantly, it may just help save the human race from going completely extinct."

"Well, now that you put it nicely like that, go ahead. Hey, I think that's a pun, get it?"

Pam shook her head and continued to smile as she stuck the electrodes on his head. "You know, Ray; maybe you should put a post-hypnotic suggestion in Tim. I was thinking something like every time he even smells alcohol, he has to vomit."

Tim closed his eyes, "Very funny, I'll be sure to throw up all over you every time I do."

The whole process took a few minutes to set up, but within seconds of turning on the machine, he appeared to be sleeping. Max stood back with arms folded, "OK, Ray, it's your show."

Ray moved in close and grabbed his hand. "All right, Tim, you're now in the Torrus flying here to the Majestik. Your captain today is Alicia Martin, and you're about to take off from Lemuria. Have you finished the pre-flight tasks?"

"Yes....same old stuff."

"Did any of the passengers talk with you before you got on the ship?"

"No, quiet group."

Max quietly interrupted, "Try going back further. How about a week before that flight."

"Tim, listen to me. Where were you one week before that flight? Were you home or on a base?"

"Stationed at fuel depot. Had a layover. Hate that place....no women."

Ray looked at his two companions. He knew that his suspicions were about to get confirmed.

"Tim, did anything happen to you at the fuel depot that was unusual or different?"

Tim rolled a little to his side, "I'm....I'm not sure. I don't know what they want from me. I was walking, exercise time. Damn they're short little freaks." He became quiet and opened his eyes. Then he sternly raised his voice, "I can't go off base, why won't you listen!"

Ray continued, "Who were they? Did they take you somewhere?"

"Looks almost as if they're wearing......masks. I can't see their mouths move, but.... I hear them in my head. I can't say no. I ... can't say no! I.."

"Tim, listen to me! You are safe. Relax. Where are you now?"

"I don't know. Another cold table. I can't move.... Not having fun, boys. I need to be back in my barracks, please. Please! Don't come near me with that thing! You little fucks, I'll kick your a...."

"Tim, you're safe again in your bed now, breath deeply for me."

Pam moved in, "Ray, stop now, his brain wave pattern is going crazy! I'm not able to stabilize him!"

Ray immediately pulled the electrodes from his forehead. Tim instantly settled to a calm sleep. Ray looked down at his hand still clutching Tim's. He turned to Max, "Sounds like a million other abduction stories we've read about over the years."

"Yeah, but now we know what they may have been doing to all those people. We have physical proof in our possession." He walked proudly over to the bench where the sample was stored. Suddenly he let out a startled scream, "Ray, its disintegrating!"

Ray bolted over to the bench and pushed Max away from the sample dish, "Let me see that!" He looked up, his face ashen with surprise, "The goddamn thing self-destructs too?"

Pam tried to calm them both, "Listen to you two! We have an alien abduction case and a brain implant that yielded us a complete DNA profile. We're even pretty sure how they got it in him, so losing the sample is not the end of the world. It's not like we've got nothing at all."

Max and Ray looked at each other simultaneously, nearly muttering the same words, "The DNA record!" They both ran over to a computer terminal. Max immediately opened the file of the sample. In seconds they both breathed a deep sigh of relief as the information flashed up on the screen.

Pam walked over to them, "You actually thought they have a way of erasing our files? And I thought I overreact at times!"

Ray rubbed his hair back as he returned to Tim's bed. "I guess we just got a little paranoid there for a moment. However, Max, I want triple back-ups on that file, stored outside this clinic."

"Can do boss. On it now."

Pam joined Ray on the other side of Tim's bed. He was now leaning on the side rail with his outstretched arms, head hanging. He said to her, "You know, I kind of miss that fuel research stress, this is too much for an old man's heart."

Max chided back from his terminal, "Listen, old man, you're only fifteen years older than me. We're in this together all the way! Now, what's next?"

Ray looked up at Pam more confidently as he answered Max, "Well, if we have a small bunch of people walking around with brain tissue implants, it would be nice to know who they are. The list of names you generated is probably a good place to start. This Victor Seeb character told us who is loyal to Dove, so the others would logically be potential Vor followers."

Pam interjected, "Or zombies." She then had an idea, "Wait a minute, Ray, remember Tim Ward's name wasn't on that list. And secondly, that list is a compilation of social probabilities; some of those people have to be innocent of being involved in either of these groups."

"OK maybe, but how many are now on the Majestik within the remainder of names?"

"If I remember correctly, about a dozen."

"Easy enough. Now, the way I see it, we probably have only one way to decipher who's who of that twelve. I'd like to get Victor Seeb questioned again, but with Alicia Martin in the same room to really get some insight on those names."

Pam looked puzzled, "How's that going to work?"

"Well, this Seeb guy has proudly proclaimed to be a Dove member, and Alicia is part An-...., well, erhh, you remember her reaction two days ago when she saw that list. She has....good E.S.P. We can make it work for us on this. I know her input can get us the most likely people to throw in the brain scanner for the definitive look!"

Max looked at the time as he finished the last back-up, "Why don't we try that tomorrow, the day's nearly gone."

Ray agreed, "Fine. I'll go talk to Alicia tonight about this, that way she can prepare herself."

Max stood and patted him on the shoulder hard, "Get her sort of psyched-up, you mean?"

"I suppose you could say that. Why don't you go contact Bernie Parker and set up a time for tomorrow with Seeb. He *is* still technically under house arrest."

"Bernie, huh? Is that what the B stands for?"

Ray grabbed Max's shoulder firmly, "He'll kill me if he finds out I let it slip out. But yeah, I discovered he's actually a real softie under that scalp."

"I'm glad someone figured him out." Max then bravely walked over to Pam, "Miss Pamela, as it is apparent that I am heading to Chairman Parker's office, would you care to come along and keep me company? We could grab a late snack afterward."

She thought a moment as she finished adjusting Tim's monitors, then looked right at Ray and smiled, "That sounds great Max, let's go."

Ray watched the two of them leave. Max swung one quick grin over his shoulder as they went through the door. Ray went back to his specimen dish and held it up to his eye level. The now liquid mess bubbled subtly, giving off a foul odor. "Damn, I hope you can't do that in someone's head." He tossed the sample back to the bench top. After a moments thought, he grabbed it and threw it into the disposal furnace and watched as it disappeared in the flames.

*   *   *

Hayden was sitting relaxed on the edge of his bed when the doctor arrived. He looked up as the man silently approached him. "Good to see ya, doc! Kind of late to be making rounds isn't it?"

The doctor looked down at Hayden's legs swinging rhythmically to an imaginary beat. "Mr. Green, I think you know why I'm here today."

"They want me out of here, don't they?"

"For what it's worth, it's against my recommendation. It's only been three days."

"But, what our king commands, the king gets."

The doctor picked up one of his legs and extended it out to palpate the muscles. "Governor Payne is a stubborn man. I believe he thinks you're a criminal. He has no patience for threats to the order of things."

Green pulled his leg back angrily, "Well, he ain't seen nothing until all hell breaks loose in a few days. My life will be insignificant then."

"Hayden, is there something you can tell me to prevent his moving you?"

He lowered himself slowly onto his back, and then let his head sink into the pillow. "No, it seems I'm just a small pawn in it all. He knows everything important enough to know right now."

"Then I'll have to move you first thing tomorrow to the small clinic at the runway complex." Green hardly flinched when he heard his destination, "So, that's his plan, use me as bait."

"I can't say. I think you'll be safe there. I'm just worried about a relapse of your symptoms."

"What would happen if that occurred?"

"You'd have to be shipped right back here again."

"Hmmm. What makes you think I'll be safe there? I'll likely be killed in no time flat."

"Killed? By who?"

Hayden now rolled over completely on his stomach, "Oh doc, it doesn't matter, you have enough to worry about with all your patients here. Just let me have one more night alone in peace."

*   *   *

Payne waited impatiently as the connection to Mars finally stabilized. The operator reappeared, "Sir, station Shepherd is coming online now." The screen flashed on with an unusual clarity, revealing Jaden King's exhausted face.

Otis didn't hesitate, "Sorry to bother you so late, Jaden, but you did say you would have more information on your samples by now."

"I said tonight? What the hell was I thinking!" He sat back and took a long sip from a mug in his hand. "It's been productive today......Pete has been invaluable as usual. He never ceases to amaze me about what he can coax out of a computer."

"Jaden, before you go on, is Peter busy right now? I'd like to bring him in this conversation."

"He's asleep. First time in days for the man. I really don't want to wake him. Insanity can come easily up here."

"That's fine, it can wait till tomorrow. So, as you were saying."

"We still have no idea what the gold-based substance is made from. It behaves like gold, but has unusual properties. It's as if it has an element in it that we have never seen before. Or there is a unique blend of known periodic elements that are matrixed in. If it's an unknown element, it's not anything we've found in this solar system."

"OK, but do you know what it was doing entwined in the structure?"

"The estimates of the total quantity and a likely pattern of distribution in the pyramid both point to a coil configuration. And if it was a coil, then it was capable of focusing or concentrating some force. And where it was focusing that unknown force would likely be downward."

"Does that explain the magnetic fields you are measuring coming from the planet's core?"

"Indirectly, maybe. Whatever the coils help focus is likely in the quantum realm. Either we are seeing a compression of inner planet elements, or a sort of repulsion factoring."

"Explain please."

"Simple laws of physics whereby opposites attract and similar's repel. If there are repulsion forces being focused downward by these structures, it might be enough to start some sort of rotation within the planet's core."

"Amazing! Almost like a giant motor starting to turn."

"More like a generator."

"Do you think that this was the original purpose of these pyramids?"

"Well, it's obvious intelligent life was on this planet long ago. At first we all thought the Andromedians had done this. However, as you know they denied building them. Pete and I discussed the possibilities of their being behind this acceleration of our project. He talked me out of that idea, however."

"He did? What exactly did he say to convince you of that?"

"What do you mean? He didn't say anything based on fact, just good old-fashioned deductive reasoning."

"I see. So, if it's not the Andromedians, who or what then? Those coils of gold just don't have a switch on them. It seems to me as if something had to have been activated in the energy outside them. Outside the planet even."

"We may never know unless they tell us. Give me another day or so to pursue the coil theory. We intend to go back down to the two remaining pyramids and kick them around a little."

"Jaden, please don't risk anything! I'm taking a lot of flak down here!"

"No one's going inside them, so don't worry. Why don't you get some sleep, you look as bad as Pete did. We must have patience, my friend."

"Patience; not one of my virtues. Listen, Jaden. In two days our shuttles have to be back in the air. There's a scheduled departure for your station with new crew. I would sure feel better if I could delay at least that one flight."

"Sorry, Otis, I need people to replace my lost crew, and we need those supplies, especially food. The planet may look and breathe like Earth, but we haven't begun any agriculture experiments yet. As a matter of fact, we'll need even more people coming out here now. There's a whole new world waiting for us, full of mysteries and potential. Pack as many people on that ship as you can."

"You'll get the bare minimum, especially since we're not sure if there'll be more quakes, or if the energy fields will die down enough to be safe."

Jaden sipped again from his mug, finishing the brew. "All right, Governor, I'll be patient as well. Good night."

Payne got up slowly and stretched. He walked over to his bar and poured his drink. He turned and leaned against it as he slowly rolled the glass in his fingers. He looked past the glass at his reflection in the mirror. "Tomorrow's the big day mister, it's do or die." He then toasted himself and gulped down the shot.

CHAPTER TWENTY

Alicia was led into the committee conference room by Ray. They stopped in the doorway and surveyed the people already at the tables. Victor Seeb sat in the middle of the room again, opposite Chairman Parker and Ms. Najib. Max stood by the door chatting quietly with Pam. He gave his usual big smile when he saw Ray and Alicia. He quipped cheerfully, "Good morning, folks, welcome to the Dove showdown, where beauty goes against sheer pigheadedness."

Ray was not amused, "Thanks for arranging this Max; I guess I'll owe you again for this one."

Alicia interrupted, "Where do you want me to sit, Ray?"

Max quickly went for a chair and slid it right next to Seeb's seat. "Over here, Captain, best seat in the house."

Seeb shifted nervously as he tried to look casually around him. "What's going on here? You told me you didn't need me anymore! What's she doing here?"

Parker leaned back in his chair, "That was wishful thinking, mostly on my part. Sorry about the confusion, Mr. Seeb. Actually, you really don't have to do anything today to possibly help us, Victor."

Najib leaned over to comment quietly to him, "Sir, I must protest this method of interrogation. You could just as easily use the clinic hypnosis machine to get more information from him. Besides, this woman single-handedly ruined my ability to interrogate the co-pilot. How do you know for sure she's not working for the enemy? She is on that list!" Before he had a chance to answer, she continued, "Also, why are you pursuing this fantasy alien line of questioning? It can't be right."

Parker tried to ignore her as he watched Alicia adjust herself in the chair. When he saw she was ready, he turned to his aide, "Your remarks have been duly noted, Ms. Najib. Trust me."

Ray plopped himself next to Parker, "Ready anytime, Chairman." Alicia nodded her readiness as well. Max handed the now-famous list to Seeb again.

Parker cleared his throat. "Mr. Victor Seeb, Captain Alicia Martin, I thank you both for coming here today. This will be very simple. Victor, will you distinguish for us from that list, the Vor recruits here at the Majestik?"

Victor's voice reflected his frustration, "Remember I was going to tell you before who was likely with the Vor, but you scared me out of it!" He grabbed the pen in front of him and went slowly down the list, marking x's next to a few names on each page. "There, that was easy. I hope I'm not too late."

Ray looked at Alicia, "Captain, would you please." She took the list from the table and rested her hands flat on it against her thighs. She closed her eyes and breathed slowly. Her face remained expressionless. Finally after several minutes, she opened her eyes. "There are more."

Parker stood up to extend his sore back, "So, Victor, you still hold back on us. Who are you leaving out?"

"I have no reason to hold back. I gave you all I know."

Alicia quickly interrupted, "He's telling the truth. Let me look at the list again, but I need Victor to hold it while I concentrate."

Everyone remained quiet as the two of them looked at the rows of names. Alicia reached for the pen and put an X in front of one more name. "This man is under Vor control."

Seeb shoved the papers away, "That's impossible, I already showed you he was a Dove contact! In fact, he's our point man up here."

Pam joined in from the side of the room where she had remained standing. "Don't you see it makes perfect sense? The Vor have infiltrated the Dove organization!"

Seeb was the first to respond, "That's impossible, we are all loyal to the cause of Vor destruction, not supporting them!"

Ray corrected him, "Mr. Seeb, perhaps your organization doesn't know everything there is about your enemy. Do you know about the brain implants?"

"The what?"

"We've come across a man who had a deep brain implant. Our sources tell us this was a Vor device."

Seeb shuddered in his chair, "We had some suspicions they got into your head somehow, but no one ever had any proof it was so literal."

Najib leaned over quickly and whispered to Parker, "Is this Tim Ward you're talking about? Is that what happened to him?"

Parker pursed his lips and answered quietly, "Yes. Tell me, have you recovered any lasers yet?"

"None. The flower stand had nothing."

Now his voice was loud enough for everyone to hear, "I want you to get a security detail to every one of the Dove people on this structure. The weapons have to be in their possession. I will personally accompany security to the double agent's room."

She protested, "Sir, that's not necessary, it could be dangerous."

"Ms. Najib, I appreciate your concern, but I feel I have to step up at this critical stage. We have no room for error now." He grabbed his gavel and was about to slam it down when Seeb interrupted, "What about those other people, the ones I just gave you? Are you just going to leave them be?"

"I am starting where the weapons most likely are. But just because you didn't hear me give any orders regarding the Vor followers, doesn't mean they aren't being dealt with." He then pounded the gavel excitedly, "Thank you everyone. Dr. Phillips, I'd like to talk with you later today about the shuttle flights resumption tomorrow. Captain Martin, I hope you'll be back in the pilot's seat again soon, pending Dr. Phillips' clearance of course."

Alicia smiled a thank you as she stood up. Seeb stood up quickly as well and blurted out, "I hope none of your people get trigger happy. If you find those weapons, the people holding them aren't going to be happy when you attempt to take them. Try to remember, we're on the same side!"

Ray came over to him, "Just what do you all think the Vor are planning next up here?"

"All any of us knew was that we should pay close attention to the shuttle and main computer operations. Maybe some of the people you round up today have more information. I hope you people have a better plan than we do!"

Max commented as they walked past him, "Oh yeah, we've got it all planned out." With that he gave Ray a look that was not his usual grin.

*   *   *

Otis Payne sat in the make-up chair where the artist worked the moisture brush lightly across his face. His eyes were intense, deep in thought, as he looked behind him to see one of his aides enter the room.

"Good afternoon, Governor. We're just about ready to go on the air with your announcement."

"Very well. Have you confirmed Green's move to the base?"

"Yes, he arrived there an hour ago."

"Good, and the communications hacks?"

"All in place. Also, all passenger flight facilities are on alert."

Otis' face tightened as he gently pushed the hand of the make-up person away. He stood up like a great general, "Let's do it. Lead the way." They walked to another section of the building, surrounded by his security team. The camera crews were selectively placed between the rows of his entire delegation assembly. Many whispered anxiously about the upcoming speech. They quieted as he took his seat in front of them. Payne tugged at his shirt to straighten it while he watched the technician count down.

"Three.....two.....one."

"Ladies and gentlemen of Africa, and the world. I have much to say to you this afternoon. Since it is my responsibility to head the all-governor inner body, it is also my responsibility to report to you decisions made by that body. While most day-to-day vote outcomes are available electronically, this is one that needs to be heard from the top. The entire shuttle system has been grounded for the past nine days due to concern over the causes of loss of the Lemurian fuel depot, the shuttle Torrus, and most recently the attack at our spaceport runway complex."

"During this time we have worked to solve this crisis. We have pursued several lines of forensics, ranging from simple accidents to hostile actions. Because we will resume flights tomorrow, you must now know what we have accomplished so far. We have no choice but to fly again, since our supplies dwindle quickly at many facilities. If this were not the case, I assure you those ships would still be grounded!"

"Earth has a militant organization called D.O.V.E. Many of you may already know this. They appear to have originated with intentions of protecting the planet. They unfortunately have become misguided in their goals and appear to be responsible for all three incidents. We have obtained invaluable information from one of their members, who we captured at the runway attack. His name is Hayden Green. Mr. Green is in protective custody at our runway base. He finally cooperated with authorities when he realized how far off the Dove belief system had become. I am warning any other members of the Dove sect that we know who you are. We know where you are. We will not harm or disturb you or your families as long as you discontinue these dangerous games. I encourage any member to provide information about the organization's leader. This person cannot be ignored and there is a reward for his or her capture. Please call the number we will display at the end of this address. You will remain anonymous."

"So, remain calm and be on the lookout for suspicious behavior. All we have among us survivors is our trust in each other. Use it. I have nothing else I can provide you with at this time, because the investigation is far from over. Hopefully, in a few days we will have enough new leads to give another briefing. Good day to you all."

*　　*　　*

Max sat with Pam over iced teas. They were quiet as they watched the people flow in and out of the small cafe. Pam thought aloud, "You know Max, it seems foolish to only round up the good guys. What is Parker planning to do with those possible Vor followers? Oh, for God's sake listen to me, I'm now talking as if everything comes down to an evil gang of aliens we don't even know exist!"

"I know something's out there. That brain implant was real."

"Yes, but how do we know it wasn't put there by someone on our side?"

"Now that's more of a conspiracy than just some bad-ass aliens! We need to find and get more data on another implant first and foremost."

Pam pressed her hands down on the table and sat up straight, "Max, that's it! We could get Parker to approve our brain scanning all of those people Seeb identified today. Wouldn't that make it simple?"

Max took one last swallow to finish his glass, "I think we might want to get them scanned anyway. You know, just in case Bernie hasn't planned for it by shuttle take-off tomorrow."

"How would we get them down to the clinic?"

"Oh, make up something, with Ray's approval first. Tell them they've been exposed to something in their rooms. You know, a 'just to be sure' kind of request."

"It sounds perfectly illegal, but I don't know why we shouldn't try. Where's Ray now?"

"At the lab. He's getting supplies ready for his trip to Earth tomorrow."

*   *   *

Ray worked methodically at his calculator, while Sarah packed essential equipment in a transport crate. She eyed a strange apparatus and walked it over to Ray. "Doctor, what's this for?"

He looked up from his glasses, "Hmmm, oh, that's just a beefed-up thermal output probe. We had to measure extreme temperatures in the combustion chamber, but were having trouble getting through the magnetic pinch-bottle." He went back to his work as the woman walked back to the crates, still turning the device inquisitively in her hands. Just then the viewcom jumped to life, using the emergency channel. Ray yanked his glasses away as he rolled his chair in front of the screen. Jerry was looking intensely right out at him, holding a handset in one of the hotel's suites.

"Doctor Phillips, we need you immediately. Level five, sector seven. It's Chairman Parker. He's dying." Ray jumped from the chair and ran from the room. Sarah stood there with her hands still reaching in the container. "Doctor Phillips, what's wrong? Can I help you?"

He yelled back at her without losing a step. "Just keep packing!"

*   *   *

He was at Jerry's location in less than five minutes, shoving himself past the small crowd of onlookers and emergency personnel. Before him on the floor lay Bernie Parker, his eyes coldly closed, clutching the mounds of bloody gauze on his chest.

Ray dropped to his knees next to the dying man; then looked up at Jerry, "What the hell happened?"

"He took a direct laser shot in the chest. They were searching this room, and his two guards never saw it coming. There's not enough anatomy left in the wound site to save him. I'm surprised he's not gone already."

Ray lifted the packing away from the wound and grimaced his head away at what he saw. "Oh Bernie, you didn't have to play soldier. Not at this time." He looked up at Jerry again, "Goddammit, don't just stand there, get a stretcher! I want whole blood transfusions set up immediately! I want the heart-lung machine ready, now!"

As several medics darted from the scene, Ray sat on his heels and lifted the chairman's head onto his lap. His voice now weak and shaky, "Listen, Bernie, I know you hear me. You're going to make it through this. I won't let you die!" He wept out, "Has he been given pain control yet?"

One of the medics nodded as he replied, "He feels nothing now, I can assure you, sir."

Suddenly the lifeless man opened his eyes the tiniest amount to see Ray's face inches from his. His mouth slowly opened as he gurgled in a feeble breath.

"Bern, don't try to talk, save your strength."

Slowly a faint sound materialized on his lips, as each breath carried with it a growing chill. "Ray, how's your.....door....working?" Ray wiped the tears from his face with his sleeve, "My door? My door's fine. Why would you.....you, you had my door fixed!"

Parker forced a feeble smile as he closed his eyes again. Ray wiped a trickle of blood from the corner of the man's mouth. "I always liked..... you...Ray. It was....the...leas...I coul....do." He then coughed in a strange horrible way as he drifted into unconsciousness.

Ray screamed, snapping his head up, "Where's my stretcher?" He grabbed Bernie's hands and pressed them harder onto the wound packing. "Bern, listen to me! We're going to stop them, do you hear me? You helped us get this far, now stay alive, dammit, to see it through!"

Jerry squatted down as the stretcher was thrust next to his body. "Dr. Phillips. He did say one thing to me while we awaited your arrival. He said to tell you to take care of the Majestik. He said she's all yours now."

Once they lifted the stretcher up, Ray walked beside his friend and held his hand. As they entered the hallway he felt the pulse of life disappear. The room was left in stunned silence as the crowd reverently maintained a circle around where the chairman's body had lain. In the next room, on the floor, were the smoldering remains of the man who had killed him.

CHAPTER TWENTY ONE

Hayden sat propped up in bed, looking out the windows of his small room. He had just watched the governor's speech and was emotionally numb contemplating the consequences. He knew Payne was going to do something, but he couldn't have imagined he would be used as bait in such a damning way. He tried to understand where things went wrong in his life. He fought off the thoughts that taunted him, the ones that said his whole life was a waste. Even worse, the thoughts of someone from his own group killing him based on a total lie by his own government.

Within the hour, hundreds of armed personnel were saturating the grounds outside the clinic. He watched in disbelief the efforts Payne was apparently taking to protect his life. Somehow their presence started to make him feel like someone important. A sudden knock at the door startled him. Instinctively he froze his breathing, trying to listen to whoever was on the other side. He wasn't sure he should answer the knock; after all, why would someone knock? The door slowly opened as a tall man stuck his head in first.

"Hayden, it's me Tom Ivory. Mind if I come in?"

Green grunted subtly as he slowly stood up from the bed to greet the man. "Since you're already in, I guess I'll say yes. So, you're the last person I expected to see on this fateful day. How's the old backstabber doing today?"

"Come on, Hayden, you know I'm just doing my job."

"Your job? Your job was to help us. I thought you were on our side!"

Ivory walked over to the windows, working his hands into his tight pockets. "Hayden, nothing's changed, I still believe in the fight. As a matter of fact, I think Payne is becoming a believer as well. It's been hard to pretend I didn't know what's going on this past week." He returned to Hayden's position near the bed, "Payne's not so bad when you get to know him."

"Yeah sure. He has about as much sympathy as a robot." He shuffled over to a window himself. "So what's going on out there? Is all that for me?"

"Just about. They're also beefing up for tomorrow's incomings."

"You know those shuttles aren't safe without our protection."

"Hayden, do you really think your people understand what they're up against? The governor and I reasoned it out. If anything is going to frighten this Vor of yours, it has to have much more firepower than this ragtag group of mercenaries."

"What more can the human race come up with, other aliens?"

"That's not a bad idea; we've been tossing that one around. If what we now know about other humans acting as warriors for the Vor is true, you have some difficult choices to make."

"How's that?"

"Well, on the one hand they would be easier to deal with than some superior life form, but on the other, if you had to kill them, you're killing a fellow human."

"If they give us no choice, then we'd do what it takes to survive."

"The real question is, how many people could this eventually destroy? I was informed earlier just such an event has already occurred. The chairman at the Majestik was killed today by a laser blast from an alleged Vor supporter. The assailant didn't do too well either, they're autopsying his remains now."

Green sat down, shaking his head sadly, "So it begins."

Ivory patted him on the back as he started to leave, "I was told to come here today by Payne. He wanted me to wish you luck, and not to worry. He doesn't believe anyone will actually show up to get you. At least, not right away."

"Wonderful, just when I was beginning to feel important."

*   *   *

It was late in the day when Max completed his examination of the remains. He sat at the computer screen watching the reconstruction of the DNA profile. Pam walked up to him and put her hands on his shoulders, gently but deeply squeezing his tight muscles.

"Relax, Max; you haven't stopped for air all day. Aren't you even hungry?"

"That'll have to wait. We almost have our answer. Just a few more seconds....that's it! Look at that, a perfect match!"

She could see the overlaps on the nucleotides from five feet away, "It's the same DNA fragment you found in Tim Ward's specimen. Max, we have to get those other suspects brain-scanned fast! There's no telling what they're being made to do up here!" Max rolled his chair back as Pam walked over to the autopsied body. She lifted the sheet cautiously, "If this was the Dove organization's point man here at the hotel, I wonder about their leaders at other sites. Are those people under Vor control too?"

He just sighed in agreement as he switched off the screen, "By the way, how's Ray doing? Is he still in his room?"

"Yes, I've never seen him so upset before over someone's death. It's not like him to be this emotional. I want to go to him and offer some help, but I don't feel right about it. I don't want to say the wrong thing and ruin my friendship with him. I don't have some poetic lines to give him like Alicia would probably console him with."

"He'll be fine. Remember he just got a double whammy. Parker wanted him to carry on the chairman's responsibilities. So he must be wondering who will take over the clinic if he accepts the role. He can refuse, of course, but he'll have to be just as involved for awhile in selecting the successor to the chair. I personally will bet he stays with our team. Anyway, I'll check on him shortly, I need to tell him these findings."

"Max, he has to go down to Earth tomorrow, this couldn't have come at a worse time. I think I should go with him."

"Well, I'll ask him. He's the boss."

*   *   *

Ray lay on his back in the quiet darkened room, pierced only by the soft music flowing through the walls. His clothes were still stained by Bernie Parker's blood, his mind still saturated with painful emotion. He hardly noticed the persistent door tone in the background.

Max used his master access card to enter the suite. He stood for a moment trying to accommodate to the darkness, but decided to turn on a small light. He saw Ray on the couch and walked over, grabbing a small chair to sit near him. He said nothing for several minutes as he looked at his friend lying there with his eyes closed.

"What do you want, Max?"

"Wasn't too hard to guess it was me, huh? Ray, I didn't come here to give you a pep talk. Death is hard, that's all there is to it. I know you'll be fine; you're too strong a character to let this eat at you. I guess I came here because I want to know what you want us to do. You're kind of in charge of everything right now."

Ray seemed oblivious to his friend's words, "We don't even have a heart-lung machine up here."

Max seemed puzzled, "Of course we don't. What is that supposed to mean?"

"When Bernie lay there in my arms, I yelled out for the heart-lung machine. We don't even have one!"

"I would have reacted the same way. With all our training, you do what you're trained for. You knew what it would take to save him. You didn't have the luxury of knowing our inventory at that very second!"

"Why did he have to go on that raid? It's almost as if he knew he would be killed. I don't think he was depressed or suicidal."

"Maybe he had a plan, maybe someone else had a bigger plan for him, we'll never know. He said he wanted to meet with you later today; perhaps he wanted to share something that might explain why he did this. Maybe he had something new on this Dove/Vor thing."

Ray sat up slowly and looked down at his shirt. "Look at this, the bastard really fried him, what a horrible way to die."

"You should see what we had to autopsy of the other guy. That's another reason I'm here. The DNA in the double agent matched the implant pattern. But I guess that's no surprise to you. Oh, while I'm thinking of it, has Najib's group been successful in getting the other Dove suspects lasers?"

"Yes, she called a few hours ago. Everything went smoothly, unlike Parker's team. They retrieved three weapons. She still wants to interrogate Tim Ward. I rescinded that order."

"Why?"

"At this point he won't be able to tell us much more, even under hypnosis. You and I know he was the most likely suspect for planting the explosive on the Torrus. What am I supposed to do with him, put him on trial here? It would be the equivalent of an insanity plea. I will recommend we never let him on a shuttle again in the cockpit, but beyond that?"

"OK, but let me get back to the laser question. Are we sure we have rounded up all the lasers Seeb delivered?"

"Who knows? Seeb's not sure how many were in his package. I suppose I should start to lose some sleep over that little tidbit as well."

"Listen Ray, Pam and I have an idea. We know our non-invasive brain scans can pick out those alien implants. We'd like to look over the people that Parker said he was dealing with, or hinted he was going to deal with. I need your permission to bring them in, tonight if possible."

"Why the hurry?"

"Tomorrow we fly again, remember? Are you still planning on going back to Earth?"

Ray got up with a deep sigh and started to remove the stained clothing. "I suppose. I do have to try this fuel experiment, and hopefully get Payne to let me talk with Rashad Ansarid."

"That's Peter Ancerid remember."

"Well, let's give it the benefit of doubt until I have something official directly from the governor."

Max got up and pulled out Ray's special bottle of whiskey from a small cabinet. He poured himself a small shot, but held it in front of him. "Pam wants to go with you tomorrow; she's worried you can't take care of yourself."

Ray came up to Max as he zippered the new garment closed. He reached out and grabbed the drink from him, shooting it down quickly, "I'm not surprised. I told her I wanted her to stay here. There are too many reasons she's not going with me."

"That's what I was hoping, but I told her I would ask anyway."

"Does it bother you she still worries so much about me?"

Max was quiet a second, then poured himself a shot. He wasted no time in drinking it. "It bothers me she doesn't see how much I want to be there for her."

"Trust me, she notices. It's nothing against you; it's just that Pam's not sure what type of man she needs. Max, I think you two are right for each other. Make her understand that. Be a little more persuasive."

"Persuasive, how?"

"Pam's a physical girl if you haven't noticed yet. Why don't you just kiss her?"

"Just like that, kiss her?"

Ray laughed as he turned on the main light, "You'll know the right time. Just remember your dating days, what was it like when you first kissed your wife?"

Max's face dropped as he thought of his lost love. Ray bit his lip as he tried to console him, "I'm sorry, I shouldn't have brought that up. I know how it hurts you to think about her."

Max turned to him and forced a smile, "No, it's OK. I need to deal with it. I know she'd want me to move on." He put the whiskey away, "So, as I asked originally, what's next boss?"

"How about getting those people to the clinic for scanning. How many are there?"

"Four, so far."

"That's not bad; I think we've got them outnumbered for now. I'll see you in the clinic in about an hour."

"Where are you headed now?"

Ray was now walking to the door. He stopped and looked at it reverently before commanding it to open. "I have to see Alicia. She has some answers I need."

*   *   *

Ray arrived at Alicia's suite, and stood outside her door before ringing. He dropped his head in thought for a brief moment, then sharply knocked on the metal door. There was almost a minute more of silence, so he started to knock again. Just as he raised his hand the door slid open, revealing Alicia garbed in a beautiful floral robe.

"Hello Ray, I was wondering when you would get here."

"You mean you didn't know? What's the matter, slipping a little?"

"Come in, I know you have a heavy burden." She led him to her couch, then sat close to him. "You learned a lot from Chairman Parker, he mentored you years before you ever realized he was on your side."

"I knew you could help me understand what I was feeling. That's why I'm here. Alicia, I couldn't save him. I've never felt so helpless in my entire career."

"The medical team called you not because they thought you could do something they couldn't. They called you because Bernie needed you there, as a friend."

Ray sighed deeply as he sunk back into the cushion, "Even still, his death seemed so preventable, so unnecessary. He didn't have to die to get my emotions going."

"Don't flatter yourself too much, all life requires death. Death always requires faith to get through it. Your logic is sometimes the enemy of faith. Parker did have a choice, and it was his to make."

He folded his hands behind his head, "I still don't know how you know these things, other than that part-alien brain perhaps. However, your point is well taken, and for that I am grateful."

"Wow, more human qualities coming through. I really believe there's hope for you yet, Ray Phillips." She got up and walked to the window, "Are you ready to leave tomorrow?"

"Yes, I believe I am. Are you still concerned about my safety?"

"Nothing's changed, Ray. If anything, the situation is even more dangerous after what Governor Payne did today."

"What did he do? I haven't looked at any news today."

"He's challenging the Dove organization by blaming them for everything that's happened in the last 10 days. This is a dangerous game he's playing, Ray."

"Why do you call it a game? It reminds me of something you said in the restaurant."

She didn't hesitate, "When an animal gets too scared, it gets desperate, and that makes it dangerous. He's leading us into an offensive move but has chosen a path that is full of great risk. I don't think he has thought ahead enough of all the possible outcomes."

Ray stood up and rested a hand on her shoulder. "Right now I have to think about something more pressing. I have to get down to the clinic; we're scanning the potential Vor people today. I need to be there when we do this. And don't worry; I'll have security down there with us."

She almost didn't hear him, "How are you going to deal with Governor Payne? You two are very similar. That could be a recipe for conflict."

"Any suggestions?"

"Whisper, don't shout."

"Alright, and how about for right now?"

"OK, say you find some implants, tell me what will you do to those people?"

"I was hoping Max and Pam will have some suggestions for me, after all, it's their idea. At the very least we'll search their rooms for weapons, and likely lock them up till we have some more answers."

"See, simple and logical. I like it."

"Great, then I'll get running. Oh, I almost forgot. When do you want to get back in the pilot's seat again?"

She turned to him excitedly, "If they had a ship here I could fly, I'd be the first one on tomorrow!"

He smiled a big grin back, "OK, Captain, I'll take that into consideration too!" He nonchalantly gave her a quick little kiss on the cheek, "I'll see you later." She held back a surprised smile as she watched him leave, her fingertips lightly touching her cheek.

*　　*　　*

Payne rubbed his temples as he looked over the pile of reports on his desk from frightened Dove members. Each one of them gave a different description or location of their leader. He even had communications from several space facilities, stating the leader was hiding there. He shoved all the papers aside in frustration. He didn't know which one to believe or where to start. He slammed his finger on the intercom button, "Send the rest of the staff home, we're not going to get anywhere on all this tonight. Has Mr. Ivory returned yet?"

The woman's voice sounded tired as she replied, "No, sir, nothing's changed since you last asked me fifteen minutes ago. Shall I put a call out for him?"

"No, just go home. He'll get here sooner or later. That road can be rather challenging to navigate at times." He slunk back in the chair and put a hand on his rumbling empty belly. He reached over to the light switch with the other hand, dimming the room. He closed his eyes tight to release the tension in his face then tried a few deep breaths. On the third breath he suddenly felt a strong cool breeze cross his face. He deepened his eyebrows and held his breath. When he had to breathe again, he opened his eyes quickly to look about the room. There in front of him a darkened figure stood opposite his desk.

He blinked hard to make sure he was actually seeing something. As he reached for the lights, the figure quickly darted to the darker corner of the room. As the lights went on it waved an apparent arm and the lights immediately dimmed again. Otis was now on the edge of his seat. His hand reached stealthily for the alarm button under his desk. He felt slightly more confident as he pressed it. He then barked out, "How did you get in here? Who are you?"

It moved a few meters closer to him. He saw what appeared to be robes covering the figure from top to bottom. However, he could almost see through the thing, its edges were blurry and somewhat undulating. Suddenly he heard a voice, but not with his ears. The tone was deep and raspy, yet definitely human sounding.

"You wanted me, here I am."

Otis tightened his hands on the chair, wondering why security hadn't burst in the room yet. He continued to posture, "How did you get in here?"

"By the time your alarm is answered, I will be gone. I came to give you a message."

Otis got braver and stood up, "What kind of message is delivered this way, other than by criminals?"

"That was clever of you to break up my organization like that, but it doesn't matter at this point. We have already won."

"You haven't won a thing, mister, or whatever you are! I know what your game is and I assure you you'll never get out of this complex alive."

The figure was unfazed and moved even closer. "We will destroy the remaining links of humanity's survival. Your prophesies will be fulfilled, and we will not have to continue this tiring quarantine of your race. We'll extract the last valuable resources from your planet and finally be out of this miserable part of the galaxy. So, Governor, enjoy your last few months in power. I have decided to keep you alive for the sole purpose of enjoying your failure."

Otis was speechless for once in his life and glanced quickly at the still closed doors. The figure drifted back to the corner of the room and stopped. Otis had had enough and lunged from behind his desk. As he stormed toward the corner, the entire apparition disappeared into the wall. He ran up to it and slammed his palms against where it just was. "What the hell?"

At that moment the door burst open and the lights blasted on. Tom Ivory was with six armed guards. "Otis, where are you?"

Payne was now leaning against the wall in the corner, "Over here, man. What took so damn long for anyone to show up?"

"What do you mean? I had just arrived at the front door to the building when the alarm sounded. We got here in less than thirty seconds!"

"Really, I don't understand, I pushed it several minutes ago."

Ivory walked cautiously over to him while the guards searched the entire room. "Are you OK? It looks like you saw a ghost."

"Tell them to leave the room but continue the search outside for any signs of intruders." Otis went to his bar and quickly poured a strong drink. Once the alcohol hit his brain he went back to his desk chair. By now they were alone. He asked his aide calmly, "Ivory, do you think I'm working too hard?"

"Always, sir."

"And do you think I'm going about this problem the wrong way?"

"I don't understand?"

"This Vor crap. What if they were using the Dove organization instead of fighting it?"

"Whoa, what makes you think that?"

"I think I just met the Dove leader, but he, it, can't be human."

"You *did* see a ghost!"

"No, I think I saw the real enemy, but I believe we're in a masquerade."

*   *   *

Pam walked into the clinic a step ahead of Max. They made a beeline for the brain scanner. Ray walked in a moment behind them, "Right on time! Did you have any trouble rounding up our patients?"

Max smiled broadly as he pulled up a chair in front of the control console. "Nope, every one of them should be here in just a few minutes. I personally called on each one and made up some story about an escaped lab virus in their sector. They were all more than happy to cooperate."

"Lab virus? That could cause a panic! You could have come up with something less frightful."

"Less frightful? These people scare *me*! Listen, I only told them the virus could make them lose their memory, nothing more."

Ray knew he couldn't have come up with anything better, so he decided to let it go. He looked over at Pam as she wheeled another instrument to the scanning device. She smiled back, "I'm glad you're all right, it's good to see you smile. I'm so sorry about Chairman Parker's death."

His smile tightened as he shook his head in acknowledgment. "Thank you; I appreciate that, Pam. OK, let's get this show going so Bernie's death leads us somewhere."

Pam now stood next to him, "Ray, do you think these people could become violent like Mr. Ward?"

"Let's hope not, but I've got a security detail coming here any minute. They'll stay out of sight so we don't scare anyone off."

The security team did arrive promptly, and Ray directed them to his personal office. Within minutes of their arrival, three men and one woman were lined up at the check-in desk, all wearing concerned if not frightened looks. Ray immediately greeted them, grabbing a clipboard Pam had prepared with their files. He spent some time describing the scanning procedure and assuring them they had nothing to worry about. He asked the woman to go first and made the remaining three wait in the clinic atrium, behind a closed door.

The monitor jumped to life as the woman slid into the tunnel. Max immediately zoomed into the region where they had found Tim Ward's implant. Pam wasted no time in exclaiming, "My God, It's there! What do we do now?"

Ray almost put his hand over her mouth, "For one, talk more quietly! He then calmly turned off the scanner. "We do nothing at this instant. I'll send a small team to her room immediately to look for weapons. Max, you go stroll into my office and come back with one of the guards. I'm going to have him accompany her to her room. Once there, we'll put a security override on the door and quarantine her. I'll tell her the virus is present and she'll need a few days to recover."

Pam looked perplexed, "Recover? Why would she believe that?"

"Because you're going to give her the magic cure shot. Just give her a saline injection in her arm; about 3cc will do." He held her shoulders and looked her in the eyes. "But Pam, keep her here in the recovery room after injecting her until I get word that her suite has been swept."

Five minutes later, Ray went into the atrium and retrieved the next patient. As he walked the man in he noticed a familiar smell about him. He then realized it was the cologne he detected the day his room was broken into. He then tensely said to the man as he helped him onto the table, "We're going to give you a few whiffs of gas to relax you. It will help you not to squirm. It's important to lie perfectly still during the scan."

The man didn't argue as he made himself comfortable. Ray held a small mask to his face misting silently a general anesthetic. Within moments the man was completely asleep.

Max watched the whole process in amazement, and when Ray came back to the console to monitor the scan Max asked, "What the hell was that about? We don't need to sedate them."

"This one we do. He's wearing the cologne of the person who broke into my suite!" He then quickly flicked through the papers he had on the man. "Let's see, he's listed as a maintenance man, specialist in heating and cooling. Damn, he's got to be the one! Light up his brain Max, I'm on a roll here."

Max calmly rested his hands on the desk before complying, "You just anesthetized someone based on the cologne he was wearing! What are you going to do if he has an implant?"

Ray got a little perturbed, "I'll do whatever I see fit to protect this hotel!"

"Like what, kick his ass?"

"Maybe I should kick your ass."

Max sighed out loudly in frustration and started the machine, "Wow, settle down there buddy. First you go all mellow on me, now just a little manic. Should I get you some lithium ordered up from room service?"

"Very funny....I'm sorry. I got a little too vengeful there I guess. I'll try harder to control my lust for power."

Suddenly the door burst open and Alicia entered the room, walking immediately toward the two men. The front receptionist followed closely behind her admonishing, "Captain, you're not supposed to go in there. Please go back to the lobby before I call security!"

Alicia completely ignored her as she nearly knocked a chair over getting into the booth. "Ray, I need to talk to you immediately."

He looked at the receptionist standing behind her with her hands angrily on her hips. "It's OK, Marla, I'll handle this." He gently pulled Alicia behind the console screen.

"Now, Miss Martin, what's the big entrance all about?"

"The Vor are definitely here. They just visited Governor Payne."

Ray let out a sigh that almost whistled, "Max, go ahead with your scan." He then sat Alicia down. "OK, Alicia, talk a little softer, I have several people out there I don't want to scare."

"You're right, sorry about that. Anyway, I have no doubts now. You have no choice but to make Payne tell you everything; his life depends on it."

Ray raised his eyebrows in surprise, "So now you *want* me to go to Earth?"

"I'm finally starting to see this come together, and you will play a massive role in the next few days."

"Jeez, just put a little more pressure on me, won't you!"

Max interjected as he pointed to the monitor, "Hey you two, check it out. Another perfect implant. Shall I go get the next guard your holiness?"

Ray looked at Alicia as she gave him that look women give you when you're supposed to read their minds. He turned his head to Max, "Yes, we'll stick with the plan. Alicia, why don't you go over and visit Tim Ward; he should be able to go back to his room tomorrow. He's in the quarantine section, just to keep the environment safe for him."

She knew he was trying to get her out of their work but had to ask one last question. "They'll all scan positive. When can you get the devices removed from their heads?"

"They'll have to wait till I get back from Earth. In the meantime I promise they'll be made safe and comfortable locked in their rooms. So, are you up to talking with your co-pilot?"

"I suppose now is as good a time as ever. Will he be locked in his room too?"

"I don't think that's necessary. But I told Max earlier, I'm going to recommend he be permanently suspended from the cockpit."

She didn't want to hear that, but deep in her heart she knew that was the right choice. "OK, I'll go check on Tim." She quickly made her way to his bedside in the far corner of the clinic. She sat down slowly next to his bed and then tapped his hand lightly to wake him. He was somewhat startled but smiled when he saw who it was sitting next to him. She spoke first, almost sympathetically, "So, what's the great party boy doing still sleeping?"

"They make me sleep with all these sedatives." He then turned his head to look at the ceiling, "Alicia, you're the last person I expected to see."

"Well, just because you didn't come to visit me doesn't mean I have to be rude as well."

He pulled himself up to a sitting position. "I don't remember much about your visit to my room. They tell me it went really bad. I guess I kind of screwed things up. I'm very sorry if I hurt you. I can't explain why I was so horny."

She had to smile as she looked at him. He didn't understand what was humorous and asked ashamedly, "Why do you want to laugh? Didn't I try to rape you?"

"I'm looking at your two black eyes, very raccoon-like. I think one's from me, and the other from when they popped your eyeball out to cut the implant from your head."

"And you think that's funny?" He probed his fingers around his still swollen face.

"Oh come on, Tim, it's OK for you to make fun of me. Where's your sense of humor? I know that wasn't you doing all those things. Actually, I think the real you has started to return!"

He held up the small mirror she had handed him from a table near his bed. He started to chuckle at his face the moment he saw it. In moments the two of them were laughing, in stark contrast to what was unfolding in the scanning room just out of earshot.

CHAPTER TWENTY TWO

It had been ten days since the explosive turmoil began at the Lemurian fuel depot and the Majestik. Today, the shuttle system was cranking back up to life again after the suspension's expiration. Most of the citizenry of the world were calm, even relieved the ships were going to fly again. Some worried there was still reason for concern and would not board any one of the vessels. Each shuttleport that was housing a spaceship buzzed with launch activity. Security was exceptionally heavy and burdensome, but everyone knew it was necessary. On the Mars outpost Shepherd, their day was one of anxiousness as well. Today was the day they unloaded the final rock samples from the pyramids.

Jaden King was climbing out of the lander ship, carefully lowering the heavy stone load ahead of him. Pete guided the satchel onto the floor, then supported his boss as he exited the vehicle. They wasted no time in getting King out of his spacesuit, each working silently and efficiently at the various zippers and seals.

Pete bent down and pried open the bag. He immediately held up a stone about the size of his hand. He smiled as he rotated it in front of his face, "Well, that makes it official. Each of the other two pyramids has a coil gel system in it."

"Right where we expected it, under our noses. Amazingly well concealed I might add. So, what have you been able to come up with while I was busy digging?"

"Well, if you follow me to the graphics screen, I'm pretty sure I've got it figured out." He led Jaden out of the small airlock and into the even smaller, darkened display room.

Jaden watched as the animation sequence recreated an amazing visual of what the planet had just done for them. Pete watched Jaden's face for his opinion as the images told the story. What he had theorized was thought to be impossible anywhere in the universe, simply had to be what had just occurred on this planet at this point in time.

King replayed the sequence several times before commenting. "You put the center of this new magnetic field 20 percent off planetary center. It doesn't make mathematical sense why it's there and not centered, but it does fit right into the descending vertex point from a trihedral using the three surface pyramid structures as the bases."

"You know we have found many planets with lopsided magnetic fields. They have to get that way somehow; this could explain one way."

"Explain? This is now a chicken/egg issue for us. Were those pyramid coils strong enough emitters to create a reaction at this core area? Or did the forming core mass create a field effect and activate the pyramids to generate a specific oscillation? And more specifically, why now, at this late stage in the planet's lifespan?"

Pete leaned against the wall, his arms crossed; "Why not now? The nutational frequency has changed 3 percent since ice began melting, especially the caps. I say the pyramids were in the right spot to capture the core energy when the axis shifted."

Jaden straightened up from the screen. "Yes, of course. The quake, all the bizarre readings. The expanding core became more fluidic and amorphous. It could easily be distorted toward a new axial alignment, much like a damper weight. But think for a moment about the positioning of the structures! If they were located anywhere else on the planet, they may not have worked. The particle fields would have evaporated and not formed this vortex effect."

They both looked at each other in restrained excitement. Jaden continued, "It was all set up! All we had to do was cycle some water out of the solid phase. But why create such a fantastic project and not use it? Whoever built this stuff obviously intended to use it, so why didn't they? This process could have been started at anytime in the last few thousand years!"

"Yeah, but we started it, that's all that matters now. The big question is, can we stabilize it? Are we smart enough to sustain the process?"

Jaden started from the room, "Well, since one structure has been destroyed, we can assume the effect on the core has been greatly compromised. We'll have to sit back and watch the magnetic and gravitational readings for awhile before I trust the planet. I don't want anybody within a hundred kilometers of the two remaining structures until I give the word!"

"Jaden, I just had another thought. What if the pyramids were *designed* to collapse once they have done their job?"

"Well that's quite an idea. If that's the case, even more reason to stay clear of them. But if that's true, then we'll know the builder's didn't want the technology used beyond the core initiation. Perhaps once things started, the structures might pose some sort of risk, maybe there's no way to turn them off. Anyway, I'm sending the lander back down to get the rest of the crew back up here right now. I'm not losing one more person to that machine down there until it settles down."

*   *   *

Ray stood next to the composite equipment box that was temporarily housing Bernie Parker's body. It was almost time for the shuttle to arrive from the neighboring hotel. He glanced at his watch as his friend Max paced nervously about the shuttle lobby. Ray sighed, "Pam, go over there and sit Max down, please, he's starting to make me nervous."

"Well, he has good reason to be nervous. And this makeshift coffin sitting out here doesn't help anyone relax."

Ray carefully placed his hand on it, "His will requested an earthen burial. I'm not going to deny him that by a standard cremation."

"Oh, Ray, at least you could have shipped him down on another flight!"

Ray turned to avoid answering her remark. Alicia was sitting patiently behind him with some of the other would-be passengers. She got up when she saw his face. "The Hanner will be docking any minute now; she has a great captain. Standing here makes me want to be back in the captain's seat more than ever."

Ray took a deep breath and blurted out, "I have to admit something to you. As you know, I didn't give you medical clearance for today. But it's not because you're not physically ready, you are. It's because I'm selfish and want to keep you safe on this first day."

She was now looking at him with a form of anger on her face he had not seen before. "You *are* selfish! I guess all that talk in my room was just talk."

By now Pam's ears had perked up, "What's the matter, Alicia, you didn't see this coming?"

"I did indeed see myself not flying today, but not because of this!"

Ray interrupted, "Well, the ship's docking. I suppose it will take about an hour for refueling and loading, so why don't we all go get some relaxing tea in the East Lounge?"

Max jumped right in, "Good idea, I don't think I can stand around here another hour." He lightly grabbed Pam's arm, "Let's go Pam, you pick the teas, I pick the snacks."

Alicia looked at him demandingly, "I'll go with you under one condition. I get clearance to fly *today*, before you leave."

He thought about it a moment, "OK, since there are no more flights you can possibly get on, I'm OK with that."

Forty-five minutes later, they all were joking around a large round table in the middle of the lounge room. Ray looked at his watch and tapped his glass to get everyone's attention. He stood up to speak. "I'd like you all to stay here in the lounge when I go. It offers a better view of the departure, and besides, it's far enough away from the shuttle bay should anything go boom."

They all looked at him somewhat surprised, but now their moods started to sadden. He continued, "We all have different feelings about this day of flight restoration, but we all agree it's imperative. So far, there hasn't been a problem on any of the 15 earlier flights around the grid. Now I know that's no consolation, but its good enough for me right now. Max, Pam, I'll be in touch with you tonight after I've talked with Governor Payne. Alicia, somehow I know you'll know what I'm up to. But if you don't get in my head, just call me; the vidphone is a wonderful tool."

They all sat quietly, each looking at something different about them. He took one last final drink of his tea, then walked solemnly around the table to each of them and shook their hands.

* * *

Otis sat in his usual position in the back seat as the vehicle rolled into the shuttle runway complex. The driver pulled up to the pavilion entrance designed solely for high security personnel. It was filled with a mixture of soldiers and news media. "Christ, they're making a circus out of this!"

Ivory turned to him from the right front seat, "They're excited. You're the hero."

"Maybe I came across in my speech better than I realized yesterday. How long before the first ship is due in?"

"Just a few minutes. I hope they're not late."

"Is Green still OK in the clinic?"

"Hasn't asked to leave. I bet he didn't sleep too well last night."

Otis chuckled softly as the car rolled to a stop. He waited for one of his security detail to open the door. The harsh noise of the crowd burst through the door the moment it opened. He tucked his head down and plowed into the strained mass of people.

Over 20 men were needed to guide him safely through the screaming mob of questions and cameras. He made his way to an elevated impromptu speech platform and from there looked down into the crowd. One of his men handed him a microphone. Otis tapped it first before speaking.

"I am pleased to be here with you today as we greet the arrival of the Hanner. It has been a stressful 10 days for all of us, but the patience and will of the people has triumphed! As you can see, the runways have been repaired to their original condition. Every flight today has gone without incident." Sudden applause broke out as he smiled in acknowledgment.

Just then the air blasted into a deep roar as the shuttle broke the sound barrier overhead in her descent. The crowd quickly dispersed onto the open grass areas to watch the ship come in. Otis stepped down from the podium and handed the mike to a soldier. He calmly walked to his chair outside and sat down. Soon the shuttle came out of a long banked turn and settled into an effortless landing.

As it taxied up to a terminal, Payne was escorted off the outside porch and into a small secure lounge. He was to meet Ray Phillips in private immediately after the arrival. Ray had insisted Payne meet him at the shuttleport. Payne was obviously not happy with the request but was nonetheless anxious to meet the famous Dr. Phillips.

Ray unbuckled himself from his seat and took a deep breath. He smiled to the passenger next to him, "Didn't doubt it for a minute." The woman got up and replied back, "Say what you will, but I'm staying on Earth for now. I'll take the volcanic air any day over this kind of tension."

He smiled as he followed her out the door. Once in the terminal, he spied the tall man looking for him. Besides, the sign he was holding made it easy. He made his way to him, "Mr. Ivory I presume. The famous African detective."

"Oh, Dr. Phillips! I'm sorry I didn't recognize you right away."

"That's fine; we've never met in person. So, which way to Governor Payne?"

"Follow me; he's expecting you over there in that lounge."

"I must say, I'm impressed he agreed to meet me here."

"Don't flatter yourself too much, doctor; he needed to be here for the PR. You know how that goes."

Ray looked down at the man's long strides as they walked, "Yeah, I suppose I do."

Ivory held the door open once they got to the lounge room. Otis immediately got up from his chair when he saw Ray walk in. He outstretched his hand, "Dr. Phillips, a pleasure to finally meet you. I hope we can fulfill your needs while you visit our labs."

Ray shook his hand firmly as he looked up several inches to meet his eyes. "You're a lot bigger in real life than what we get to see on the screens."

"I am losing weight, doctor; you should have seen me a year ago!"

"Actually I wasn't commenting on your weight, but I'm glad to hear you're losing it. I have some great health shortcuts I can share with you later."

"Very good, I'd like to hear them, Dr. Phillips."

"You call me Ray if I can call you Otis."

Payne smiled and nodded, "That's fine. Before we go on, let me say how saddened I was to hear of Chairman Parker's death. He and I had several good conversations over the last few years. I'm going to miss them."

"I appreciate your condolences, Otis, he meant a lot to me, especially in this past week. I transported his body down with me on the shuttle for a burial. He had a son I believe on Lemuria, so I'd like to arrange for an air transport as soon as I'm done here."

"Why didn't you just wait for a shuttle that was going back to Lemuria?"

"Have you been talking to my lab assistant Pam Aquain lately? She wondered the same thing. Actually I brought him down with me because I wanted to run a test on his body with no one knowing about it back at the Majestik."

"Sounds intriguing, what kind of test?"

"Bernie's actions that led to his being killed were very uncharacteristic. We found a way to easily scan for alien brain implants, and I want to make sure he didn't have one in his head."

"That *would* be concerning, especially at such a high level of leadership! Think how that could affect policy decisions!"

"Tell me about it. He even wanted me to take over his chairmanship in his dying breaths. That doesn't sound like the man I knew either."

"OK, doctor, erh Ray, we'll transport him in our caravan back to the complex when we go. So, Ray, I understand you have more to talk to me about than just using our facilities for the fuel experiment."

Ray tried to relax as he answered, so he stuck his hands in his pockets, "Yes, I need to talk with Dr. Rashad Ansarid. But am I right in calling him Peter Ancerid?"

Payne's smile immediately disappeared. He turned to Tom Ivory and barked out, "Ivory, get the car ready, we're all leaving for my office."

Ray walked directly next to him as he headed for the door, "Seems I've hit that nerve again. You and I have got to start sharing on this subject, Otis. I won't leave this place till I know where my man is."

Otis peered back at Ray as he was helped into his coat, "I get the feeling I'm going to regret this. I will tell you where he is, but not here. This room is not secure enough."

Ray followed him out the door and into the waiting open doors of the transport vehicle. "Otis, what makes you so sure your office or this vehicle is any safer than here?" Payne snapped back as the door slammed shut, "Damned if I know."

*   *   *

The ride lasted a little over an hour, just enough time for Ray to catch Otis up on everything that happened at the Majestik. Otis listened intently most of the time, but refused to start into any details from his perspective until he reached his headquarters.

"Otis, you haven't said 10 words the whole trip. Surely you have some comments you want to share that don't involve our secret scientist."

Payne looked out his window with a steady nodding of his head, "We're almost there." Soon they were standing in the doorway to Otis' private office. He turned to Ivory standing behind them both, "That will be all for you now, Tom. Why don't you keep an eye on the flight monitoring crew, they might be bored by now, this day is going so smoothly." Otis then threw his coat on one of the hand-carved hangers and walked to the corner of the room. He placed his palm flat on the wall.

"What do you know that can walk through a solid cement wall? Is there any technology we have that can enable a man to do that?"

Ray walked over to where he was standing and touched the wall inquisitively with his fingertips. "Through this? You mean something solid, something biological?"

"I think so. Is it possible?"

"Not with anything I've had privilege of. So what happened, see a ghost perhaps?"

Payne sighed and went to his bar and poured a small shot of his usual. After savoring the burn for a few seconds, he smiled at Ray. "There have been a lot of things lately I've had to change my views on. There have also been a lot of things I've had to do recently that I didn't like. This job requires certain skills that few people care to burden, I'm sure you can relate to that doctor."

Ray remained next to the wall as he listened, but he started to become impatient, "You still didn't tell me what this wall thing is about. I'm listening."

"Indeed, indeed I haven't! Well, I honestly don't know what the hell happened. We took a gamble and blamed everything on this Dove organization in an effort to draw out their leader. Well, it seems this character has been around because I've got scared Dove members fingering him all over God's creation. Then this, this wall thing."

Ray walked over and took a seat as Otis continued from behind his desk. "This cloaked apparition comes in here yesterday, no one saw it. It says a few words to me, mostly threats. And then, like a ghost, it fades right through that wall."

Ray looked intensely at Otis as he talked. Payne waited for some logical sympathy from Ray, but all he got was a question. "Otis, what do you think you saw? Trust your instincts."

"It was real; it was in here with me. It was no hologram because I've seen plenty of those. I'll tell you what I believe. It wasn't of this world. That's all I can come up with. So, you're the scientist, who or what did I see?"

Ray got up and started for the door, "I'll tell you this. If it was an alien, it might give the Vor legend a good run for the money."

He grabbed the door handle and just started to turn it when Otis demanded, "Where are you going? Is that all you can tell me?"

"To my hotel. So far you haven't told me what I need to know about my missing scientist. I've got a busy agenda."

Otis maddened quickly and slammed his hand down on the desk, "Close the door, dammit, and sit down!" He sighed loudly as he watched Ray return to his chair. "I'm contacting him today; you might as well be in on this. You sure are more stubborn than Parker ever was!"

Ray smiled coolly as he settled back in his seat. He asked calmly, "So these two men are the same person?"

"Yes. Next question?"

"Ohhhkay, that wasn't so hard. But why the mystery, even the murder allegations?"

Payne folded his hands neatly, "Ray, you remember the Andromedians don't you?"

"It's been hard not to remember them lately. Seems a lot of people conveniently chose to forget about them when they disappeared."

"Well, some of them remained. Pete is one of them."

Ray drew his head back, stunned, especially by Otis' casualness. "Do you know how many are still here, especially those working for us?"

"Oh, just a few. Those that decided to stay behind years back were told they could only stay in the research community. The rest of the gang are out there saving some other poor civilization in the universe, I guess. We just weren't worth their time once they saw how unstable the planet and its people were."

"I think it was more that they got tired of rejection. Our brains seemed too damaged, no sense of tribe."

"That's about it. Naturally the ones they left behind were volunteers. They still felt we were worth it, or maybe we just had better food. So we allowed the scientists incredible access but strict exposure limits. They accepted the rules, some not so gratefully. That's where Peter comes in. He was a loose canon everywhere he went. There was an explosion at one of our fuel research centers after he left the Majestik. One of his co-workers was killed, another missing. The local police suspected sabotage, and the evidence pointed to Ancarid."

"Really? Do you think he had something to do with it?"

"Of course not, he was set up. And you think these recent explosions were all you had to worry about! So, I had to move him again."

"So you sent him as far away as you could get him!"

"From us, yes. But in a slight irony he's actually closer to his homeland by being at Mars. Anyway, what's your next question?"

"I need to talk with him. I'm at an impasse on synthesizing one of his fuel recipes. Ironically I'm at the point of trying to avoid killing *myself* in an explosion."

"I'm scheduled to talk with him tonight. We're in touch every day now that Mars has done so well."

"So well? What does that mean?"

Payne grinned smugly as he leaned back, placing his feet on the desk. "Doctor, you are only the third person outside of the Mars crew to hear this information. Since you are now in an important leadership position, and you are a scientist, I will tell you."

"I hope this is all good news, I sure could use it."

Otis laughed, "Every cloud has a silver lining. Let me tell you about our clouds."

CHAPTER TWENTY THREE

The Earth sunset was shining prismatically through Ray's hotel window. He stood-up tall in the relaxing light as he shut his eyes and inhaled the real air. Even though it was slightly odoriferous, it didn't matter, it was real, and it was home. It had been over a year since he'd set foot on the planet. This visit was no vacation, yet he felt as if he were in the middle of one from long ago.

After enjoying the view for several more minutes, he went over to his viewcom. In seconds the crystal-clear picture was alive with Alicia's face. "Alicia! I hope you don't mind me calling so soon."

"I was just in my room working on a report. Have you had a good day so far?"

He smiled as he marveled at her stunning features. He never saw her like this before; she looked almost celebrity-like. "Listen, Alicia, I've learned some things already that are pretty amazing. I was wondering if you could tell me anything more concerning my health down here, if you know what I mean."

"Now that you know more, I know more. You're giving Mr. Payne a lot of comfort. That's already easing my feelings."

"Interesting. Alright, what might you tell me about Mars right now?"

"Only that something profound is occurring there."

"Nothing else?"

"No, but Mars has been idle so long, it may take awhile for its vibrational signature to really change."

"So you think its changing?"

"Oh yes, and many on Earth are watching it change as we speak. Do you want to share with me what you know about it? I can tell you're just dying to tell someone."

"I can't tell you, and don't try to read my mind!"

"I don't read minds!"

"Could have fooled me. I was actually thinking of wearing a lead-lined hat the rest of my stay. Do you think that's overkill?"

She set her chin on her hand unamused, "I assume that would be to shield you from the Vor and not me right?"

"OK, apparently my joking doesn't go over well with you sometimes. So, do I still have anything to fear now?"

She thought for a second, "Right now, it seems mostly yourself."

Ray leaned away a second to catch one last look at the disappearing sun. "Alicia, how can I trust myself if I'm my own worst enemy? I'm not sure I'm going to make the right decision on what's next down here."

"Just remember the virtues of patience and instincts. All the decisions have been already made for you. You just have to pick the right ones."

"There you go again making this all sound like a TV game show."

"When you come back, I would like to share some ideas about our reality. Now is not the best time for such a deep topic. I can tell you that our talking right now, like this, has happened already."

"Oh boy, another riddle. Is that supposed to be something like past lives crossing again?"

"Not a bad suggestion, but think more in the time line concept of differing probabilities. What might you and I already be doing if there were no explosions?"

"Uhhh, I'd likely be sitting in a hotel lounge drinking tea, and you might be somewhere between the moon and earth."

"Or how about we would be sitting together on the beach getting some sun."

"OK, my mind was not ready to go quite that radical. See ,there you go again making my legs all weak talking like that."

"Better exercise those legs then, we can't have them giving out at the wrong moments now."

Ray felt himself blush so he backed away from the screen a little. "I'll say good night on that one! Thanks for your help, Alicia."

He quickly connected to Max to fill him in on Payne's apparition visit. He purposely didn't share anything about Mars yet, and kept the conversation brief as he wanted to head over to the labs and inspect the facility he would use tomorrow. After that, he planned to head back to Payne's office for the call from Shepherd.

*   *   *

The security was still very heavy at the government compound. He had to wait in the lobby until Tom Ivory arrived to escort him back up to Payne's office. "Dr. Phillips, hope you had a nice little break."

"I enjoyed the rest thoroughly, and yourself? I'm surprised to see you here this late."

"My hours are Governor Payne's hours. Sometimes it's like this, sometimes it's very nice."

"That could be pretty tough on a family man, especially getting the salary your position commands."

"Well, I'm my own family, so that's not a problem. As you know, Dr. Phillips, this office is highly respected. I do it out of a sense of pride and duty, not the money."

"So you like your boss?"

He smiled as they waited in the elevator, "Most of the time. He's a bit pushy, but he's open to criticism."

"Ah yes, a good trait to have. I'm working on that myself right now." They reached the executive floor and Ivory pointed the way down the hallway. "You'll remember, first door on the right. I'm going to check the final flight reports for the day in the operations room."

"I assume all flights have gone smoothly?"

"Smooth sailing, as us fisherman like to say. Looks like we made it through without a single incident." Ray reached the room, then knocked litely as he cautiously entered the dimly lit office, "Otis, it's me Ray. Why is it so dark in here?"

"Oh, I'm simply doing a little meditating. It's all part of my weight loss regime. Come on in Ray, have a seat over here next to me. I'm just about to get that call from Shepherd."

The two of them perched in front of the large screen. Surprisingly, the reception was no where near the quality Ray had in his hotel, but soon the interspace operator appeared. "I have a priority call from Dr. Jaden King. Please enter your security code."

Otis promptly pounded a few symbols into the computer. Soon, Jaden King appeared. He immediately saw Ray sitting next to Otis and was hesitant to talk.

"It's all right Jaden, he knows. This is Dr. Ray Phillips from the Majestik. He's going to be using our labs for some research and he needs to talk to Peter."

"I think I remember meeting you once at a conference years ago, doctor. I believe you were lecturing on artificial gravity fields and the life cycle of the potato."

Ray smiled, "That was indeed a long time ago, I'm amazed you remember. We still haven't got the damn things to taste like an Earth potato."

King proceeded, "Otis, we think we have the solution to the terraforming acceleration. We created an unpredicted nutational change by some of the polar ice melting. It was fast by solar orbital time standards, and at the wrong point in the orbit ellipse. So as perhaps luck would have it, we ended up with a measurable wobble that caused the planet's core to shift. It didn't just slide over, it rolled, and it has been spinning slowly since."

Ray asked, "That's amazing, but perfectly logical as it would have no choice but to damper the wobble by shifting."

"Yes, but here's where it gets interesting. The core has been magnetizing again, and...."

"A magnetic field is developing? Otis didn't quite give me that detail. What are you people doing out there?"

Jaden almost laughed, "Honest, doctor, we'd like to take credit for everything, but all we can claim is that most of it started once a certain threshold was reached in atmospheric density, which led to a given net quantity of freed surface water. Since then, it's been an amazing ride here, except for the quakes."

"Yes, Otis told me about your loss. I'm dealing with the loss of our chairman recently, so I know what you're going through."

King nodded in appreciation, "Well, science and mother nature can be quite heartless at times. Let's go on, I'm sure you have more questions."

"Yes. How do you think the stone pyramids generated those high levels of energy into the atmosphere?"

King stopped a second and looked at Payne, "Otis, you following all this?"

"Not all of it, but I'll have Ray explain it to me again later."

Jaden continued, "Well, the magnetic field that resulted from the core shift and its renewed rotation was at its strongest right at the region between the three pyramids. That's the part that will amaze me till the day I die, how they were in just the right locations to capture the strongest part of the field. The rocks in the structures already have a high saturation flux density, which was exponentially compounded by an exotic metallic gold alloy coiled through them. So the planet's magnetism was then turned into another form of electromagnetic energy and literally radiated right out to the atmosphere. It was built to do just what it did. Sort of reminds me of buying that special toy, but the box says batteries not included. It just took our actions to put the batteries in."

Otis asked, "So you take these huge coils and sit them on top of a giant magnet, and they come to life?"

Jaden responded, "That's it, and what a coil they were. You wouldn't believe how high the flux waves were in electron volts. It was in the billions! That's why it was messing with our instruments and causing me concerns for our safety while we were on the surface. I couldn't be sure whether the ionizing radiation was dangerous or not. It turns out it's tuned to a frequency that doesn't tear DNA."

Ray was now a little giddy as he envisioned the possibilities. "It sounds like a grand version of one of Nikolai Tesla's experiments. The one where he tried to transmit electrical energy without wires."

King smiled in memory, "Hey, I also remember reading he even tried to communicate with Mars by one of his early radio transmitters. But in all seriousness, this is far beyond Tesla, this setup looks like a pure isotropic radiator, nature's perfect antenna system."

Ray thought a moment then asked King, "So this flux is making its way to the ionosphere and changes the rates of gaseous interactions. It sounds like reverse photosynthesis."

"Yes, that's a good way to look at it. It drove all sorts of particles downward by increasing their molecular weights, especially the O2. The N2 cycle is still barely existent, but that should come up when we get the nitrogen plant cycle started by agriculture. So far, most of it has come from our bacterial friends in the soil eating dirt. I must add one more thing. There has been some return of the quakes. However, they occurred near and under the remaining pyramids. And yes, they were significantly damaged by them."

Ray interjected, "Well, that effectively shuts down the energy beams I bet. Was it all on long enough to get the job done?"

"I would say it would have been nice if they ran a few more weeks, but we're a half-century ahead of original projections."

Otis said through his grin, "So, do we have a habitable planet now or what?"

"I think in another few weeks; we'll see if anything else happens. The planet still has its wobble, but it's not much worse than Earth always had. The magnetic core field is not as strong as we would like, but we predicted a calm century for the sun anyway."

Ray asked Otis, "Can I talk with Rash-....erh Peter now?"

"Jaden, get Ancerid on the screen." A few minutes elapsed before the man appeared. Ray joked while they waited, "Hope the taxpayers don't mind these phone bills."

Pete said hello and stared blankly at the two men. Ray moved in closer, "Peter, it's me Ray! Remember, from the Makestik?"

The man sighed impatiently, "Yeah I know, what do you want?"

Ray looked at Payne embarrassed and whispered behind his hand, "I guess I was a little hard on him when he worked under me." He returned to the screen, "Listen Pete, or do you want me to call you Rashad?"

"Governor Payne, are you sure Dr. King should be in on all this?"

"Why not, now is as good as ever. The two of you have been brilliant on this whole project. It's time for no more secrets. I'll lay it out right now. Jaden, listen and don't say a word. Pete is an Andromedian. Go on, Pete."

While Jaden stared at Pete in amazement, Pete went on, "OK, Dr. Phillips, call me what you like. Neither is my real name."

"Really, so would you mind sharing that?"

The man relaxed a little, "You would pronounce it oon-nah-tay."

"I'll stick with Pete. I'll get right to it. I can't stabilize that fuel recipe you left us with. I'm down here to try it again, but I'm not sure how to regulate the thermal output in the initiation phase."

Pete folded his arms in disbelief, "You're lucky to be alive! You tried it in the magnatron chamber didn't you?"

"Where else could I try it at the hotel?"

"It's too powerful; you'll need a pinch-bottle containment field with a fluctuating parabolic combustion center."

Ray sat quietly listening and now making himself some notes. Pete continued, "There are actually two requirements for that fuel to work. Whatever hydrogen catalyst you use, it has to be resonance-phased before the high pressure injection."

Ray now was inches from his screen, "We estimated the strontium isotope would be our best bet for the main ligand on the hydrogen. Would that work?"

"Good guess, doctor! Where do you intend to get the kind of power needed to resonate the nuclei?"

"That's why I'm here. I certainly didn't have enough at the Majestik to spare."

"And you won't down there either! It was never intended to burn in a lab. The only way to get enough power and generate a strong enough containment field is from an accelerating shuttle."

He immediately saw the point, "Wow, you're talking about magneto-hydro-dynamics! We never could use that principle on the shuttles before because all our field traps were too heavy for the ships. I think it's been over five years since I last thought about that idea."

"Well, we now have the perfect conductive alloy to wire into the ships hulls, thanks to the secrets of these pyramids. Jaden and I might have a way to recreate the alloy by recycling the materials from the debris here."

"Wouldn't that be a lot of work? Why not make them from scratch?"

"Well, besides the rarity of the gold, there's an element in it not found in our solar system. We're trying to come up with a good name for it."

Ray understood and could see his former colleague was becoming more relaxed, "So, I wire up a shuttle with an exotic lightweight coil to drive the skin charge into my fuel tanks for resonance, and using the same energy field, fire up a standard pinch-bottle flux that compresses a combustion chamber in the engine orifice."

"Yes, but remember to fluctuate the catalyst nuclei to the thermal output. Your fuel will burn at least ten times cleaner, and you'll end up with a much higher thrust ratio. Now, has our supply shuttle departed for Mars yet?"

Otis joined back in, "No, we're doing the best we can to get our local routes restocked first. And I didn't want any ships too far from home on the first day. You folks have a little longer food reserve as well, so it may be another day or two before we send out your ship."

Ray was busy finishing his notes then he clapped his hands together, "Pete, you're quite special. I wish I could hop on that shuttle when it leaves to shake your hand personally."

"Thank you, you're pretty talented yourself, you just didn't know it before."

Ray smiled back, "I've met someone special recently. She's opened my eyes to a lot of things. I can really relate better to an objective view now."

"Andromedians have a way of doing that, don't they?"

"I know I didn't tell anyone about her father. Come to think of it, I never even mentioned her name. So how...."

"Say no more Ray, you're letting doubt back out again from your beliefs!"

Otis looked somewhat suspiciously at Ray, and then finally got his question in. "Listen, Jaden, Pete, this exchange of information is extremely interesting. My God, you three have figured out the process to accelerate the formation of a new atmosphere on a dead planet and perhaps a practical application for more efficient shuttle propellants. But, like I said to you before, Jaden, we may not be able to enjoy those fruits. So, in all honesty Pete, I need one simple answer. Are there aliens in this solar system called the Vor?"

Pete's face became very concerned at the question, "For all our sakes, I hope not."

"So you've heard of them?"

"Yes, but like many things in this universe, their real name is not what the humans have decided to call them."

Ray interjected, "Any easier to pronounce than yours?"

"Their planet is called Ply-reez-ee-uh."

Otis sighed, "Well, that's not even close to Vor! What else can you tell me?"

"They have a history of occasional interactions among my people."

Ray couldn't restrain himself, "Interactions? Do you mean wars?"

"No, not quite. They're a powerful race, even have the ability to rearrange their molecular structure to the extent that it enhances hyperspace traveling."

Otis answered, "Would they be able to walk through a wall?"

Pete laughed, "That would be the easy stuff for them!"

Ray asked again, "But, let me get this straight. They never engaged your people in any actual fighting?"

"That's not how they operate. For their race to grow, they seem to thrive on the negative emotions of those around them. They may start trouble, but it wouldn't be their style to just go in and wipe out everything."

This time Jaden got into the conversation, "I should be in shock now listening to all this. But somehow after watching a planet metamorphasize before my eyes and now finding out my co-worker is an alien, this all sounds like another day at the office. So, Pete, if your race didn't leave this pyramid set-up on Mars, is it the Vor's?"

"I doubt that also. I think it's too clever for them. It also would have taken too much labor. They usually come in and take the spoils, not build for the future."

Jaden continued, "If you never went to war with them, how did you get rid of them?"

"Oh, you never get rid of them! I imagine they'll always be keeping an eye on you once they find you. They'll wait for a mistake or a new opportunity. No, we just proved we were smarter than they were. We joined together like never before. The positive emotions were too much for them. Actually, they elevated our society to new heights of moral and social values, just the opposite of what they expected."

Ray rubbed his chin and asked, "Pete, do you know about any brain tissue implants they were using?"

"Yes, it's how they control life forms with their thoughts. They actually project and materialize a part of themselves right into the brain of the victim."

Ray shook his head in disbelief, "Boy, did I get it wrong. I thought they surgically implanted the things with nanobots."

"Doctor, that's way too primitive for them."

Payne got back into the conversation, "All right, we have a real bad enemy here. How many are there? Am I dealing with a hundred or millions?"

"We don't know. It appears they are a relatively fragmented nomadic race of life now. It was very hard for us to mind-link them. Only as a whole society could we begin to understand their goals and fears."

"What are their fears? Is there anything out there they really respect?"

Everyone was silent a moment, then Peter offered, "Whoever or whatever built this mechanism on Mars might be a candidate."

Otis sighed slightly optimistically, "If so, that won't be one bit of help. It looks as if they're long gone."

On that note, all four became lost in thought for a few minutes, and the conversations then drifted into personal topics. Soon the men said goodbye to each other, each with a lingering sense of uneasiness. Ray and Otis decided they were done for the night, and they headed for their respective beds outside the compound.

CHAPTER TWENTY FOUR

It was morning on the Majestik when Alicia sprung up in the bed from a deep dream, her face soaked in nightmarish perspiration. She sat there in the dark, breathing heavily, fixated on the mental image that wouldn't stop flashing before her eyes. She jumped from the bed demanding, "No, no, it can't happen this way!" She slammed her hand on the door sensor and sprinted out into the hallway when it popped open.

She slid to a wobbly stop just outside the door and looked down at her body when she felt the sudden cold of the corridor. She was totally naked from sleep and instantly covered herself with her hands as she retreated to her room. As she shut the door she glanced back out to see an empty hallway. "Damn, always something you forget, bloody clothes!" She quickly dressed and grabbed her ID badge. In moments she was in the elevator and impatiently waited for a few others to get in. As she stood there she noticed in the mirror she had put on her pilot's uniform. It was the first thing she could grab in her closet. It felt like an old friend. Her floor was first and she nearly shoved an old lady aside as she made her way out of the elevator. She ran down the corridor until she found the suite she wanted. It said 'Pam Aquain' on the door ID. She leaned on the doortone.

Pam opened it after thirty seconds of constant ringing. "OK already! What's the probl—Oh, hi Alicia."

Alicia walked right in as Pam stood there expecting a reply, "Good morning to you, Pam, sorry to wake you so early."

Alicia stammered right back, "Pamela, there are going to be some terrible things happening today to the shuttles!"

Pam folded her arms indifferently as she walked back in the room. "How do you know, more ESP?"

"I know, I just know. I've never felt this strong of an image before in my whole life. We've got to stop all the shuttles from flying today!"

"Why are you telling me this? Why not call Ray?"

"He won't be convinced to do it without your consent."

"I didn't know he needed my permission to make decisions. You do know he can't make that kind of decision alone, it'll need the governor's OK, too."

"Whatever! Will you contact Ray with me now to get them stopped?"

"All I have to go on is your word. I'm not even sure I trust you yet."

Alicia grabbed Pam's shoulders with a steel grip and stared intently into her eyes. "Your life is about to change so fantastically it's beyond your dreams. You will find love and with that love you will be responsible for being part of starting a new world!"

Pam couldn't believe what she was hearing, but part of her couldn't help but break into a smile. "Oh yeah, why should I believe that?"

"When you call Ray right now, tell him you'd like to go to Mars."

Pam's smile instantly dropped from her face, "Mars? Now I know you're full of it. That's almost a punishment sentence for most people; it'll be a dead miserable planet for God knows how long."

By now Alicia had let go of her shoulders and had taken her hands, "Pam, do you remember anything unusual about Mars lately?"

Pam thought a moment, "Well, come to think of it, we did have a hard time getting through to them when we were looking for Dr. Ancerid. Max said it was as if all their computers were busy on some big project." She then raised her eyebrows in heightened interest, "All right, maybe something *is* up; let's see what Ray has to say then."

Alicia pulled her to the door, "Can we do it from the computer operations room? And bring Max, he can help us too."

*　　*　　*

Less than ten minutes later Alicia and Pam arrived at the computer operations room, dragging a half-asleep Max with them. He flashed his ID badge to the door sentry, and they were let into the center. It was occupied only by two other night shift technicians. They both gave baffled stares to the threesome as Max and Pam pulled chairs up to the nearest terminal. Max asked, "OK, ladies, what do we do first?"

Pam started, "Let me get Ray's room on Africa; he should be up by now anyway. Max, why don't you get into flight operations." The process took several long minutes, accompanied by an unusual amount of static interference. Ray appeared on Pam's monitor and was pleasantly surprised to see three familiar faces huddled together to greet him so early.

"Well, well, you guys look like the three musketeers for some reason this morning. To what do I owe this pleasure?"

Pam wasted no time, "Ray, what's going on at Mars? No secrets, lives may be at stake!"

Ray furrowed his brow as he looked at Alicia, who simply shrugged her shoulders and said, "Yes, Ray, this is all my doing. Do what she says please."

"I can't say specifics over this unsecure line. You'll have to take my word for it, Pam, that something fantastic has and is occurring there."

Pam smiled and said, "That's all I needed, go ahead, Alicia, tell him what you told me."

"Ray, you have to stop today's flights, all of them. There are going to be more explosions."

His face immediately grew concerned, "Max, when are the first flights departing today, and from where?"

Max was just ahead of him as he commanded the system for the data. "Oh boy, two are already in flight, both inter-hotel jaunts."

Ray instantly replied, "Can you tap into their flight tracking; it'll be from ground radar. How far are they?"

It took less than a minute and he had what Ray needed, "They're both about halfway into their flight paths. What do you want to do?"

"Send a warning to them on the emergency frequencies. Tell them to shut down their engines and establish geosynchronous orbits. It's too late to turn them around and probably too dangerous. How much time before any other ships are in flight?"

Pam worked her terminal, "None for hours, Ray. Shall I contact those terminals?"

"Not yet, I'll let governor Payne know what's going on, and he can decide. We'll stay focused on those ships in flight."

Max updated, "Both ships have just acknowledged our transmission and are awaiting further instructions."

Ray looked to Alicia, "Well, what can we do? Any ideas where the threat comes from or what it is?"

She leaned in to look at the two blips blinking on the screen. "I'm not sure; it's very different than with the Torrus, I didn't have any real sense of danger with that incident." She now was touching the screen when Pam exclaimed, "Did you see that? One of them just disappeared from the screen!"

Ray spoke sharply "Max, speak to me buddy, is it still there or what?"

Max's hands were a blur as he opened a second tracking system. Suddenly the second blip disappeared as well. He screamed in frustration, "Ray, I think we're losing them; it's not a computer glitch! There's just no data stream coming from the ship sensors and the radar signature is either gone completely or just too small to capture."

Pam was now suddenly filled with fear and shrieked to Ray, "We've got to do something! There are hundreds of people on board those ships!"

He yelled back in frustration, "What the hell am I supposed to do? I'm hundreds of miles away! Max, get ground control on the line, see what they have for us!"

Everyone waited in silence, now joined by the two other technicians working in the room. A minute later Max hung up the receiver slowly after hearing what they had to say. "They've confirmed the two ships have disappeared as intact targets. All they're tracking is debris. However, one of the ships is still in a very large piece and tumbling out of control. It appears to be heading straight for our hotel."

Alicia tried to remain calm, "Max, try to contact that ship, the cockpit may still be intact."

He immediately complied, "I'm sure flight control is trying that, I'll just listen in." In moments they could hear the line chatter, ".........repeat,..this is ground control, do you read?"

Suddenly a weak transmission came through the speaker, "Repeat, I repeat, ...hit by....energ....bolt. No...controls working........Fire outside everywhere.....We're decompressing.....oh no, we're.............."

Ray could hear everything as well. He just dropped his head into his palms and closed his eyes. No words could come this time.

Pam buried her face on Max, sobbing. He sat there shocked, yet still studying the screen as he wrapped an arm around his friend.

Alicia held her temples with both hands as she spun away from the picture. Suddenly she turned back and commanded at Ray, "Chairman Phillips; requesting permission to take the utility shuttle on an immediate intercept course to save the hotel from impact!"

He looked up, "How do you plan to do that? That ship has no defensive lasers; it won't be able to stop it."

"There still might be people alive in the fuselage. It's designed to withstand an engine explosion. I can use the shuttle's loader arms to catch it and pull it into a safer orbit."

Max looked up at her in amazement and doubt, "That's way beyond design limits, you'll kill yourself trying."

"Do you have a better suggestion? If that ship hits this hotel it could be a total catastrophe!"

Everyone was silent again as they pondered any other possibilities. "That's what I thought! I have enough time to do this. Pam, call Tim Ward, get him at the shuttle bay immediately. He's going to redeem himself today."

The two of them watched dumbfounded as she streaked from the room. Max gave a gentle jab to Pam as she sat up with a glimmer of hope, "Well, what are you waiting for? Call Tim Ward." He looked back at Ray, "You'll need to warn the shuttle bay personnel she's coming."

*　　*　　*

Alicia was running across the main lobby as she neared the shuttle terminals. She slammed to a halt in front of a boarding agent, "Which gate is the utility shuttle docked in?"

"Number Two to your left, Captain, is there something wrong?"

"No time to explain!" She dashed away as fast as she'd arrived. Just as she barreled up to the gangway door, two technicians were opening it from the other side. One of them spoke immediately "Captain Martin, we're here to help you do the emergency preflight check-offs."

"That will take a half-hour. I need to be out of here in five minutes!"

They protested, "This ship was supposed to go through a yearly tear-down when it arrived yesterday. We can't guarantee everything is working."

"I don't need everything to work. I need it to simply fly. Now, let me down there." At that moment, Tim came running up.

"What's up, Captain? They just told me to be here immediately or I was going to jail!"

She looked at him with a slight grin as he followed her down to the ship. She asked through her breathing, "Let me guess, Pam Aquain called you."

"Yea, I still think she likes me."

"Tim, if this doesn't work, going to jail might sound like a great option. We've lost two shuttles in the last half hour. One of them, at least a big part of it, is heading right for the hotel. We're going to stop it."

"Oh God, there must be no survivors!"

"Maybe, but I'm moving this fast because there might be some still alive."

She turned to the two men following them, "I have no time to do the usual float out. So when I signal, clear me out with the emergency seal blow procedure."

Tim informed her as they entered the airlock doors, "That's never been done before on a ship this size. It could be dangerous."

"That might be the easiest part of this rescue. Come on, in we go!"

The techs sealed the doors behind them and ran out toward the windowed docking control room to monitor her flight. No sooner had they reached the room than her voice barked through the speakers. "Clear me now, I've barely got six minutes to go once I'm out!"

They looked at each other in amazed concern, but obediently followed orders. With a quick sequence of switches thrown, there was a jolting explosive lurch of the ship as it blasted out of the bay backwards. They both held on to the control top as the room shook from the inertia shock. Their viewcom cracked on and displayed Ray's face.

"You people in the control tower, I told you to leave all connections open!"

"Sorry sir, we're doing our best under the circumstances. We just launched Captain Martin out of the bay. She should be starting the main engines now."

"Good, I want a direct audio line to that shuttle. Do you have my signal coordinates to do that?"

"Consider it done. She should be able to hear you in just a few seconds."

"Good. Now, Max Rogers is in the computer operations room mirroring your tracking. I want one of you to go help in the evacuation of the outer rims in your sector. We're sounding the general alarm in thirty seconds!"

One of the men started for the door then turned and asked, "Where should I start?"

"Start with the nearest support cog corridor. Our tracking operations people can't predict exactly where the impact might occur other than your half of the hotel somewhere."

With that the man was gone from the room. In seconds, alarms began to sound everywhere in the hotel. The other technician remained nervously fixed to his screen displaying her progress.

Ray tensely pulled his seat close to his room's viewscreen. He took a deep breath then spoke, "Alicia? Can you hear me? This is Ray."

She calmly replied, her breathing back to normal after all the running. "Good to hear from you again, Ray. This may be the last time we get to talk. I've got a visual already on something. I'm coming up on it fast. Tim, give me a 30° pitch down and open the bay doors."

"Let me know when you have a confirmation. It looks like you're almost on top of it from what I'm seeing."

"The computers can only be so accurate; I can just make out the ship. I'm turning on the work lights. Oh no, Ray, it's a total loss. The side of the fuselage is burnt open and it's all dark. No one could have lived in there with direct exposure to space."

"Did the ship carry any spacesuits?"

"No, they're too bulky to store and take too long to get in."

Ray swallowed hard then continued, "I'm sorry, Alicia, you did everything you could to warn us. If only we'd had more time."

Tim interrupted, "Excuse me, but don't we need to stop that thing from hitting the hotel?"

Alicia shook her head to clear her mind, "Of course we do. Ray, there are self destruct features on all shuttles aren't there?"

"Yes, we generally don't let anyone know that."

"How do we activate it?"

"Our man in the control tower needs to push a special button while I send in a coded signal from my terminal. You there in the tower, are you getting all this?"

"Yes, sir! I'm touching the button as we speak! I assume it's the red one."

"Alicia, are you far enough away to withstand a blast like that?"

"No! Tim, yaw us 180° immediately! Ray, give me 30 seconds to get up some speed then go for it."

He stared at his watch and then said, "OK, I'm sending the code signal to you right now, control." They all waited for the moment of truth, but it never happened.

Alicia spoke first, "The circuits must be too damaged. Tim, bring her 180° back again and roll us so we're looking down on the fuselage from above it. Ray, it looks like we're going to have to try it the way I thought. I'm going to grab it."

Tim continued while he eyed the instruments, "We should be right over it in one minute."

She watched from the window, "Easy, I'm building retro thrust in mark five. Just a little more, Tim, and we're right on top of it. OK, Tim, man the cockpit, I'm moving to the robotic arms control station."

Max interjected, "Alicia, you've got two minutes till impact. If you don't have it in 90 seconds, get the hell away from her. We can't have your ship hitting us, too."

"Understood. That should be enough time. I'm extending the arms now."

Everyone stared at the trajectory monitors as the blips moved ominously toward the Majestik. Pam had a firm grip on Max's thigh as she bit the nails of her other hand. He hardly noticed the pain of her grip. None of them in the operations room paid attention to other monitors displaying the screaming anarchy of the hotel's inhabitants running for cover. It was no surprise people reacted so primally to the alert sirens, why should they react any other way? At least there was humanity left in them, as people did stop to pick up fallen children and elderly. At this moment none of them knew what was wrong, but they knew it wasn't a drill. No one needed special mental powers to know how to act this fateful morning.

Max cautioned another warning, "Thirty seconds to go captain." There was no reply. "Fifteen seconds." Suddenly the speakers came to life. "We're latched. Tim, fire the main engine **now** and get us out of here!"

Ray stood and paced nervously as he watched the now-unified blip slowly start to move away from the hotel, then suddenly accelerate away. Pam jumped up and ran over to an external window just in time to see the bright blue glow of the engine shoot the ship and its lifeless cargo into the darkness. The image reminded her of a mother cuddling her young to safety; in spite of the fact her offspring was no more.

She jumped up and down with a simple restrained clap, "Oh Max, she did it, she did it!" He remained in his seat, staring at the screens. "Alicia, your new orbit should be transmitted to you shortly from ground control. How does the ship feel carrying a load that size?"

"Definitely heavy. I'm back in the cockpit now. It's going to take two of us to fly this thing properly back down to a lower orbit before releasing the fuselage."

Ray continued, "Alicia, when you let the damaged ship go into a decay orbit, I want you to return to the Majestik. Don't try to make it down to Earth, understood?"

It was now Tim's turn again, "Dr. Phillips, I hate to be the bearer of bad news, but seems someone forgot to fill up this ship with fuel before we left. We ain't going back to the hotel."

Alicia quickly looked at the gauges. "He's right, Ray, we'll have to glide down to Earth. Someone please calculate which landing site we'll most likely make. And just so there's no confusion, landing in the ocean is unacceptable." Several minutes went by and then a voice from ground control, "Dr. Phillips, Africa is their best shot."

Max replied, "Do you have thruster propellant reserves?"

"Yes, but we're not sure how much will be left after we release our parcel."

Ray was now smiling in spite of the emotional pain he felt, "Alicia, if I didn't know better, I'd swear you planned it this way. Africa!" He then directed himself to Pam and Max, "You two have been spectacular. I guess I've knocked one more off on what I owe you both." Max tried to be light, "Give it up, Ray, you'll never be able to repay me."

Suddenly Alicia came back on. "Guys, I have another problem. I just noticed a signal warning coming from the robotic controls. It is warning of stress overload on one of the arms. I'm using the external camera now to inspect the situation." She worked the images for a few minutes then reported, "One of the arms is twisted like a half pretzel. It must have happened when we had to accelerate so fast. Anyway, it won't move in that condition."

Ray swung his fist in disappointment, "I knew this went too easy! Alicia, is the other arm undamaged?"

"Yes, the instruments say it has full range of operation."

"Good! Now listen to me carefully. Isn't there a cutting laser in the emergency tool box for that shuttle?"

"I think so. Let me go look." She made her way two chambers aft, carrying her mike piece. "I see the tool box. Just taking a look inside now. Well, there appears to be something that looks like a laser gun, but it looks too small for the job."

"That's it. And size doesn't matter for this job, that thing is powerful. Now, one of you will have to go out and cut the arm off at that fuselage or at your ship."

Tim overheard and immediately volunteered. Alicia made her way back to her seat as she passed him hurrying to get into a spacesuit.

"No heroics out there Tim, just cut the bloody arm off."

"Seems to me just going out there is pretty heroic. And to think just a few days ago you guys were drilling inside my head! I guess you didn't quite get all the crazy out."

Pam was sitting next to Max again, listening intently to the conversation, her head down solemnly with her hair shielding her face on both sides. Yet she too started to smile with what she was hearing.

Max looked at his gauges, "I need to remind everyone you're going over 20,000 miles an hour, and you're starting to pick up some thermospheric heat. I'm guessing you've got just over 10 minutes before you're in fireball state."

Alicia replied, "I'm using thrusters now to change the descent angle and roll. That should buy us a few more minutes."

Max reminded, "Yea, but will you have enough to maneuver the cargo away?"

"I'll have what I need, nothing more, nothing less."

Max covered his mic and looked at Pam, "What does that mean?"

She sighed, "It means stop worrying."

Ray came back in, "Everybody, I just got word that Governor Payne has been brought up to speed on the situation. He has agreed to immediately stop any remaining flights. Alicia, how far along is Mr. Ward with that laser?"

"This is Tim; I'm wired in to everyone, so no off-the-cuff remarks. I'm about a minute from reaching the control arm base. I'll cut it there, it'll take too long to get to the other end. You know, it's very spooky out here being right next to this damaged piece of shuttle. I can almost feel everyone still in it."

Alicia added, "You should feel what it's like in my head right now. Their energies are bringing back to life many long since departed. Many memories have not been fully erased."

Ray questioned, "Alicia, what do you mean? You keep alluding to this information that is out there. What does that have to do with our lives?"

"It's just a theory the Andromedians have and taught to some humans. It's based on the concept that our universe is nothing more than an amazingly well-built quantum computer simulation. I find comfort in that theory, that's all. It keeps me from being angry at God."

Tim came in, "That's pretty wild, Captain, I'd love to discuss that over a few drinks."

Ray shot back, "How's it going, Tim? Are you at the arm yet?"

"Better than that, I'm almost through it. You're right; this little laser is a nasty son of a bitch."

Alicia managed a smile, "Make sure you stay clear when it gets all the way free. We have no idea if the fuselage will shift when it breaks." Suddenly Alicia felt a measurable jolt go through the ship. She turned to the monitor to see what had happened. There was no sign of Tim or the robotic arm. She rotated the camera until she could finally see the fuselage again, extended completely out of the cargo bay range, yet still hanging on to her ship by the good control arm. And then she saw him, way out on the end of the long cut off control arm. He was hanging on with his body suspended out away from the ship.

"Tim, can you hear me? Are you OK?"

He came right back at her, "You should see the view from out here. The earth almost looks pretty again."

"Can you make it back in? We've only got one or two minutes to go."

"I'm tugging my way back. I had no time to tether myself on, so I have to be a little slow right now."

Max had to contribute, "Any light coming off the ship's belly yet from the atmosphere?"

"I was hoping you wouldn't notice. Yeah, it's getting quite bright."

Max turned to Pam, "I don't see how he can get back in the ship in time. She's got to jettison that fuselage very soon. If she doesn't she may not make the re-entry, or even if she does she'll have no way of landing safely until that arm lets go of the payload."

Alicia calmly guided Tim, "Tim, I want you to know you're the best co-pilot I've ever flown with. I know you can float back a few dozen feet in time, it's nothing for you."

"Hey, Captain, I'm already at the base of the working arm now. I'm going to release the fuselage from here, since I'm right here. You never know if this thing will work from the inside remote."

She agreed, "Hurry."

He pushed the control signals, but just like clockwork, the arm failed to release the cargo. He tried it several more times, but still no response.

"OK anybody listening. It's unresponsive. What's the plan now?"

Ray immediately came in, "Young man, get the hell back in the ship now!"

"OK, and then what?"

"Give me a minute!"

Pam was once again chewing her nails, "God, Max, I feel as if that's my sister out there. I can't stand this."

He nodded back, now somewhat nervous himself, "They're doing some pretty amazing stuff right now. It's hard not to root for both of them. But this is definitely bad."

"This is Tim, I'm back in. Give me a minute to close the hatch and re-compress."

Alicia came in, "The ship is starting to shake violently. What has my brilliant scientist come up with? It's now or never, Ray!"

"Alicia, you said you have some thruster fuel left?"

"Yes, what about it?"

"Is there enough to make a complete 360° roll?"

Her face immediately lightened, "I see what you're thinking! You think we can create just enough torque to snap the arm off the ship!"

"Yes, what do you think?"

Tim jumped right in as he emerged from the air lock, "I think that arm will never break with a simple roll. However, if you fire a full roll burst for two seconds instead of a steady 30-second micro, it might do it."

Max then added, "That's definitely doable, but you'll need an opposite burst once it's free to stop the ship from going into a deadly corkscrew."

Alicia asked Ray, "Ray, can Tim's idea do it?"

He didn't hesitate, "Honey, its gotta!"

"OK, I'm going for the full roll thrust bursts, hang on, Tim Ward!"

Just before she did the ignition, Ray came back on, "Alicia?"

"Yes, Ray?"

"I love you!"

She gritted her teeth as she fired the thruster rockets at full power. The ship moaned violently as it twisted from the force, throwing both pilots sideways in their seats. There was a massive jolt and immediate bang as the robotic arm snapped off its base. The joined ships were now two again! The lifeless fuselage drifted quickly away from the shuttle, instantly igniting in the atmospheric friction. She looked over at Tim and gave a teasing sexy wink to him. He wanted to reply but he pointed to the gauges, "OK, now what about this crazy spin we're in, do you mind if I bring her back in control?"

"Be my guest, but switch seats with me, it'll be easier from here."

He unstrapped and swapped seats with her. As he slipped down into the captain's seat he stopped and put his hands respectfully on the chair arms and stroked them. "This is nice, thank you, Alicia."

"Just stop the spin, Tim."

He looked at the instrument panel in front of him, "Ah, captain, I'd like to but it says we're out of thruster fuel."

She closed her eyes and commanded, "Fire the rockets anyway."

He complied and much to his surprise they ignited perfectly. "How about that, who would have believed!" Within seconds the ship started to slow its rotation, until he expertly had the belly solidly down into the merciless atmosphere fighting them. In no time at all, fire was shooting past their windows as the ship began the final stages of the descent.

Alicia's eyes were still closed as she touched her mike "You really meant that, didn't you Ray?"

He wiped a small tear of joy running down his cheek, "Well, I had to motivate you somehow."

She laughed back as she opened her eyes to check her instruments, "Still think quite a bit about yourself, doctor. Are you going to meet me at the runway?"

"Oh I suppose I can fit it in my schedule. I have no idea what we're all going to do now. We can't stand to lose more lives and ships like we did today."

Pam and Max stood side by side as they listened. He looked down and saw she was holding his hand. "I'm happy for them, Max. I really am. Ray really knows what he wants in life this time, I can tell."

He looked at her intently, "How about you, do you know what you want?"

She leaned back to take a broad look at him, then looked into his eyes, "Well, I'm starting to get a better idea everyday."

She then reached her arms around him and hugged him, gently at first, then intensely. Tears flowed as she thought of the people killed. He felt her emotion envelop him and pour deeply through him, until it drew his own tears from the depths of his soul. After several long, lovely minutes of two humans saving each other, they looked again into each other's eyes. He had no more doubts, no more fears, he just simply kissed her lips gently then cradled her head against his chest. The room was quiet as the workstations began to fill with technicians. The two of them didn't notice. They would not let go of each other until they had the strength to go on, no matter how long it took.

Ray switched his viewscreen back to the hotel's operations room, but he immediately saw Pam and Max standing in their embrace. He smiled contently and respectfully turned off his monitor. He left his room and headed for the government complex. There was much to talk about.

CHAPTER TWENTY FIVE

Hayden Green was getting into his street clothes as fast as he could. The radio was on in his room, blaring the news of the recent loss of the two shuttles. He listened intently as he finished dressing, his emotions welling with anger at Governor Payne. He pounded on the door with his open palm, "Let me out of here, I need to talk with the governor!" He persisted for several minutes until it opened. The guard was not in a good mood.

"What's your problem, man?"

"If you don't get me to the governor's office immediately, there won't be any shuttles left by the end of the week!"

The man studied him suspiciously, then left the room without saying a word. He returned in a few minutes. "Looks like they want to talk with you, also. The governor's transport is already on its way here. You'll get your chance real soon, Green." With that he slammed the door as he left.

Hayden sat down somewhat satisfied, no longer noticing the redundant voices of the news announcers in the background. He thought about what he was going to say. There were no more nerves, no more fears. He was more than angry and he had to do something!

Fifteen minutes later he was startled by the sonic boom of an incoming shuttle. He bounded to the window for a glimpse. No spectators or families were waiting. He was confused. He wondered where the ship was inbound from. He then spied the governor's aircraft taxiing up to the hanger adjacent to his room. He leaned against the glass and watched it pull to a stop. Governor Payne got out, but Hayden didn't recognize the next man out of the door. Payne hastily made his way toward Hayden's building while the other man walked briskly toward the runway fencing.

Hayden was waiting at the door. As Payne opened it, Hayden instantly began his rant: "You murderer, you knew those ships were in danger! *You* killed those people!"

Otis stopped in his tracks and looked silently at him, his face somber. He calmly took off his hat and walked defeated to the edge of Green's bed. He sat cautiously, "I made a mistake. I need your help, Hayden."

The stunned diplomat walked slowly up to him, not sure he heard correctly. "Wait a minute, are you apologizing to me?"

"I need fresh input, including yours, to figure out a better way to stop this Vor."

Green was unsure of himself again; this was not how he expected it to go. "You want me to help you stop the Vor? What makes you think I trust you? Maybe you want to make me bait again?"

Otis looked intently at him, "I'm sorry I put you through that, but you have to know the facts. Your Dove leader was an alien, probably one of the Vor higher-ups. All the Dove chapters were likely infiltrated by it or them. They used you all; they even stole your minds in some cases. Now I need you to help me better understand how they think. You're the only one close enough to me to trust on this. Of course before we proceed, we'll need to give you a quick brain scan to make sure there's no implant in your head."

Hayden reeled back a little by that comment. "OK, have they scanned you and Mr. Ivory yet?"

"If that's what it takes, we'll all get that done today."

Hayden walked to the window. "What shuttle is coming in? I thought we had no ships scheduled here today."

"This is a utility shuttle that was just docked at the Majestik for maintenance. It's being piloted by some very brave people who risked their lives to steer away one of the damaged shuttles from a collision into the Majestik. They had no choice but to land here; they're out of fuel."

"Hum, that's some fancy flying then! Who's waiting out there? Who came in with you?"

"Dr. Phillips from the Majestik. He helped coordinate the diversion mission. He'll join us as soon as they land."

"Phillips? Ah yes, I heard his name on the news when they talked about the chairman up there getting killed. He's the acting chairman now, isn't he?"

"Temporarily, yes. He's a good man for the job right now." Otis joined Hayden at the window. Together they watched the shuttle glide in for a perfect silent landing. Otis turned and surveyed Hayden's body up and down and asked, "You feeling better? Doesn't look as if you were ever injured."

Hayden looked back at him unbelieving, "You don't care, so stop trying to make conversation."

Otis chuckled softly, then put his hat back on, "Come on, let's go out there, you could use the fresh air."

As they walked out together, Hayden added, "Governor, I'd like my gun back."

*   *   *

Max sat back in his chair and put his feet on the table in front of him. Pam was leaning against the station computer bank next to his feet. He watched her as she silently picked at her nails, her face expressionless. Her mind was too distant for Max to stand another second. "What's wrong? It was just a little kiss."

She looked at him, her face conveying the guilt she felt, "Max, you know it's not that. It's all those people, we should have been able to save them."

"How? We did the best we could considering what we're up against."

"I should have believed her. I wasted valuable time this morning trying to show her up or belittle her. Also, she said something to me earlier that really got to me. Now, I'm not sure how I should react at this point."

He got up and moved closer to her, "Care to share?"

"She said I would be responsible for helping start a new world with the love I would find."

Max grinned proudly through his puzzled look. "Well, I had hoped to enhance your life a little, but start a new world? Where, and why?"

"She had me ask Ray about Mars."

"So that's what this all comes down to, Mars? What the hell is going on out there that's connected to all these Earth events the last 12 days?"

"She made it sound so positive, almost as if it will balance out all this horror somehow."

Max took her hand to lead her from the room, "Let's go to the clinic, we have some work to finish there. They may also need a little extra help if there were many injuries during the evacuation. After that, we need to take our turn going through the things that were confiscated from those people's rooms."

"I want to talk with Ray again. I need to know what we're going to do now. We're back where we started from, you know."

Max replied as he checked over the now-empty room one last time, "Oh no, we're not. They may have hit us hard, but now it's our turn."

"But how much time do we have before people start dying? You said at the meeting we couldn't survive without our shuttles. How will everyone feed themselves, how will anything get done without them?"

"We can still do it at this point; we have twelve remaining ships. With enough cooperation, it can be done."

She put her arm around him as they walked from the room, "You sure have more confidence than I do right now. Oh Max, did you lock the door?"

He didn't even look back, "I'm sure I took care of everything."

*   *   *

Payne, Ivory and Green had gone directly to the medical center for brain scans. Hours later, they were all satisfied each was still a trustworthy human. They made their way to the government offices to do a brainstorming session. Tim Ward was delegated to a room several floors below them, where an armed guard stood outside his door. Otis still needed to keep an eye on him, based on Ray's conclusion of his role in the Torrus' destruction. He didn't want to confine him, but protocol dictated it.

Meanwhile, Alicia and Ray were back at his hotel. She stood by Ray's side as they watched another murky sunset from the room balcony. He took her hand, his mind dancing in hundreds of directions. "Alicia, what am I going to do now? We're up against a real enemy, one we can't see and one that seems to prey upon the Universe looking for trouble. The human race is a sitting duck if they thrive on negativity! We've got enough of *that* emotion to fire up a star."

She was silent as he continued to think out loud. "If they succeed in eliminating the shuttle system, we're surely history. All this struggle, all this rebirth and regrowth for nothing! Maybe you're right. Maybe it *is* just a big computer game to someone or something out there, just for amusement."

She tightened her grip on his hand, "Well, you're certainly negative tonight; this is just how the Vor want you to behave."

He let go and turned his back to the sunset, "Dammit, we all can't be as confident as you! This is the curse of humanity; disconnected from each other, and, even worse, disconnected from our creator!"

"These emotions arise from fear."

"Duh! Yes, I'm scared; shouldn't that be a luxury now?"

"Wouldn't it be better to make your enemy afraid?"

He walked back into the room and flopped on the couch. She followed behind him and sat next to him. He looked at her, "What could they be afraid of? Pete said the same thing in essence. He thought whoever built the Martian, and the Earthen pyramids for that matter, might be a good candidate. But they're long gone. The Andromedians might have given them a challenge, but nonetheless, the Vor went after them in the past as well. And we humans have got nothing right now I can see that would scare a fly away!"

"Use the people you are surrounded with. You're all in the right places to do this. I think we should have a meeting."

"A meeting? Like a committee meeting?"

"No, not political. Just me, you, Max, Pam, Otis, Green, and the people at Shepherd."

He thought about how he could arrange that when the viewcom signaled. He got up and turned it on. Max's face appeared. He was holding a stack of papers and smiling. Ray leaned in closer, "Is that what I think it is?"

"Yup, all your stolen pages on the fuel research. We found them buried in a suitcase of the maintenance man's belongings they confiscated."

Ray asked, "By the way, how are those four taking their confinement?"

"They're tense, but a little angry at us more than anything. They're angry because they *believe* the infection story we gave them and naturally they're blaming the lab personnel for being careless."

"Better not tell them that those same people will be burning implants out of their brains in a few days!"

Max laughed as he squared up the paperwork, "Now what? I've reread the papers but I don't see what we can do with them."

Ray was sitting in front of his screen, "I don't know why the Vor would want that data, I don't think they have a need for rocket fuel. And those studies haven't anywhere near the potential of what Dr. Ancerid has come up with."

"Maybe they didn't want to leave any easy options for substitutes in case we never got Ancerid's work figured out."

"OK, so it seems obvious the strategy is to cut off the shuttle lifelines, and if running out of fuel wouldn't do, just blow up all the shuttles and fuel depots. It also makes sense that they would try to pin a murder charge on Ancerid. If they could discredit him, no one would want to be associated with any research he did."

Max crunched his face as he pondered, "It's scary to think what would happen to the human race in general if we lost all our abilities to get back and forth to space, and especially to Mars. I can envision not only everyone dying who's not on Earth, but the remaining people on the surface withering back to the stone age."

Pam had now joined Max and stuck her head into view, her face somber, "Ray, when are you going to tell us more about Mars?"

"Pam, nothing's changed since we last talked! This is not a secure channel and what's going on out there has little to do with our predicament!"

She was mad now, "It has to you boob; use your head!"

Alicia couldn't help but laugh a little out loud, "She's right you know, there has to be a connection."

He sat back and folded his arms, then looked directly at Alicia. "I want to share everything with all of you, but our enemy has ears everywhere. If we were all here on Earth, I'd literally take us out to the middle of the desert to talk about our next move. I obviously can't get everyone together safely right now, so you two up there will have to trust us just a little longer."

Pam didn't like what she was hearing, but knew he was right. She conceded, "We can handle the shuttle aftermaths from here, you stay focused on those aliens."

Max watched her walk away, then turned back to his monitor, "She'll be OK, Ray, we'll get things taken care of. Call when you have something."

Ray still sat with his arms folded as the screen went black, then determinedly reached forward and dialed Payne's office.

"Otis, can you, Ivory and Green meet us tonight? Say in one hour."

"Where?"

"Let's start in the hotel parking lot, then we'll go to a more secure location from there."

*   *   *

It was now dark as the government hovercar glided into the far end of the hotel lot. Ray and Alicia stood waiting next to their vehicle as it approached them. Ray went to the window of Payne's vehicle and stooped over, "We'll go in our vehicle; leave your goons here, or they can follow us, but not closer than two kilometers."

Otis didn't hesitate as he and the other two climbed from the vehicle. Otis instructed his security to stay where they were. They protested, but he quickly won that argument. Soon, all five of them were speeding out of town to the darkness of the desert.

Thirty minutes later, Ray pulled off the road and went several kilometers farther into the sandy weeded plains. Once he was satisfied, he stopped and turned off the engine.

Hayden Green was the only nervous member of the group, but it was understandable. They all climbed out and stretched their legs as the cool night air breezed past their bodies. A few stars were actually visible through the haze, something few got to see on Earth anymore.

Ray began, "I feel we can figure this out, here and now, if we let go and hold nothing back. Otis, what did you three come up with today?"

Otis leaned on the vehicle, "Hayden has been very helpful. Why don't you summarize what you told me earlier, Hayden?"

Without hesitation he began, "As a sworn Dove member, we were never allowed to talk with each other about our tasks. We were never able to see the face of our leader. We were led to believe that he was the top man in the organization, not just our local group."

Ray asked, "Didn't that strike you as odd that he could be in so many places so easily?"

"As I said, we talked very little among ourselves, so we thought we were special to have the entire movement's leader at our division. We had no idea who directed the other divisions' meetings."

Alicia asked, "Why did everyone believe in him so unquestionably?"

"Well, I guess he said what we all wanted to hear. He said he was directed by an astral guide. You know, sort of a multidimensional entity, an angel if you will."

Ray drew a deep sigh, "Hayden, did this thing ever say anything about Mars?"

"Mars? Not that I remember. But he was almost obstinate about the need to guard the shuttle system, including the Mars transports. Why, what's happening at Mars?"

"Mars has taken a dramatic lurch forward in the terraforming project. It is basically about ready to support humans on the surface without protective gear."

"Wow, how'd they do that? That's not supposed to be near done for another half-century or more!"

"Let's just say that good science and gut instincts played a role. However, we're giving ultimate credit to the three pyramids we discovered on the planet.

You must remember those discoveries. They were 70 percent buried, which is why they were never found until we got people on the surface exploring the anomalies the orbital probes picked out."

By now Tom Ivory had to say something, "Well, Otis, you kept this secret very well these last few days. Aren't you worried the Vor built those things long ago precisely for this moment? Maybe it's part of a plan for colonizing our solar system."

Ray shook his head, "No, our Andromedian contacts say it's not their style, too much work, I think they said. And *they* certainly deny building them as well, which includes the Earth pyramids I might guess."

Alicia added, "I think it's very conceivable the Earth and Mars pyramids were built by not only the same race of beings, but at the same time. Knowing what they were able to do on Mars, I think they may have done the same thing here on Earth long ago."

Green contributed more, "So if they did work here on Earth long ago, they may have kept them intact for possible use again. Then the Earth rips apart on us and either crumbles all of them or submerges the rest under the oceans. I guess we never figured out how to get them cranked up again."

Otis revealed, "Don't think the world's governments didn't try. They let the public continue to believe they were burial chambers. From what I was privy to by studying old records, we couldn't start our pyramids in time to stop the Earth from ripping apart because we didn't have certain parts or elements to activate the mechanisms. So we did the next best thing by building antenna arrays in multiple locations to broadcast certain frequencies to the outer atmosphere. They experimented with them for decades."

Hayden acknowledged, "Yes, yes, especially the ones the Americans maintained in Alaska. The public fought for disclosure on that but never could get the truth. Now I know why. It would have let every human on Earth know that our scientists were suspicious of a coming calamity."

Otis got off the vehicle he had been sitting on, "If we're trying to connect the Mars events to all this destruction, it seems simple to me. The Vor were monitoring everything we humans were doing, including off-planet activities. They saw the Mars project coming to life and had no choice but to accelerate their plans to finish off we humans."

"Before we could get full colonization started!" Alicia proclaimed proudly.

Ray took her shoulders and looked into her face in the near total blackness. "That's what they're afraid of? Humans getting a fresh start on Mars?"

"It makes sense, doesn't it? They know as much as we do, although the original builders are likely long gone. What else can drive them away faster than the positive emotions of a new beginning for the entire human race? Can you imagine the global excitement when people know they may not have to spend the rest of their lives on this smoldering shell of a planet?"

Ray dropped his hands and grabbed his chin in thought, "That brings us back to our problem; how are we going to get people out there safely?"

Otis came in, "Dr. Phillips, can we build into our shuttles those engine modifications that you and Pete talked about?"

"Yes, I'll have to get from them the secrets on manufacturing that gold-like coil. I was thinking we could use the moon base facilities to do it. We could get easy access to anything Mars sends us from their salvage, plus the low gravity makes it ideal for such a project."

"OK, but what is going to stop the Vor from attacking *those* attempts?" Hayden jumped right back in, "Tell the world right now about Mars! No more secrets remember?"

Otis asked while trying to hold his emotions, "Does everyone here think that can do it? Will the happiness on Earth really be enough to make them stop trying to wipe us out?"

For a moment everyone was silent. Then, starting with Alicia, each simply nodded or said yes. The last to agree was Tom Ivory. He finally concurred when he felt Otis standing inches from his face waiting for his answer.

Ray slapped his hands together excitedly, "OK, we tell everyone Mars is the new home for the human race. We start a cautious shuttle flight renewal, and emphasize getting materials from Mars to the moon to soup up all our remaining shuttles. Any other ideas, anyone?"

No one had any more to add, so there was a ritualistic handshake among the five and they drove back to the city lights. They all felt part of some monumental thing the human race was about to do— or do over again.

CHAPTER TWENTY SIX

The day after the desert meeting brought a huge dust storm on Mars. Jaden and Pete stood by the observation portal watching the action on the planet. Pete stepped away and tried to be philosophical, "Well, it figures; we bring on an atmosphere and now we get winds. I can only imagine what the weather is going to be like from day to day as this thing equilibrates."

"I'm not too worried, my alien friend. During my flyover yesterday, I saw a large body of water starting to form on the other side of the planet from the rains. We need to bring plant life down there soon to stabilize things. When do you think we'll get a shuttle?"

"After the two we just lost yesterday, I'm not sure we can count on any getting out here soon enough."

"What about our food supplies?"

"Well, water won't be an issue, but we'll all have to go down to the surface and stay soon for access to the hydrators. Otherwise to answer your question, we may have a week. We won't have enough fuel to keep up these salvage jaunts for more than a few more days. The recovery of coil material is eating our lunch in fuel."

"I know, I know. I'm thinking we should move the salvage extraction to the surface as well. Have you figured out a way to synthesize the coil from what we're extracting?"

"I think so. I'm just playing around with various ways to reconstitute it. It may be no more complex than using a foam extruder under vacuum and then cooling it to just the right temperature to allow it to be malleable."

Jaden left the window and sat at a computer monitor, "Excellent. I'm sure Otis and Ray will be happy to hear that." At that moment, an interspace communication came in from Governor Payne.

"Good morning, doctors, I have some big news." Pete walked up behind Jaden to see what was happening.

Otis continued, "After a high-level meeting, it's been decided to tell the entire human population about what we've accomplished on Mars. I'm making a formal announcement later today after I inform the other governors privately."

Jaden quickly replied with a big grin, "That's OK with me, I told you we need lots of people out here soon."

Otis cleared his throat before continuing, "That's where things get tricky. We are hoping these bastard Vor creatures get the hint that we're not scared of them and we will not sit by and let humanity die in this part of the galaxy."

Pete questioned, "That sounds good on paper, Otis, but you have no guarantees, do you?"

"Of course not, do we ever when it comes to this kind of thing? If your people got them to leave you alone by uniting, we can too. Now, what do we need to send out there on the shuttle mission? And before you answer that, Dr. Phillips is hoping to get a shipload of raw gold material for the trip back."

Jaden answered, "You mean besides the usual crew changes, food, fuel cells and repair parts? Oh, how about a few tons of seeds! We need to get this place starting to green."

"I'm going to get one your way in the next week."

Jaden despaired, "Otis, we can't wait that long, we'll be out of food for too long by then. We needed a ship sent yesterday!"

Payne got close to his monitor, "Doctor, we'll all remain happy and calm during this period. I know you'll find a way to get through without all starving to death. I don't want to say any more, we cannot trust any communications methods to be free of snooping."

Jaden looked at Pete as he answered, "Understood, your highness. We'll come up with something. And count on a few tons of coil materials for the trip back." The monitor went black as his last word came out. Jaden stood up and began preparing for the day's activities as he continued the conversation with Pete.

"I'm not sure we'll be as lucky as your people were in the past. I can see what they're doing, working the human emotional angle. I think we need something bigger to keep the Vor away. You mentioned they'd be afraid to come near us if the folks who built these pyramid generators were back in town."

"It was a passing thought. Last time I checked, I didn't see any special beings floating around out there."

Jaden clenched both fists in excitement over a sudden idea, "What if we faked them out? What if we fooled the Vor that the makers had returned?"

"How would we do that?"

"It would be easy. Just send a message back to Earth that they've returned because of some signal the pyramids sent out when they cranked back to life!"

"If we were to send such a signal to Earth, we would have to fool them too, since Otis said all transmissions were likely insecure. That kind of lie could set some things in motion at central command we couldn't predict."

"You may be right. They might even decide *not* to come out here so quickly until they knew it was safe."

"So, we would lie as we go; make up all kinds of shit just to buy some time? We would need our whole crew to be in on it. I don't know if we could pull that off."

Jaden returned to his seat to think. "What if we were all unable to communicate after we sent word of the aliens return?"

Pete stood right in front of him, hands on hips, "Just what are you cooking up there, old buddy?"

"We could all take Stasipro shots sometime after we send the message. There's enough onboard for everyone."

"If I remember, that's in the medical kits for emergencies. Isn't it supposed to put the body into deep hibernation?"

"Yes, for any medical emergency we couldn't handle out here. It would possibly buy the sick or injured enough extra time to get to a cure."

"OK, let's say we all take the drug and go sleepy-by. Earth then can't reach any of us, so they try to figure out what happened. They'll try to probe all our databases for an answer. If they see us all in our beds in stasis, what's to make them think our nonexistent aliens didn't harm us?"

"Well, they do know we'll run out of food, so they could also think it was a survival strategy. And, we'll leave a clue behind, encoded in the database. I know the people at the Majestik will find it. Besides, all they'll do is make the supply shuttle flight a rescue mission if they remain concerned. That just means bringing some weapons along. I think it would work, the Vor would stay the hell away from the shuttle for sure if they knew the pyramid builders were back!"

"So if we do this, how can we be sure the Vor won't come racing here to see who the builders are?"

"That could be the wild card. I guess we've reached a point where taking a vote with everyone can give us the confidence we need to try it or not."

Pete walked around a bit and went back to the portal, "Jaden, did you ever really study all the theories of how the Earth pyramids were possibly built?"

"I think so, at least most of the mainstream ideas."

"How about the giants?"

"The giants, you mean big people?"

"Yes, really big people. Some legends had them over fifteen to twenty meters tall."

"Wow! Hell, you could pick up those big stones like simple bricks all day long if you were that big!"

"Exactly. My people believed that story the most, based on the evidence. You know how the universe goes; it's all a matter of perspective. Size is so relative."

"So, what are you saying, we need some flair in our message, tell them they're freaking giants?"

"Couldn't hurt."

"Alright then. So let's get all the crew together later today when we've fin-ished our flights, and see how they like the idea of a long nap."

*   *   *

The sun had gone down hours before at the African headquarters. Otis was exhausted; he had made the dreaded conference call to all the other gov-ernors. He was still amazed how cooperative everyone was with the news. He took that momentum into his worldwide announcement. He had his staff create colorful graphics, with Dr. Phillips' input, explaining how the Red Planet had transformed so magically. He wasn't sure how many understood the theories, but *he* certainly had a much better understanding of what had hap-pened. The announcement couldn't have come at a better time, as the latest shuttle disasters had pushed people's emotional confidence to the breaking point. Now, however, it was time for the ritual evening drink. He leaned on his intercom with his free hand.

"Tom, you out there anywhere, man?" There was no reply. He walked over to the door and peered into the darkened hallway past his two guards. He mumbled to himself, "The one time I want to share a drink with someone, I'm all alone again."

A repeating ring tone interrupted his pouting as he made his way back in the office. It was interspace communications. Otis sat down first before opening his screen. Jaden King was on the other end, and of all things, holding a drink.

"Otis, I see you've got your usual poison in your hand, you can see I'm joining you! I'm calling to tell you something amazing since this morning's conversation!"

"I see you're smiling, too, so lay it on me."

"I should have called earlier, but it's been a whirlwind day. Here goes; the pyramid builders have returned and I can't wait for you to meet them!"

Otis nearly fell out of his chair as he lunged forward, "What! And you're sure it's not that Vor gang fooling you?"

Jaden got a little more serious, "Damn sure, they said they got the signal from the pyramids' transmission. Turns out they never really were too far away. They say they have a different dimension they now exist in, but their home worlds are overlapping our solar system."

"I can't believe this, what do they look like? Is one there with you now in the Shepherd?"

"Ahh not exactly. There's one little thing I have to mention right away. They're a little big."

"How big?"

"I'd say about 25 meters tall. Yup, we look like little baby midgets next to them."

Otis sat back in his chair trying to picture them. "What are they here for? Did we piss them off by messing with their pyramids?"

"No, not at all. They're quite impressed we figured it out. As a matter of fact, they want to meet everyone involved with solving the mystery. But, they can't come to Earth; too big. They lived on Mars because the lower gravity was easy on their massive weights. They're going to just keep a few representatives on the surface while we begin the next phase of terraforming. So for now all I can do is send a ...."

The screen suddenly went black with no warning. Otis was furious, "Come on you piece of shit!" He slapped the side of the monitor a few times to no avail. He then dialed the operator in, "What happened to my transmission?"

"I'm checking now, sir." The woman worked several minutes trying to re-establish the link. "I'm sorry, governor; it looks like the transmission was interrupted out at station Shepherd."

"Well, can you contact them any other way?"

"I'm trying, but unless you have made arrangements for a secure laser line, I don't think there's anything else I can do. We'll keep trying the rest of the night. Should we wake you if we get reconnected?"

"Damn right you will. Thank you!"

He grabbed his hat and coat and walked out the door. As he entered the hallway his two guards joined him immediately. He asked routinely, "Is anyone else in the building yet?"

"Only one, sir, Mr. Ivory is down in the communications room doing some research."

He looked at the man surprised, "Really, hmm."

"Do you want us to get him for you?"

"No, just wondering. Let's take me home, I'm damn tired."

*   *   *

The next day marked the two-week point from when the fuel depot was destroyed. Alicia and Ray were having breakfast at their hotel when a waiter came up to them with a com-tablet.

"Dr. Phillips?"

"Yes, that's me."

"I have a call from Governor Payne."

Ray took the screen and wondered aloud, "Kind of early for work already, I hope nothing's wrong."

"Ray, is Captain Martin there with you?"

He looked up and smiled, "Yes, she is, do you need to talk with her?"

"Yes, if you don't mind. It won't take long."

Ray handed her the tablet, "Captain, I had an interesting call last night from Mars. It gave me certain new questions and ideas."

"Go on."

"That shuttle you flew down to Earth the other day is now the biggest one we've got left. I need to get a huge load to Mars ASAP. I want you to fly the mission."

She looked up proudly at Ray, who couldn't overhear the conversation, "Yes, I'll do it. Can we discuss details later?"

"Yes, I need both of you at my office by lunch, I have something else to update you on that may drastically change our plans. See to it that Dr. Phillips is on his toes."

"Good day, governor." She smiled as she placed the pad gently on the table. He looked at her waiting for something, "Well, what the heck was that about?"

She just blurted it out. "I'm going to Mars ASAP."

He waited for more, but she purposely remained quiet to watch his reaction.

He looked down as he slightly pursed his lips, "Well, if the Governor has ordered it, I guess I can't stop you."

"Also, we have to meet him by lunch today for an important update."

"OK, so that gives us the rest of the morning. What would you like to do?"

"Well, it's very strange out there in everyone's minds. They have such mixed feelings about the new Mars and yet the tragic deaths of the latest shuttle explosions will linger forever in many memories."

He wiped his mouth with his napkin as he listened, then leaned forward in a sudden serious tone. "Have you flown the Mars route ever?"

"Only twice; its four days of mostly boredom."

He continued, "If you have to go all the way to Mars under these conditions, I'm going to say this now while my *unpleasant* memories of what happened the other day are still lingering."

She could feel he was getting emotional. She reached across the table and took his hands.

"Alicia, I won't lie. I'm afraid to let you fly yet, but I know that's wrong. I have no right to stop you, especially on a mission of this magnitude. Besides, you did magnificently getting that debris cleared."

She felt she had to interrupt him, "Ray, why am I so special to you? Is it my Andromedian half? Maybe because I'm a woman pilot? I can't believe it would be my intuition you've fallen for; that seems to frustrate you."

He thought as he stared at the table, "I love you because of all of that. I'm just going to say this right out, crazy as it seems. I want to marry you."

She immediately became uneasy and let go of his hands and looked away. He didn't have to wait long for her to explain.

"I'm still married, Ray; my husband and little girl may still be out there."

He gently reached for her face and turned her chin toward him, brushing aside her hair, "When we first talked, I didn't know much about you, yet I tried to console you about your family and..."

"You really didn't believe they were alive, I remember."

He let go and began to fiddle with her napkin, "I really believed what I said at the time. It was for no other reason other than what I felt. You brought that out of me. I had no ulterior motives in saying those things. But now, honey, after twelve years, with that sense of yours, surely you must know in your heart whether or not they're still alive. There should be no doubts where they are."

She remained quiet, looking at his hands cradled in her napkin, then put her hands to her face as she began to weep. He immediately got up and sat in the chair next to her. He put his arm around her and became a partner in her release. She began to cry louder and louder as she confronted the reality of acceptance. Ray looked around at the few remaining patrons in the cafe and smiled assuringly to them.

After she was finally done, she looked at Ray, her eyes red and swollen. Her true beauty was now evident, more than he had ever seen in any human. He laughed at himself when he noticed the tears that were flooding his eyes. She smiled as she reached her arm around him and placed her head on his shoulder, "Thank you Ray, I never thought I'd have the courage to admit they were gone. I forced myself to believe they were still here. I know where they are. I have to be patient, that's all."

He understood. "You had no choice. We all need things to believe in to keep us going every day."

She looked at him deeply after wiping her eyes. "I love you too, Ray."

He restrained his smile as he took her napkin to wipe the last tear from his own face, "Does that mean you'll marry me?"

She touched his lips anticipating what he would say, "Not right now. If the Mars trip goes OK, and I'm still here, in this, when I get home; then I will seriously consider saying yes. I just don't want any more from life right now. It's perfect for what it is." He spoke anyway through her fingertips, "I think I follow that, and I *will* be waiting for your answer when you walk out of that ship."

She straightened her blouse as she sat up tall, "Good. I think we should go for a long walk around the city. I just want to feel real gravity the way it was meant to be. Is that OK with you?"

He smiled as he pushed his chair back. "I'm ready to go wherever you want to go."

*   *   *

Pam rushed to finish her morning clinic chores while Max was busy in a meeting with a small committee. He had put it together for shuttle disaster surviving family members to aid them in communicating anywhere they needed. In no time the committee deeds had expanded exponentially. It wasn't anywhere near what the survivors deserved from the government, but they knew it was earnest.

Max looked at the clock as the last detail of the meeting was finalized. "OK then, Ms. Najib is focusing on surviving minors in space facilities, and Mr. Brounes' group is handling room contents getting packaged for shipping to surviving family on Earth. I think that covers everything for now. I thank all of you once again for doing such a wonderful job under very difficult circumstances. We'll meet again in two days, same time."

Max waited for everyone to leave before calling Pam at the clinic. "Hey, beautiful, is today when I get a smile out of you again?"

She sat down and pulled her black hair behind her ears. "I do feel a little better on the inside today, but it's still hard, Max. Are we supposed to call Earth today?"

"Yes, Governor Payne's office wants a conference at noon. I'll do it from here and you can join us from the clinic since it's almost noon."

In just a matter of minutes both of them were connected to Earth, where they saw Ray and Alicia, Payne, Mr. Ivory and Hayden Green all involved in the discussion. Otis began, "This has to be done this way, secure channel or not. I had a late call yesterday from Dr. King and he floored me with a single sentence. He said the pyramid builders had returned, and he was certain they weren't the Vor."

Alicia was the first to comment. "I don't feel that kind of presence at all! Do you believe him, governor?"

"I have to at this point, and so will all of you. The problem is, I lost communication with him before he could finish filling me in on the details. As of today, we still can't raise a peep out of anyone at Mars."

Pam quickly asked, "Do you think anything's happened to them? Did the pyramid builders harm them?"

Otis responded, "From what he was able to tell me, I'd say if anything hostile happened, it was not from them. I need to find out what the hell is going on out there. So, the Majestik is to use every bit of its technology to get into their databases. I have other outposts trying to assess the planet's status."

Hayden sided with Pam. "I think something's wrong, especially the way you were cut off so abruptly. Are you planning on going out there? Surely they drastically need supplies!"

"Yes Hayden, Captain Martin will be the pilot and I'm assembling a team for the usual rotation of personnel. We will add security, and most importantly according to Jaden, we need to bring lots of seeds."

Max listened intently then asked, "If they've suffered injuries or illness, some form of medical personnel have to get out there too."

Otis agreed, "You're one step ahead of me, Dr. Rogers, so, who from your station do you want to complement the person I'll recruit from down here?"

Max looked at Pam with his eyebrows raised as he held back a smile. He said, "Oh I think I can come up with someone very easily."

Pam came closer to the screen, "Alicia, what do you think, should the Majestik risk sending someone or should they get both people from Earth?"

Ivory now had to say something before she could answer, "What does the captain's opinion matter?"

Alicia simply looked at him as she replied, "I think the Mars outpost definitely needs someone familiar with spaceborne tech. I would nominate Pam Aquain for the task."

Otis looked at everyone before focusing on Pam, "Very well, do you accept the job? Before you answer that, let me add this is all voluntary."

Pam could see Ray was getting a little fidgety all of a sudden, "Ray, you know I'd be the last person to volunteer for a trip to Mars. But with what's happened out there, who wouldn't want to go and have a look." She asserted herself, "Yes, of course I'll go. So I assume the ship will come up from Earth, pick up the rest of us here, and head on to Mars."

Otis confirmed, "That's the way I would guess."

Ivory had more to say, "I want to go on record as opposing this mission until we have firmly established what the conditions are out there."

Otis consoled him, "Relax, Tom, it will take days for the ship to be prepared. We should know a lot more by then. We'll also need a full delegate meeting to finalize a new flight restoration plan. Otherwise, I won't say anymore about what Dr. King discussed unless I'm in person with one of you. We'll have a daily morning briefing as we go. So, let's all get to work."

As he shut off communication from his office, Otis knew the three in his room would have lots of questions. "OK, let me just tell the story exactly as it went from yesterday. Then, I want ideas on anything that comes to mind. No question is too stupid unless I say it is."

CHAPTER TWENTY SEVEN

Five days had elapsed since the plan to send a rescue ship to Mars was conceived. The African parliament had approved a new overall flight schedule exactly as Otis Payne had recommended. Ray Phillips was to ride the utility shuttle back up to the Majestik and immediately begin preparations with the moonbase manufacturing facility for the shuttle coil program. His expertise was also needed to complete the removal of the implants from the four remaining hotel personnel.

Max and Pam stayed busy working with various science and research stations trying to decipher what had happened to the Mars team. They had managed to access the Shepherd's computer systems and life support controls. There was still no word from any of the station's inhabitants. This day began with that fateful accomplishment.

"Max, I finally got through to the biometric databases. I don't understand what I'm getting here; can you come over and help me?"

He rolled his chair energetically across the floor. "Let's see what you got. Well, that's certainly a live feed, and you've managed to bring up all the personnel monitors. I see why you're confused. You're not getting any data simply because they aren't on the station."

"None of them? But where are they? If they had all gone to the surface then why did I find yesterday that their shuttle is still docked at the station?"

"Really, I guess I didn't catch that when we reviewed the day's data. OK, we know that ship can be remotely controlled. The question is, can it be controlled from the planet's surface. And if so, why would they want it back up at the mother?"

"What if they felt it was safer for it to be docked in space rather than at the surface?"

"You mean the weather, perhaps storms that might damage it?"

"I don't know, it sounds like a logical option. Max, we're due to get Alicia and Ray back here tomorrow, then I'm supposed to join Alicia and the rest of the crew and head out there. These last few days coming up with no answers are starting to give me second thoughts."

He flashed his predictable big smile, "Don't be silly, we've learned quite a bit. We know the planet is still improving daily, based on the readings. We know the station is still intact. We know they must be on the surface, and can you blame them?"

"And we've learned they all might be abducted or dead!"

He sighed a slight agreement to her point. "Let me ask your help on something I've found." They went to his monitor. "See this database from the gold reclamation studies Pete was working on?"

"Wow, that's a lot of data, five terabytes? How could he have generated so much information in just a few days?"

"My question too. Surely he knew we would be interested in this stuff more than anything right now. Yet the file was not encrypted the way all research data should be stored."

She rolled through a few pages. "It all looks like valid research, but I see multiple mathematical expressions in almost every line that have nothing to do with the thought process of the experiment."

"I saw that, but if I take out that intermittent math and analyze it, it still doesn't make any sense against any known decipher program."

Pam stared at the screen for a moment. "You said it wasn't encrypted or compressed?"

"Neither."

"OK, what if we encrypt and compress the nonsense math and see what type of file it generates?"

"I didn't think to try that; it shouldn't take but a moment to find out."

They both watched eagerly as the program zipped along. Finally it was done as the new data package displayed. Both of them stared in amazement at what was before their eyes.

"Max, how could all that data be compressed to a single sentence?"

"The algorithm continuously deletes redundancies and nonsense. It took quite a mind to think of this."

"So, what does it mean? 'Big friends are nice to have, but there's no place like home'. Is it a riddle?"

"I guess so. The fact that he put this in there, no matter what it means, tells me they didn't want to come out and just say something over the unsecure lines. That tells me they are worried about the Vor discovering something."

"Discovering what Mars is doing? Surely they know that already. They must also know that the pyramid builders are back. What else could they be trying to keep from the Vor?"

"Maybe the gold coil data itself? If this huge file has this secret message in it, maybe it was put in there not to say anything special, but to make it unreadable to any snooping?"

"OK, but then where is everyone, including the returning builders?"

He got up and stretched, "That's why you're so excited to go out there, you love a mystery! Come on, let's get some chow."

She got up after closing the programs. As she walked with him she repeated, "There's no place like home, there's no place like home. Max, that's from the Wizard of Oz!"

"Why, I think you're right! I guess the Andromedians have watched one of the reruns. Some movies never go out of style, do they?"

She repeated the same words silently, her lips mouthing them rhythmically. Then she exclaimed, "I get it Max, I get it! The whole point of the movie was there never was a wizard! There's no aliens out there Max, they're bluffing!"

He smiled as he walked, but thinking deeply about her idea. "Let's keep this between you and me for now. If you're right, we had better keep our mouths shut if we want no more shuttle explosions."

*   *   *

Otis sat in the computer operations room at the government complex as they watched the successful docking at the Majestik. "Well, Tom, that's the last ship to account for today, and when you consider yesterday's successful flights, it looks like we're back in business."

Ivory was unusually quiet as he sat next to Payne watching the live feed. Otis jovially punched his shoulder, "Come on, my man, join me in my office for a toast to our success."

"It's time to go home, Otis, and I think Dr. Phillips would want you to lay off a little on the liquor. Besides, why would you want to celebrate, you may have lost everyone at Mars, people you care about."

"I have complete confidence in their ability to survive. Besides, if the pyramid builders are truly there and have harmed them, then the Vor have as much to worry about as we do."

Tom folded his arms in an unusually defensive manner while he listened. He then mumbled defiantly under his breath, "You humans never give up do you?"

Otis was stunned by what he had just heard and turned to look at Ivory, "What did you just say?"

Ivory responded by standing up slowly, yet remained silent. He then put his hands on his face and rubbed them downward back onto his shirt. Otis watched in bewilderment. "I asked you a question, Tom, why would you say that?"

Then, Ivory just disappeared before his eyes in a brief flash of light. Otis jumped up and grabbed at the empty space where Tom had been. "What the hell. Guard! Come in here now!"

Both men burst through the door brandishing their lasers. Otis yelled, "Search this room and the rest of this floor, something's happened to Tom.

And give me an extra weapon!" One man ran through the door into the dim corridor while the other started to peer into the adjacent storage rooms. Otis sat down and stared at the laser in his hands. "Good God, what have I done! Please don't let Tom be harmed."

The man in the room reported back, "This room's clear, I'll post at the door while reinforcements arrive, sir."

Otis waved the gun at him, "Very well, leave me here while you wait." He looked up at the monitors, all still displaying normal readings and pictures. Then he heard a voice behind him call his name, but inside his head once more. He turned to look anyway. There, in the dark corner, floated the same figure he had seen before. "You again! What have you done with Tom?"

This time it remained where it was as he walked defiantly to just a few meters from it. The voice, now deep in his thoughts, went on in a synthetic texture, "You humans have a disgusting tenacity for this level. We don't understand why. You survive for thousands of years on a constantly hostile planet you have called Earth. Why? It has killed over a hundred billion of you over time from its endless attacks on your homes, foods and bodies. It has limited resources that always lead to wars over their control and some form of pollution to your environment, endlessly weakening your immune defenses. You have no hard proof of your God and yet you never stop begging him for help in trying to stay alive."

Otis couldn't swallow what he was hearing. He had to talk out loud to collect his thoughts, although he felt an incredible urge to reply in his thoughts. "I can't believe what I'm hearing! Why should you care, you obviously don't belong here either!"

"Don't you know yet? You're no help to us alive. We can make better use of some of your resources than your pathetic bodies can. We don't know who brought you humans to this particular planet, but it seems a rather cruel deed for whatever reason."

"Brought us here?"

It laughed in a bizarre buzz in his head, "You have learned so little in all these years. So much time being spent on survival."

"I'll tell you what we have learned, you bastard! We never stop trying precisely because of the fact we *don't* know who the hell we are. So get the hell out of my building and get off my planet!" With that he angrily blasted the laser at the alien. It lit up the figure in a ghostly green glow that flashed a distinct facial image under a hooded robe as it lurched backward. Much to the shock of Otis, he thought he saw his own face before it suddenly thumped to the ground. Otis yelled for the guard as he squatted over the body. He rolled it onto its back and was shocked by what he found.

There was the face of his trusted aide, Tom Ivory. His eyes were closed but there was still a faint breath. Otis then realized there was a huge oozing hole in the man's chest from the laser.

"Tom, oh Tom, what have I done? What were you doing?" Suddenly there was an interspace call ringing through into the room. Otis became angry and screamed at the guard now standing over him, "Answer that goddamn call, will you, man!" Otis continued to kneel next to the body. He laid the laser down next to him as he began to weep when he saw Tom stop breathing. The guard interrupted, "Governor, it's from Mars."

Otis froze in his breath as he couldn't believe his ears. "Mars! Who?"

"I think you should see for yourself."

Otis climbed painfully up his own legs and made his way cautiously to the screen. He wiped a tear from his eye to focus on the screen. Once he sat down, he rubbed both eyes in disbelief, "Tom, is that you?"

"Otis, you're not going to believe this, I'm at the Shepherd space station. I have no idea how I got out here! One minute I'm home in bed, the next bam, I wake up on the floor here! Hey, you should see this planet, it looks like it's livable down there. What's been going on?"

Otis still could not fathom what he was seeing. "Wait a minute. You had no idea Mars was at this level of development?"

"Should I have? Last I saw you before I went to bed, we had nothing special going on out here."

"Tom, how many shuttles have we lost?"

"Lost, what do you mean? Has there been an accident?"

Otis jumped from the seat and went back to Tom's body on the floor. Only now, his face was unrecognizable as human, just a smooth sphere of flesh-tone. He reached cautiously to touch where the face was, but his hand simply went right into a haze of light. Within seconds there was nothing left. Otis waved his hands back and forth where the body was. He looked up at the guard standing, "Did you see what I did? Where did he go?"

"I have no idea. I'll say whatever you need me to say, sir, but that obviously wasn't Mr. Ivory."

Otis returned to the screen and sat down again, "No, it wasn't." He composed himself before turning his mic back on. "Mr. Ivory, is anyone there with you?"

"Give me a few minutes to search the ship."

Minutes later he returned, "No sir, no one on board; sure is eerie."

"Listen to me, Tom. There will be a ship arriving in about four days with supplies and medical personnel and security. Until they arrive, I want you to call back hourly with status checks on what you're doing. I'll have the Majestik people call you tomorrow when they get up."

"Otis, I just woke up here like you wake from a dream. How many days have I been asleep?"

"Oh, I'd guess a few weeks, a few months, give or take a little."

"What? How could that be! I just saw you yesterday!"

"Tom, I have an amazing story to tell you, but we'll save it for tomorrow. For now, don't break anything, carry a laser at all times, and keep an eye out for some very big friendly aliens."

"How big is big?"

"Bigger than life right now, Tom, bigger than life."

*   *   *

Alicia worked the morning preflight checklists as the ship prepared for its departure from the Majestik to Mars. She looked over at the man who was assigned her co-pilot for the trip. He was military all the way, even wearing a sidearm. Her thoughts drifted to Tim Ward back on Earth, awaiting a trial at the African complex. She quickly turned her focus back to her work.

Ray was busy in the cargo area supervising the loading of medical supplies with Pam. He had many things he wanted to say, but for some reason, he remained businesslike as they worked.

Pam cleared her throat, "Ray, there's something I need to talk with you about before I leave." She looked around suspiciously at the other personnel in the bay, "I need to say this to you in private."

He put the clipboard at his side, "If it's about you and Max, I want to say right now I encouraged Max to express his feelings to you."

She looked at him surprised by raising her eyebrows, "Well, that's not exactly what I needed to talk to you about, but thanks for sharing that."

"Oh, maybe I should keep my mouth shut till we're done here." Then, his voicecom buzzed. "Excuse me, Pam, looks like Payne's office."

"This is Phillips, can I help you?"

"Just a moment, doctor, I have Governor Payne for you."

"Doctor, good morning! How're the preparations going for the Shepherd trip?"

"It'll be a tight fit. But we'll get it all in there."

"Good; I need to have you join your top guy Dr. Rogers in a secure conference call as soon as possible."

"Can it wait till after we get the shuttle out?"

"No, it affects this trip tremendously."

He looked at Pam, who could overhear everything, "OK, I'm on my way to the communications room." He shoved the device in his pocket. "Well, Pam, if you follow me, will that be private enough talking in the hallways?"

"It'll have to be. Let's go."

Once they were in a remote part of the hall, she pulled him into an empty side corridor. "OK, Ray, Max doesn't know I'm telling you this, but he's not the one getting on that ship this morning." She took a breath and nearly whispered, "We deciphered a hidden message in the Shepherd's gold coil research database from Dr. Ancerid. It was a sort of rhyme, but we believe it was trying to tell us there are no pyramid builder aliens out there; it's all a lie."

He stuck his head into the main hall to verify they were still alone, "I can see why you have to keep this quiet. I don't know what to say. There's no way we can get this info down to earth safely right now."

"I know, but I felt if at least you knew, you might be able to make some changes on what we put in the shuttle."

"Let me think this over. Come on, follow me to the call. Maybe Otis has something big for us as well."

"I don't know what he could say that would top this."

Once they were at the communications room, Max was just rounding the corner to enter. "Hey, guys, I got a call from Governor Brickman's office telling me I had to take this urgent conference call."

They made their way together into the conference chamber. Ray pondered as they pulled up their seats, "I guess Otis is bringing in all the governors?"

"I don't know, but seems every time we're all together it's more bad news." Max made the connections and in just minutes all screens were on. Otis spoke first. "You folks at the Majestik, I have the rest of the Earth leadership linked in. We again acknowledge limited security, but things need to be said. Last night I was visited again by the mysterious alien. I can only assume it was the one portraying the Dove leader. The only thing is, after it got done telling me how pathetic we humans were, I shot at it. The next thing I know it's morphing its appearance; first into a damn good impression of my face, then it died as Tom Ivory, my lead assistant and delegate."

Ray asked very worried, "What do you mean Ivory" If the alien was mimicking him, where's the real Ivory?"

"That's why I needed this call. He immediately appeared at the Shepherd station and has no idea where he's been or how he got there."

It was Governor Brickman's turn. "Congratulations Otis, you had an imposter in your inner circle for who knows how long! Why didn't that brain scan you all took show anything?"

Ray answered this one, "Because it will only pick up humans who have been abducted and tagged. If this was actually one of the Vor, it apparently was able to mimic a complete human form, inside and out."

Otis went on, "Yes, but that form completely vaporized after it apparently died. I don't know, hell, it all seems like magic illusions at this point, I don't know if it ever was in my office! What I'm hoping for from this meeting is some understanding of who or what plopped Tom Ivory into that space research station."

Pam questioned, "But you can't be sure he's even the real Tom Ivory!"

Otis shook his head side to side, "Thanks for bringing that up. For all I know that creature simply changed locations at the blink of an eye. If it did, it apparently wasn't afraid to go and face the pyramid aliens who are now supposedly out there."

Ray saw the dilemma, "And if there's no fear of that race, we may still be vulnerable to pot shots at our shuttle system."

Max tried to bring the confidence back, "Hey everybody, don't get so down so fast. The aliens returning to Mars is just gravy on the stew! We're a happy race of humans now, remember? Let's show them we believe in ourselves! We've got ships to upgrade and people to bring to Mars."

Everyone was silent as they thought about his words. Finally Otis continued, "He's right you know. Let's get that ship on its way to Mars and find out what happened to my people! Dr. Phillips needs his materials to get started on the propulsion coils and Dr. King needs his seeds to get some green on the surface. Does anyone else, especially you other governors, have any better ideas?'

They all mumbled for a moment or two, but none could disagree. Max looked at Pam, ever so subtle, but she refused to acknowledge him. Otis then finished the call, "Very well, let's proceed as planned. I will implement a detailed search of Mr. Ivory's quarters and try to verify if that's really him out there. Otherwise, departure is what time, Dr. Phillips?"

"Six a.m. our time. Now, we have to get back to the port; there's much to do yet." After closing the viewcoms he sat back and said to Max, "You go back with Pam and finish the inventory; I have some thinking to do."

"OK, boss. Come on, Miss Space Explorer, there's packing to be done."

*   *   *

Ray stood the next morning in the shuttleport lobby as he watched the two women in his life board a rescue ship to a planet he had never been to himself. He had flashbacks to the trip he had just taken down to Earth and the emotions he felt. This time there were no friendly rounds of drinks, no long goodbyes, no lectures. He turned to Max at his right side, "What have we got ourselves into, 'ol buddy?"

Max plopped his arm on top of Ray's shoulders, "They'll be fine. Besides, they're highly motivated to make it back in one piece."

"Really, how's that?" He looked at him surprised, "Us, you fool! They can't live without us!"

Ray laughed, but he knew that's what Max wanted out of him. "I suppose that's one way to look at it. Alicia said she felt no bad vibes, so to speak, when she got up this morning."

Just then the final departure warnings sounded. They went to the portals to watch the ship pull out. It was a sight they had seen countless times before, but now it was different. Now it was perhaps the most important shuttle flight that had been flown since the planet had taken so many lives. When the shuttles flew again after those first few months of turmoil, they gave a tremendous ray of hope to everyone still alive. Today, the remaining humans knew the stakes were even higher. This time the enemy wasn't nature.

*   *   *

Four days later, at the Majestik, Ray had finished removing all the implants from the four unhappy hotel detainees. They were never told what was really in them until the operation was over. They didn't protest anymore once they got a look at the things that were in their heads. And, just like the one removed from Tim Ward's head, the implants promptly disintegrated after a few hours of exposure.

Ray had mixed emotions over the brain scan on Parker. It came out negative. Ray also finalized the return of Chairman Parker's remains to his last family on Earth. He never had the time while he was on the planet to fulfill his promise to supervise the burial. Otis promised Ray that Bernie would be shipped promptly to his hometown.

The shuttle arrived into Mars orbit right on schedule. The trip was uneventful in all ways. Ray was in the tracking control room the minute the shuttle dropped into orbit. He couldn't wait to hear what they had to say. They had Tom Ivory involved the whole time in their arrival. He was anxious to see real people again, and was getting quite a bit hungry with the little food that remained on board.

Ray spoke as soon as the mission control chatter would allow it. "Alicia, how much longer till you dock?"

"Five minutes. Ray, please get a monitor on so I can feed you a view of what the planet looks like."

He looked at one of the technicians who nodded at the appropriate monitor to watch. In seconds the planet appeared. He smiled like a child seeing the stars for the first time in all their glory. It was so different, so alive, it took his breath away. "Hey, I think I can see some water bodies down there!"

"Yes, I see them, and look at all the clouds! Ray, have any of you back there made contact with the crew out here yet?"

"I won't lie to you; no."

"I'm feeling some incredible things out here Ray. I feel so alive, I feel like I did when I got my first trip into space. I can't explain it, I..."

Ray quickly looked at the tech. "What happened, why did she cut out?"

"Just a minute, there doesn't seem to be anything wrong with her signal. Try again doctor."

"Alicia, Alicia, come in...."

"I'm here, Ray, sorry about that. I had to stop a moment. Seems something caught my eye on the other side of the space station."

"Like what? What do you see?" After a moment of silence she came back, "There's a large ship out there Ray."

"A ship? Is it their shuttle?"

"No, it's way too big for that. I've never seen anything like it. I'm going to circle around for a better look."

"Be careful! It could be the Vor."

"Don't worry; the military people are already buzzing about on the ship. My co-pilot is making me go very cautiously."

"Alicia, I feel I need to say this again: I do love you."

"Ray, thank you, it's nice to hear, but I really need to concentrate. Let me check in after we decide whose ship this is."

Ray looked to the personnel around him, "How come we didn't know about that ship? Didn't Mr. Ivory see it the whole time he's been out there?"

One of them responded, "He may not have been able to see it, sir, the station does have blind spots. And, Mr. Ivory is no mission specialist; he wouldn't know how to read many of the station's instruments."

Ray flopped back into a chair as he stared at the monitors. "Dammit, this is just great. If I could just be at that station right now!"

There was a sudden flash of light in the room; enough to make several of the technicians turn to where Ray was sitting. They all looked puzzled at what they saw. In the chair Ray had been, sat a bewildered Tom Ivory. He was touching his chest while he looked feverishly about the room.

"Where am I?"

One of the men answered as he pushed a button calling security, "You're at the Majestik; where did Dr. Phillips go?"

"Dr. Phillips was here, in this chair?"

"Yes sir, but we didn't notice him leave. You just seemed to appear right there out of thin air. Who are you?"

Ivory got up, "Nice to meet you fella's in person. I'm Tom Ivory. Is Max Rogers here?"

*   *   *

Ray picked himself up off the floor of the Shepherd station. He couldn't believe he was exactly where he had just moments ago wanted to be. He tapped his hand down on the nearest table top to assure its solidness, then ran for a portal to see if he was really over Mars. He darted from one end of the station to the other trying to see what was happening outside with the shuttle. All he could see was either the blackness of space or the wonder of the new planet below him. Frustrated, he lunged for a com microphone and set the frequency for the distress bandwidth. "This is Dr. Phillips, can anyone hear me? Alicia?"

"She is fine, Ray," answered a voice that resonated in his own persona. It was as clear and real as if it came through a headset, yet drawing from every corner of the room.

His eyes darted in all directions, "Who said that? Who's here?"

Suddenly a glowing, white, misty cloud materialized in front of him, mixing onto a background of beautiful colors that flowed kaleidoscopically in a slowly spinning vortex pattern. He froze in wonderment at its beauty. He wanted to be fearful, but he began to understand what Alicia said she was feeling. His apprehension disappeared completely as he approached the cloud, wanting to reach out and touch it as he asked, "What am I doing here on this station?"

"You wanted to be here, so you are here." Questions now poured into his thoughts, "Did you build those pyramids?"

"We taught the builders many things."

Ray felt himself weakening with each second and realized he was now sitting on his heels, actually kneeling on the floor. An overwhelming sense of humility enveloped him and he almost couldn't look at the swirling energy before him. "Can you help us all get to this planet safely? Can you tell me where the Shepherd crew is?"

"We know all of your questions, we will answer them all, as one."

He hung his head lower, "I want to understand you, but I don't know what that means."

"You are all part of a powerful consciousness, one that has been forced to suffer in this part of existence far too long. This is finally the time for coming back. We now see you have done better than expected for what has blocked your way."

Ray swallowed hard, but had to ask, "Are you God?"

"We are all in God for now until we rejoin the level of our creators' realm. This universe is not far from that moment, and this will be your starting point. We have missed you greatly and will give your return the majesty it deserves."

"Why now, why did it take so long? We have suffered so much without a presence."

"Your time is nothing and always but the present. You never really left."

The feeling of love now coursing through Ray's body was so overwhelming he had tears running down his face. He hung his head in his palms and wept softly from the flood of emotions. When he had finally released the sadness and joy of what felt like the entire human race channeled through him, he looked slowly back up to the light. It was gone.

He dropped his head and stared at the floor to compose himself. Then, when enough of his strength returned he climbed up to the microphone, "Alicia, I repeat, Alicia, can you hear me?"

Her voice suddenly came over the speaker, "Ray, I hear you."

"Alicia, you won't believe where I am! What's the status on that ship you saw?"

"Hang on a moment, I'm climbing back into my seat. Ahhh, I can't see it anymore. Ray, we're all just coming back to reality here. I know you're at the Shepherd! We all just saw and heard everything you just did! It's as if we were all one person. I've still got chills. You should see the look of my co-pilot!"

Suddenly a voice came through the speakers from the surface channel, "Shepherd One, this is Jaden King, is anyone up there?"

Ray jumped over to the window as he held the microphone, "Come in Jaden, this is Dr. Phillips. I hear you. Where are you?"

"Hello, Ray. We seem to be down at the planet in the main base building. Last I remember we went under stasis on the station, so we have no idea why we're waking up down here. Everyone seems fine, however. I assume you came out here on the supply shuttle?"

Ray looked at his hands again to verify he was really there, "Not exactly. You might say I had quite an unusual ride out here. That shuttle will be docking any minute now. We see your shuttle is docked up here as well. I assume that's right where you last parked it."

"As far as I remember, yes. How about sending it down when you get a chance, I can't wait to get up there and get a mouthful of some of that fresh food."

"We'll have plenty of that, and I hope *you* have plenty of my gold stuff."

"A few tons enough?" The speakers then switched channels, "Ray, this is Alicia, I'm coming into mooring. You shouldn't have to do anything, so don't touch any controls while we dock."

Ten minutes later the airlock opened, and Pam was the first one out. She had a look of relief on her face as she smiled at Ray while shaking her head, "No fair, you just magically pop out here and I had to take a four-day ride!" He took her hand, "Glad you made it, come on in; the place needs a woman's touch."

"Ray, that energy, it was so beautiful! I never felt so safe and loved before in my life! Do you think whatever it was has chased the Vor away? And whose ship was out there? I don't think something that powerful needs a spaceship, do you?"

"I don't have answers for those questions Pam. But somehow I don't care, I feel no fear as well, for the first time I can even remember. I don't know how we're going to convey this entire encounter back to Earth, but it should be interesting."

She went immediately to the large portal window and looked at Mars, "After what just happened, I'm not sure we got it right about the giant aliens *not* being here."

"That entity we just experienced said *they* taught the pyramid builders, so I think you and Max were correct; it was a bluff. I think it was working well till that ship showed up outside to take a look. I'll bet that was the Vor, so we should be damn grateful the entity gave us this visit."

Her attention shifted to another window as she curiously ventured further into the station. Ray continued to greet the rest as they entered the station. He patiently waited for the most important traveler to exit. Finally, Alicia appeared in the hatchway, her face aglow with energy, her hair glistening like starlight. She wasted no time in hugging him. After a long embrace, she reached for his face and kissed him passionately. Then she leaned her head back and looked him straight in the eye. "You said you would be waiting for me when I walked out of this ship. I bet you didn't think it would be out here."

He was about to say something when she interrupted, "Yes, Ray Phillips, I shall marry you."

He just grinned back, "I thought you wanted to be through with the mission first, back at home."

She led him to the window and looked at the planet. Then he heard her voice in his head say, "I am home."

Ray's hand jumped to her shoulder as he excitedly exclaimed, "Alicia, I think I just heard you in my mind! Did you say 'I am home'?"

"Well, well, it seems as if you have made a major leap. Yes, I did say that."

"I gotta tell you; it's a little spooky. I hope I don't start hearing everyone's thoughts; that could get crazy."

"Don't worry, I'm probably the only one you'll be able to hear for awhile."

"Honey, why now, why did these entities finally come back for us?"

She reached around his waist lovingly, still looking down at the planet, "Think about the people that were buried under that rubble down there. When it happened, everyone on this station knew *roughly* where they were, but they were faced with limited time and resources to do a sweeping dig and rescue. However, if they'd had just one little sign of life from the stones, especially at a specific location in the pile, they would have tried a rescue with the tools they had available. Without that sign of life, they couldn't or wouldn't risk it."

He nodded as he asked another question in his mind, "So where did the entity go?"

Alicia graciously replied into his thoughts, "Oh, they're still right here!"

He looked around him quickly, but saw nothing except the flight crew. He smiled, "Our saviors, so to speak, had to get a fix on us somehow? And now that they know where we are, we're home free? Is it really over, just like that?"

His mind now raced everywhere so he regressed back to his voice, "I know the universe is vast, but I heard it say something like we never really left. What does that mean?"

"This universe exists because we exist. It is here because we are here. Without our consciousness, all of this is not real to anyone else not here. The layers of reality are indeed vast."

He actually understood this amazing concept without further question. He gently turned her to him and gave her a kiss. As they looked into each others eyes, you wouldn't believe what they both were thinking!

THE END,
or
THE BEGINNING?